# Huge Fathomless Blue-Violet Eyes Met His . . .

Vesper was the most beautiful woman Cord had ever seen. Her hair was a burnished river of ebony that framed a pale face, silken to the touch. Her rose-petal lips, now slightly parted, unknowingly enticed him with their intriguing blend of delicacy and sensuousness.

Instinctively he drew her to him and felt her tremble within his grasp. Vesper did not resist. His nearness had a paralyzing effect on her, the heady warmth of his powerful masculine body sending strange shivers through her slender frame. She had never encountered a man like him, so powerful, as free as the wind from the prairies.

Their lips grew achingly close . . .

Dear Reader,

We, the editors of Tapestry Romances, are committed to bringing you two outstanding original romantic historical novels each and every month.

From Kentucky in the 1850s to the court of Louis XIII, from the deck of a pirate ship within sight of Gibraltar to a mining camp high in the Sierra Nevadas, our heroines experience life and love, romance and adventure.

Our aim is to give you the kind of historical romances that you want to read. We would enjoy hearing your thoughts about this book and all future Tapestry Romances. Please write to us at the address below.

The Editors
Tapestry Romances
POCKET BOOKS
1230 Avenue of the Americas
Box TAP
New York, N.Y. 10020

# River To Rapture

### Louisa Gillette

**A TAPESTRY BOOK**
PUBLISHED BY POCKET BOOKS NEW YORK

Books by Louisa Gillette

Glorious Treasure
River to Rapture

Published by TAPESTRY BOOKS

An *Original* publication of TAPESTRY BOOKS

A Tapestry Book, published by
POCKET BOOKS, a division of Simon & Schuster, Inc.
1230 Avenue of the Americas, New York, N.Y. 10020

ISBN: 0-671-52364-3

First Tapestry Books printing November, 1985

10 9 8 7 6 5 4 3 2 1

POCKET and colophon are registered trademarks of Simon & Schuster, Inc.

TAPESTRY is a registered trademark of Simon & Schuster, Inc.

Printed in the U.S.A.

To Phil and Tom
and nights in Marin

# Chapter One

VESPER LAWRENCE'S HEART POUNDED AS SHE knocked on the deeply grained oak door to her father's study. Earlier at dinner, her father, Senator Frederick Lawrence of Virginia, had demanded her presence in no uncertain terms. Vesper was afraid she knew all too well what the subject of their discussion would be.

For three social seasons she had been paraded before the eligible bachelors of Washington, D.C., and not one had offered for her hand. Vesper was secretly pleased, for she had yet to meet a young man she either liked or respected. Sometimes she wondered whether there was something wrong with her. Her younger stepsister, Roxanne, seemed to fall in love at every ball.

"Come in, Vesper," boomed a hearty voice.

1

Her father, a tall, elegantly dressed southern gentleman with graying hair, stood behind his massive marble-topped desk. Behind him were row upon row of legal books bound in the finest calf-skin.

"I won't mince my words, Vesper," her father began. "Sit down, daughter. Sit down," he repeated impatiently, waving her to a dark umber leather settee. "Your stepmother and I are greatly concerned for your future."

Vesper's heart sank. She had been right.

Lawrence sat down beside her and put his arm around her shoulders. "Don't look so crestfallen, my dear. You know we only have your best interests at heart."

"I know, Father, but . . ."

"You are the only child of my blood, Vesper. Your mother and I had hoped for many more, but I lost her and your newborn brother at the same moment. You are all I have left."

Vesper was touched by this reminder of her mother, who had died when Vesper was four years old.

"You know, Vesper," he confided, "I miss her every day of my life. I look forward to the time when your children will bring her back to me."

When he seemed to stifle a sob, then look out of the corner of his eye at her, Vesper stiffened. Once again he had invoked the name of her mother to weaken Vesper's resistance. His patent insincerity irritated her. After all, he had married Belle, her stepmother, before the first six months of mourning were over.

"What is it you want from me, Father?" Vesper demanded, angry at his manipulation.

Her father left her side and lodged himself behind his desk.

2

"You've known from childhood that my political career requires you to make an advantageous marriage."

"Isn't my happiness of any importance to you?" Vesper questioned.

The senator frowned. "You're too young to know what will make you happy. A woman's happiness comes from helping her family, her husband, and her children. All the rest is sentimental nonsense."

"Then all I have to look forward to is being an ornament in some man's drawing room?"

He snorted derisively. "You wouldn't make much of an ornament, the way you keep yourself. Belle tells me you've done nothing to make yourself attractive. Look at you!"

He gestured toward her disparagingly.

"You insist on wearing these dark shapeless dresses, no matter what Belle buys for you. You slouch as if you have something to be ashamed of. You never smile; you never talk to people; you never encourage any of the young men around you."

Vesper had to admit to herself that he was right. She made no effort to flirt and simper as the other young girls did. The female artifices of dress and ornamentation had never appealed to her. Nothing could have made her into the tiny, delicate porcelain doll that her contemporaries so prized.

In fact, her five-foot-nine-inch frame could never look doll-like. But she was wrong in assuming herself plain. Vesper could have been breathtakingly beautiful, yet her drooping shoulders and unassuming walk veiled the grace and majesty she might have displayed. Her habitual downcast expression effectively disguised her extraordinary face.

Vesper's huge eyes, the exact shade of gentian violets, were thickly starred with long black lashes.

She had a small, straight nose, and her high patrician cheekbones accentuated her alabaster-cream skin. Rich cascading waves of shining blue-black hair were tied back severely from the perfect oval of her face. Her mouth was a study in contrasts, with its thinly elegant upper lip and sensuously soft and full lower lip.

At nineteen, her tall, angular body had blossomed into soft womanly curves. Under her severe plain gowns, her breasts were full, even lush, and a man, given the chance, could have easily encircled her waist with his hands. Her rounded hips flared provocatively, and she had long, classic legs. She possessed all the gifts that should have made her a statuesque beauty, but no one could see it, not even Vesper.

The senator stood and glared at his daughter.

"Vesper, listen to me! What do you think will happen to you? Do you want to spend the rest of your life as an aging spinster in another woman's household? Or do you prefer to end up like your Aunt Lucinda?"

Although Vesper loved her mother's spinster sister, Lucinda Moore, Vesper knew she would hate running a shabby boardinghouse in order to keep bread on her table. Nor could she live with Belle's hypocrisy the rest of her life.

"Mother was a schoolteacher when you met her. I could be a governess to a family here in Washington."

"Do you think I'd allow a daughter of mine to be taken on like a servant in another senator's household?" Lawrence roared.

Vesper winced inwardly, realizing that she had gone too far. He would never let her choose her own life, especially if her choice were at cross-pur-

4

poses to her father's political ambitions. What was she to do? Was there any way to be free of his shackles?

Perhaps dear Lucinda could help her. Vesper would disobey Belle's edict once again and secretly visit her aunt tomorrow.

"I'm sorry, Father. I have no answer for you," she murmured, her eyes lowered.

"Then I'll provide the answer," her father boomed, the false heartiness returning to his voice. "You leave it to me, my dear. I'll find your husband for you."

Moving to her side, he patted Vesper patronizingly on the shoulder. He raised her from the settee and kissed her wan cheek.

"Now off to bed with you. You need your beauty sleep."

Mutely Vesper left her father. Alone in his study, the senator pulled a sheet of vellum from a desk drawer and dipped a quill pen into his gold-chased inkwell. With a triumphant grin, he dashed off a note to his closest friend and longtime political crony.

Dear Augustus,
    Congratulations! Vesper accepts your suit, making me the happiest man in the world. As you will be dining with us tomorrow night, it occurs to me that it would be the ideal moment to announce your betrothal to my daughter.
                                    Yours ever,
                                    F. L.

Lawrence called for Hadrian, the family's black-skinned butler, to have the note delivered immediately. Lolling back in his wingback chair, he lit an expensive cigar and puffed contentedly, congratulating himself on a job neatly done.

The next morning, in the pearly half-light of an April dawn, Vesper tiptoed cautiously down the central staircase on her way to her clandestine meeting. She winced as a floorboard creaked, and held her breath. When no one stirred, Vesper crossed to the foyer and threw an anonymous gray cloak over her plain indigo-blue gown. The cloak's heavy hem almost overturned a silver tray for calling cards that perched on the edge of a dainty Louis XIV stand. When it did not fall, she breathed a sigh of relief and reached for the latch on the oversized mahogany front door.

Before she could reach it, the door was flung open and there stood her half brother Taylor, his cravat askew and shirttails dangling at his waist. His equally inebriated and disheveled companions were only partly successful in keeping Taylor on his feet. Like many young bloods of the city, they spent their nights drinking and carousing, moving from posh hotel saloons to the rougher taverns of Washington's poor section. Vesper tried in vain to hush the last chorus of their bawdy ballad.

"C'mon," Taylor slurred. "It's a good song!"

He slung an arm toward his half sister's shoulder but missed. Vesper stepped back, stymied for the moment. She would not be able to reach Lucinda if she could not get past these idiots whose expensive pearl-buttoned shirtfronts were stained with liquor.

"Where're you goin'?" asked one of Taylor's rowdy friends loudly. "Why don't you stay with us?"

"Yeah, sister," prompted another. "Yuh got a better place to be than with us?"

She endured all their teasing remarks in the hope that she would elude them before they woke the family or the servants. But the drunken lot did not tire of their game, and Vesper's patience came to an end.

"This is quite enough, gentlemen," Vesper announced firmly. "Kindly let me pass."

A round of drunken laughter met her demand, and she straightened, her magnificent eyes flaring angrily. In a shaft of morning light Vesper's beauty was momentarily revealed. The men stared, open-mouthed.

"Why, Miss Lawrence, your beauty confounds me," stated one of Taylor's friends, tugging ineffectually at his tight wool evening coat. Before she could stop him, he had taken her hand and placed a wet kiss upon it.

Another young blood smoothed his elaborate mustaches and bowed low before her, offering his undying affection. A third took her other hand in his, embarrassing her further. He murmured throatily, "Your eyes slay me with violet arrows, O cruel goddess."

Vesper was helpless. How could she escape? No one had ever paid her such compliments before, and she did not know what to do. Her eyes darted to Taylor, pleading for help, but he was watching the scene with as much amazement as herself.

Vesper's inability to flirt back encouraged the young men to become bolder. One snaked an arm around her waist and whirled her to his companions, who took up the game with great enthusiasm. Vesper became dizzier and dizzier as she was passed from man to man. Her chignon loosened, and rough hands pulled out the remaining pins. When one of the excited group rudely caressed her tousled raven locks, she pulled her hair angrily from his grasp, only to fall into the arms of another who was intent on pressing a kiss to her face. Helplessly she struggled.

Rescue arrived in an unexpected form. Vesper's blond, voluptuous half sister Roxanne appeared at the head of the stairs, clutching a lacy dressing gown to her body.

In a practiced flirtatious voice, she called, "My oh my, whatever is goin' on here?"

She batted her long golden lashes the requisite number of times for a popular debutante.

"What a ruckus you all are making!"

Descending the stairs, Roxanne stopped, shocked as she discovered the object of all the males' attention. Mousy old Vesper, who had never had a beau, was being lavished with attention. Instantly jealous, Roxanne artfully turned all eyes to her.

"Oh, boys! Whatever would your mamas say if they saw you? I do declare, if my daddy knew you were here, and making such a fuss, he'd forbid you the house."

She paused for a dramatic sigh that caused her ample bosom to quiver.

"And I'd just hate that. I'd miss every one of you . . ."

She moved her sky-blue eyes meaningfully to each one.

"Now hurry on home," she said, dismissing them.

The young bachelor who had tried to kiss Vesper stepped forward.

"Oh, Miss Roxanne, I do apologize for our unpardonable behavior."

The others echoed his sentiments, shamefaced. Then, to Vesper's grateful amazement, the drunken troop sheepishly turned to the door and left. Taylor, ignoring his sister's disgusted look, weaved up the stairs to his bedroom.

Roxanne walked up to Vesper, who towered above the five-foot-two-inch blonde.

"Where do you think you're going at six o'clock in the morning?" she demanded harshly.

As always, Vesper was struck by Roxanne's ability to change from honey to vinegar in the blink of an eye. There was no mistaking her for anyone but Belle's daughter. Artful practitioners of social manipulation, they matched perfectly her father's wheeling and dealing in Congress. Vesper's silence angered Roxanne.

"I'm going to get Mama right now . . . unless you tell me."

The last thing Vesper wanted was to provoke another tantrum from her calculating, self-centered stepmother. If Belle knew what Vesper planned, she would fill the house with tearful recriminations and make Vesper's life a misery.

As Roxanne climbed the stairs she taunted, "It can't be a man. No one would look at you . . . unless he were drunk. So it must be that dried-up old bluestocking aunt of yours."

She noted with satisfaction Vesper's unconscious start. Smugly Roxanne said, "Mama will be absolutely livid!"

Her face suffused with color, Vesper ran up and grabbed Roxanne's wrist.

"You won't stop me, and neither will your mother. You can't chain me to this house like a disobedient slave!"

Releasing her stepsister, Vesper marched furiously out the door. Roxanne, her face twisted with frustration, rushed off to her mother's bedchamber to tattle on Vesper.

# Chapter Two

IT WAS A GLORIOUSLY FRESH SPRING DAY IN WASHINGTON, D.C. The economic depression of the late 1830s had finally run its course and now, in the mid-forties, the capital was bursting with unbridled optimism. From every avenue, the city sang with the pounding of hammers and the rasping of saws. Carriages dashed down the spacious but unpaved boulevards, and the air hung full of dust from the energetic hooves of the horses. Fashionable politicians and their polished families rubbed elbows with humble tradesmen dressed in practical homespun clothes. The city's four open-air markets were doing a brisk business as peddlers enthusiastically hawked their wares.

Pennsylvania Avenue, the hub of the city, had recently acquired gas street lamps and was looking very modern. The most elegant building on the broad thoroughfare was the Executive Mansion, known unofficially as the White House, with its classical Georgian facade. The avenue ended at the Capitol with its copper-covered wooden dome. Foreign dignitaries, secretaries with satchels overflowing, and hustling journalists swarmed over the building's magnificent marble steps. Through the busy throng strode an extraordinary pair of men. They made their way up Pennsylvania Avenue, oblivious to the unabashed stares they were receiving.

The white man, well over six and a half feet tall, was dressed in beaded and fringed buckskins that did little to disguise his rock-hard, massively muscled body. His shoulders were immense and his biceps bulged forcefully through a thin deerskin shirt. The golden pelt on his broad chest glinted through the rawhide lacings of his Indian shirt. A knotted belt holding a sharp Bowie hunting knife encircled his lean waist. Weathered deerskin trousers covered strong thighs and long, powerful legs.

Determination marked every inch of his rugged, handsome face, darkened to sienna by the wind and the sun. Thick bronze hair, held back by a narrow beaded headband, was touched with gold. His skin was taut, emphasizing the strong angles of jaw and cheekbones, and under wide golden brows startling leaf-green eyes blazed.

Cord Travers, from the Minnesota Territory, was his own man and answered only to his own conscience. To Cord, the confining demands of polite society, with its double standards and underhanded dealings, made it impossible for a man to say what he thought and do what he had to.

His companion and foster father, Chief Running Wolf, looked every inch the serene and noble warrior. His war bonnet, thick with wild turkey feathers, attested to his many feats of bravery. The supple animal skins of his war shirt and leggins were elaborately decorated with designs in elk teeth and porcupine quills. A necklace of bear claws clicked as he walked proudly through the gawking crowds. His impassive face was painted with symbolic designs and his deep black eyes seemed to look through and beyond this white man's world.

As the two men walked, Cord Travers grated, "Every one of those senators smiled at us and lied through their teeth. The government used to be the Indians' friend and protector. Now they have no more interest in the Santee Sioux other than to pay us lip service . . . and steal the land."

The older man's eyes softened as he listened to the growl of harsh frustration in the white man's deep voice.

"You have fought well, my son, but your white brothers are greedy and words will not reach them. The hearts of the committee are closed to us. They will no longer send protection for our lands."

Travers' jaw tightened. "I won't see you ripped from the land of your ancestors."

Looking into the distance, the Indian chief said, "For five summers and five winters, our alliance has worked. The elders have never regretted letting you claim our lands in your name. It kept the white man from our land, and our herds and people together. But the time has come, as we knew it would, when the white man can be held back no longer."

Cord heard the truth in Running Wolf's words.

"I had selfish motives too, my father. Living among you, honoring your ways and making them my own, I hoped to protect my place among the Santee Sioux. The Indian Woods have become my home, too."

The chief stared hard into Cord's unhappy green eyes, as if sending fortifying strength to his adopted son.

"You won our trust long ago, Fierce Bear, and you are one of us for as long as your heart lies in the woods."

Angry despair reappeared on the young giant's face.

"If we could just find one man in Washington who would keep his word . . . Perhaps we could sidetrack the settlers long enough for the tribal elders to plan their next move."

Off on a side street, the two men heard a rumbling crash of falling bricks, followed by the sickening sound of a whip lashing human flesh. A burly Negro slave had stumbled beneath a bone-crushing load of masonry strapped to his back. His portly redheaded master shouted imprecations as he belabored the poor man with a cruel whip. The two men from the frontier stared as a tall, regal figure in a plain gray cloak interposed herself between master and slave.

"Stop, please!" begged the beautiful young woman. "Can't you see you've given him too much to carry?"

"Get on now, missy," grunted the slaveowner, and pushed her away forcefully.

But she clung to his sweaty arm. "You must stop beating him," she insisted.

Furious, he shoved her to the dusty street and raised his whip over her threateningly. Before he could strike her, a bronze-haired giant of a man loomed over her and, with one expert move, wrenched the whip from the assailant's hand. Who was this man, Vesper wondered, who moved to protect her in spite of any danger to himself?

Her pulse raced as her buckskinned rescuer twisted the man's arm behind his back and snarled, "Cowards strike women, and men in chains. What you need is a taste of your own whip."

He cracked the whip above the sweating owner's head.

The man cringed, stuttering, "N-n-no . . . no, don't hit me!"

Disgusted, the brawny young man released the slaveowner, who scuttled away, followed unwillingly by his slave. Cord knelt in the dust and gently raised the young woman to her feet, admiration for her courage in his face.

Huge fathomless blue-violet eyes met his, and before he could say a word he was drowning. She was the most beautiful woman he had ever seen, and in his twenty-seven years he had been with many. Shaken loose by the ruffian's violence, her hair was a burnished river of ebony that framed a pale face, silken to the touch. Her rose-petal lips, now slightly parted, unknowingly enticed him with their intriguing blend of delicacy and sensuousness.

Instinctively he drew her to him and felt her tremble within his grasp. Vesper did not resist. His nearness was having a paralyzing effect on her. The heady warmth of his powerful masculine body sent strange shivers through her slender frame. She was overpowered by the demand in his hungry eyes. She had never encountered a man like him, so powerful, as free as the wind from the prairies.

Washington dissolved around them. Their lips drew achingly close. It was only Running Wolf's dispassionate reminder that recalled them to where they were. Dazed, Vesper retreated from Cord's arms.

"Thank you, k-kind sir, for your h-h-help," she

stammered confusedly. She nervously repinned her hair. "I . . . must be going. They will wonder where I am." Before he could even learn her name, she had darted away.

Running Wolf rested a hand on Cord's shoulder, and Cord found the old Indian's words heartening.

"Your paths will cross again. She is the woman whose spirit is equal to yours."

Tripping up the short brick walkway that led to her father's front door, Vesper felt light as air. She had met a man straight out of a heroic saga, forceful, just, and, she admitted to herself, splendid-looking. Now she could understand and sympathize with the girlish sighs and midnight confidences so common among Roxanne's friends.

Vesper felt as if she had been lifted by a great wind and carried aloft. She was no longer tied to the sticky stratagems that pervaded the world of the capital. She momentarily forgot her father's threat of an arranged marriage and the disappointment of finding her aunt away from the boardinghouse. Lost in her reveries, Vesper failed to notice the perturbed expression on the face of Belinda, the chocolate-skinned downstairs maid who greeted her in the foyer.

"Where you been, Miz Vesper?"

Belinda peered into Vesper's flushed face.

"Lawdy, you are lookin' pretty as a picture. Miz Belle, she been lookin' for you all mornin'. She be on de warpath!"

Vesper's heart sank. Her moment of transport had been all too short.

"She's waitin' fo' you out on de verandah, chile."

With heavy steps, Vesper apprehensively approached the verandah, where she could see her stepmother reclining on a white wicker lounge, being fanned by a ten-year-old slave. At thirty-eight, Belle Lawrence still retained her hothouse southern beauty, preserved by ceaseless attention to all the details of her toilette. Her pale pink afternoon dress was trimmed fetchingly with priceless ivory Honiton lace. The bodice of her redingote came to a sharp point, emphasizing her still-tiny waist. Turning her head with conscious grace, Belle gazed disapprovingly at Vesper's heavy gait and arched an eyebrow.

"Can't you pick up your feet, child? A lady should always appear graceful . . . even if she isn't."

Belle brushed her lily-white brow with limp fingers. "You're making my head ache."

Though it seemed like a simple request, Vesper immediately felt clumsy and tongue-tied.

"Your father doesn't know yet that you've been away all morning. I wouldn't want him to be disappointed in you again. But you sorely tempt me, Vesper."

Belle sat upright and fixed her drooping stepdaughter with an uncompromising stare.

"You've deliberately disobeyed me," she said harshly. "Didn't I expressly forbid you to see Lucinda Moore? She encourages what I can only call your unattractive bookishness." In a lighter, more melodic voice, she added, "Young ladies should be lighthearted as flowers, bringing the breath of spring into the arduous lives of their menfolk."

Vesper had been through many scenes like this one with her impossible stepmother. There was no way to win. Any objections Vesper made were batted down with an avalanche of mock tears and thinly disguised insults. Vesper tried to distance herself, but at times Belle's barbs found their target.

"Aunt Lucinda is all I have left of my mother," Vesper said in a strangled voice.

Falling back into the cushions of her chaise longue, Belle dramatically covered her heart with one hand. With practiced tears, she cried, "Child, you cut me to the quick! I have been your mother for fifteen years, and, believe me, it has been a thankless task."

Not missing a beat, Belle turned to little Marcellus, who, wide-eyed, was still plying the ostrich-feather fan, and ordered him to fetch her a glass of freshly made lemonade. As soon as he was gone, Belle motioned for Vesper to come closer.

"Vesper, honey, you exhaust me. I wish you wouldn't be so provoking . . . especially when I have such thrillin' news to tell you!"

She paused for effect.

"Fan me awhile, honey. I declare, it's positively hot out here today."

Belle flashed her famous smile. With a sinking feeling, Vesper picked up the discarded fan and mechanically waved it above Belle's lavish coiffure.

Belle said breathily, "Your father and I have found a wonderful husband for you, a man of high repute and fabulous wealth who can give you a palace for your home, a mature man who understands young women . . . and he has great influence in the capital."

Vesper was stunned. It was only last night she had given in to her father's demands. How could he have found a husband in less than one day? She fumed inside, realizing he must have had the man already waiting.

"I was so amazed when Augustus offered for your hand!" said Belle.

"Augustus?" Vesper blurted out. "Augustus Bledsoe?"

Belle nodded. "I had the very same reaction when your father told me. After all, he's been your father's best friend for over twenty years, ever since the senator began his career in politics."

A sharp image broke into Vesper's mind of the proud young frontiersman who had saved her that morning. She was so shaken that she voiced her objections about Bledsoe out loud, forgetting that Belle would not be sympathetic.

"But he's thirty years older than I, and fat and bald. We have nothing in common."

Though Augustus Bledsoe had always treated her in a jocular, avuncular fashion, she had never overcome her instinctive dislike for him. How could she explain this feeling to Belle? Over the years, Vesper had remained polite to him for her father's sake. But to marry him? To bear his children? Vesper threw down the fan.

Belle, of course, swept past Vesper's objections as trivial.

"All young girls . . . and spinsters . . . are shy of marriage, honey. When I married my first husband, I was as innocent as a newborn lamb. But I learned, and you will too. Your husband will teach you. Now you run along, and dress yourself as pretty as you can for tonight. Your fiancé is coming to dinner, and your father has invited that backwoods hero everybody's talking about."

Belle, having done her duty, turned back to little Marcellus, who was waiting patiently with her cool drink. Vesper climbed the central staircase in a panic. How could she marry Augustus Bledsoe, with his subtle aura of unscrupulousness? Could she overcome her distaste and spend the rest of her life with the fleshy, balding financier?

Once in her bedchamber, Vesper went to her mirror and peered at the pinched, wan face before her. If only Aunt Lucinda had not been called away. Perhaps together they could have found an alternative. Now Vesper's betrothal would be made public. Father had tricked her once again, she thought bitterly. She supposed it was this skill that made him a successful politician, the ability to move people around like chessmen on a game board. After all these years, she should have known better than to trust him.

Disgusted, Vesper grimaced at her image in the mirror, thinking how unattractive she was. Why would even Bledsoe want her? She leaned her elbows against the windowsill and looked out between polished chintz curtains. If she had to marry, could it not be someone she at least respected and could learn to love?

As she watched the tops of the elms toss golden in the late-afternoon sun, her thoughts drifted to the brave giant with his leaf-green eyes. He had looked so strangely at her, with a call in his eyes she did not know how to answer. Vesper could not see herself at this moment. If she had, she would have seen a face of beauty, eyes sparkling like dew-drenched violets, her pink mouth curved in a dreamy, delighted smile. Vesper was aglow with the fresh bloom of awakened desire, hoping, dreaming, that she would see him again.

# Chapter Three

THAT EVENING IN HIS STUDY, SENATOR FREDERICK Lawrence entertained Augustus Bledsoe with a drink before dinner. Bledsoe raised his crystal glass of Spanish Madeira to the light as he savored the distinctive dry flavor of the expensive wine. Unconsciously, his large fleshy fingers tugged at an intricately brocaded waistcoat, trying to cover the roll of fat spreading at his middle.

He looked as trim as the most experienced tailor in Washington could make him appear. Years of overindulging at the table had begun to turn his husky, bearlike body soft. Still, Bledsoe exuded an intimidating air of power. He was known in Washington society as a ruthless financier.

The senator filled his own glass and joined his oldest friend in a toast.

"To Cord Travers," proclaimed Lawrence, "who

came to Washington to leave his mark but will leave only with empty promises. May all our challenges be so easily overcome."

They clinked glasses, the crystal echoing in a clear, high-pitched tone.

Lawrence added with another flourish, ". . . and to my future son-in-law and my grandchildren-to-be!"

Bledsoe acknowledged Lawrence's remarks with an approving nod. They downed the liquor quickly, the heavier man snaking his tongue to the corner of his mouth to catch the last drop.

"An excellent vintage, Freddy."

"I save the best for you, my dear Augustus . . . like Vesper, eh?"

As Bledsoe nodded condescendingly, he thought smugly that his association with Lawrence was becoming more and more profitable. Not only had this relationship provided him with direct influence in Congress, but it had also given him respectability in the community, as well as an entry into the highest Washington circles. In exchange for all these dividends, marriage to a shy, gawky spinster could be tolerated. After all, there were plenty of women who would be eager to satisfy his needs. He could afford to humor Lawrence.

"I've watched Vesper grow into a long-stemmed rose, Freddy, and now she's ripe for the plucking. She'll make me fine sons, old friend."

The two men, arm in arm, ambled over to the senator's marble-topped desk, where the tall, slender Lawrence slid into his wingback chair and Augustus sank onto the wide settee.

"But enough of family matters, Augustus. I still don't see why you wanted me to invite that uncouth backwoodsman to dinner, even if he breeds the best racehorses in the country."

Freddy was so thickheaded, Bledsoe thought. He had to be led to every conclusion.

"When Travers leaves the capital, he should be completely deluded into believing that the government will fully support the Santee Sioux in their territorial claims. He should be expecting federal soldiers to appear and guard the Indians' boundaries. In the meantime the Sioux borders will stay unguarded and our new settlers will stake their own claims. We will tell Major Stone at the fort to honor them. By the time Travers realizes he's been used, Americans will own the land and the savages will be run off."

Lawrence interrupted pettishly.

"I understand the plan, Augustus. But why does the man have to eat at my table?"

Bledsoe stifled a sigh.

"Because, my dear Freddy, it is easier to convince a man of your sincerity when he has dined with your family in your own home."

Lawrence brightened visibly.

"Ah. So charm's the trick. Well, Roxanne will cooperate. She's done it before. He won't even know what hit him."

"Good. That's just what we need. And as for that officer from Fort Snelling, he's also been cooperative. He'd make a useful territorial governor."

"You're right. Without Stone's warning that Travers was on his way, we'd have been caught with our britches down."

Lawrence chuckled.

"Actually, I'm surprised how easy it's been to control Travers. By all accounts, he's supposed to be tough as nails. It would take a slick talker to get Indians to round up wild mustangs and breed them to good American racing stock. He's made a bundle with his Travers Speed Horse. I own a couple of them myself."

"Maybe he's only clever enough to swindle redskins," Bledsoe sneered. "Give them a bottle of firewater and—"

There was a harried knock at the door.

"What is it?" the senator called.

"Excuse me, Massah Lawrence," said Hadrian, the Negro butler, his brow furrowed in worry. "Your dinner guest has arrived, suh, but he's brought along an Injun with him. What should I do, suh?"

Bledsoe and Lawrence exchanged frowns.

"You'll have to handle this carefully, Freddy," Augustus warned. "We're playing for high stakes."

The men proceeded to the foyer, where Cord Travers stood, dressed in formal evening wear and looking formidable. Next to him was Running Wolf, who had honored the occasion by coming in the full regalia of a tribal chief. The senator put on his old campaigner's grin and crossed the polished floor, his arm outstretched. He shook Travers' huge hand heartily.

"It's a pleasure to have you in my home, Mr. Travers. My family has been looking forward to meeting the man behind the legends. Roxanne, my younger daughter, has talked of nothing else."

He paused, glancing at Running Wolf.

"Our friend here will be more comfortable in the kitchen, I'm sure. Hadrian will have the cook prepare a plate for him by the fire."

He took Cord's arm as if to lead him away. "You've met my associate, Mr. Augustus Bledsoe, before. Let's go into the parlor and meet the ladies."

But Cord was immovable. His eyes had hardened to shards of green ice. Bitterness welled in his throat at this insult to his foster father.

"Running Wolf is welcome in the Senate chambers when a treaty needs signing," said Cord in a cold, rigid voice, "but he's not welcome at your table. I had hoped for more from you, Senator."

Bledsoe shot a warning look at Lawrence, who realized their whole scheme was at stake.

"Young man, why do you want to put your adopted father through an uncomfortable evening, sitting on a chair, struggling with silverware . . ."

He stopped as he accurately read the implacable anger in Travers' eyes. Cord's voice became dangerously quiet.

"The difference between a civilized man and a savage, sir, has nothing to do with table manners. It has to do with how he treats his fellows."

Lawrence bristled at the implied insult, and his voice became louder.

"Don't presume to dictate to me, sir. I will decide who is welcome in my own house."

His shrill words had penetrated the walls of the parlor and brought out Belle and Vesper. Vesper saw before her the man who had been haunting her thoughts all afternoon. Her cheeks felt suddenly warm as her heart began to pound and her breathing quickened. The man looked as natural in his elegant evening clothes as he had in buckskins. Tense, masterful, and dominant, he towered over them all in angry authority.

His blazing green eyes swept over the newcomers and returned with a shock to Vesper. Who was she, Cord wondered, and what was she doing here? He could not believe she was Lawrence's daughter, the child of a man so blatantly prejudiced. His jaw tightened as he turned back to the senator, who was still infuriated.

Lawrence expostulated, "Indians must learn where they belong in the white man's world."

Belle's dulcet tones interrupted the debate.

"Gentlemen, please! This is all so distressin'. Surely you can settle your business without shouting."

She approached Cord, cooing, "Mr. Travers, I have so looked forward to makin' your acquaintance. My friends will be positively green with envy."

Insinuating her arm through his, she added, "We have such a lovely dinner planned . . ." She gestured gracefully toward the dining room and took a step toward it. Gently Cord disengaged her arm and stood firm.

"Forgive me, ma'am, but I will not eat in a house where the chief of the Santee Sioux is sent to eat in the kitchen like a dog."

"Father," Vesper interrupted, gesturing toward Running Wolf, "only last week you entertained Monsieur LeFèvre, the French envoy. Surely this gentleman deserves equal courtesy as an ambassador from an Indian nation."

Her father began to sputter, glaring at her. Cord was impressed once again by this statuesque beauty. She had stood up to her small-minded father, and her respect for his foster father warmed him. But Cord was taken aback by the familiar way Bledsoe addressed her.

"Vesper dear, don't contradict your father. You know nothing of the situation."

The senator recovered and gruffly directed his butler to lead Running Wolf to the kitchen. Cord Travers squared his shoulders and spoke respectfully to his foster father.

"We are not welcome in the senator's house. Let us go."

Running Wolf's low, dignified voice stopped him.

"My son, the well-being of our people is more important than a single moment of pride. The words of other men do not trouble one who walks his own path."

The innate nobility of the chief impressed even those of the party who believed Indians were inferior. Before anyone could stop him, Running Wolf was gone and the front door closed. An embarrassed silence hung over the group.

Tossing her curls, Belle directed Hadrian to see that Miss Roxanne and Master Taylor joined them at table. Affecting a light tone, she led the somber group to dinner.

Over rich steaming bowls of turtle soup, Senator Lawrence addressed Travers with false heartiness. "What do you think of our fair city? She's growing day and night."

Cord glanced down at him and answered coldly and politely. Belle hurried to help her husband placate this difficult guest.

"Surely our ladies have caught your eye. From all I hear, you've certainly caught theirs."

Another dissatisfyingly brief reply followed her cajoling remark. And no wonder, Vesper thought. Did they expect Mr. Travers to forget their insulting behavior only moments before? She looked at him with warm sympathy in her blue-violet eyes and found him gazing at her.

Cord Travers was having a difficult time keeping his eyes from Vesper. Even in her simple white gown, she outshone the other women at the table. It was with an effort that he forced his attention back to the stilted conversation. Vesper's younger sister, girlish, plump, and fussily dressed, was trying to flirt with him.

"You surprised me tonight, Mistah Travers. Here I was looking forward to seein' you in your animal skins, and instead you look just like everyone else."

Roxanne fluttered her gold lashes in false alarm at her own seeming audacity and hastened to add, "Well, not quite everyone else. I hear tell you're the tallest man in Washington these days."

Her flirtatious gibes, so effective with most young men, were having no effect on this taciturn giant. She redoubled her efforts.

"Why, you're the most famous trapper of them all! How ever did you learn all those huntin' tricks so fast? I heard you made five thousand dollars in one season! And you were only fifteen when you started, weren't you? But what I'll never understand is how a wealthy young gentleman from a southern plantation could bring himself to spend whole months at a time doin' that nasty, dirty work. Why, the very thought of it makes me feel faint."

Deliberately Roxanne paused as if collecting herself and stared beseechingly into Cord's eyes. Cord reminded himself of Running Wolf's message. He must not make an enemy of this senator who could so easily turn against the Sioux. He would maintain a facade of politeness, even to this spoiled little flirt.

"Miss Roxanne, no one would expect a young woman like you to stand up to the wilderness."

Vesper had kept her eyes studiously on her plate of roast pheasant and parsleyed potatoes. Hearing the veiled irritation in Travers' voice, she glanced at him momentarily and caught him staring at her. Confused by the consuming intensity of his forest-green gaze, she lowered her eyes.

Roxanne was frustrated. All her hard work had not even earned a perfunctory compliment. She intercepted an encouraging wink from her stepfather and renewed her pursuit.

"And that grizzly bear . . . why, he must have been even bigger than you."

She turned to her brother Taylor with artificial enthusiasm.

"Have you heard how Mr. Travers here rescued a redskin from the arms of death? Well, it seems there was a young brave out huntin' and his horse got spooked by a huge grizzly bear. The boy's leg was broken, and the bear would have crushed that poor Indian to death had not this gentleman come upon the scene and shot that big ol' grizzly bear right between the eyes."

Vesper stared at Cord Travers, her heart beating faster as she pictured him pitting himself against the marauding bear. She colored at the thought of her own rescue just that morning. Her half sister was oblivious to the current coursing between Vesper and Cord. The vivacious blonde laid an admiring hand on his broad forearm.

"Now tell me the truth. Weren't you even the least bit frightened when you saw that killer bear?"

"Of course I was," he answered coolly. "Everyone is afraid of danger. But fear can make you strong when you use it to your advantage."

Cord's words gave Vesper new strength. Perhaps her worst fears of being married off to the heavy man at her side would not be realized. If she could use her fears to strengthen her resolve . . . Her fine-boned body quivered with new life, and impulsively she looked directly at Cord. On her face were written her exhilaration and the inexorable bond she felt with this man who lived by his own code.

Cord was scorched by her gaze of passionate admiration. He knew her display of feeling was innocent. She could not know that she was offering herself to him. But he knew it, and it made him want to oust everyone else from the room and go to her.

Roxanne was furious at Cord's lack of attention. He was staring hungrily at mousy old Vesper, who, surprisingly flushed, was looking as if she had been struck by lightning. If only he would look at her like that, Roxanne thought, like a panther poised to spring. Desperately she searched for a way to regain his interest, and playfully slapped his brawny shoulder with her napkin.

"And the strangest thing of all I've heard about you, Mr. Travers, is when that ol' Indian chief tried to adopt you after you saved his boy's life. Now, I just didn't believe it when I heard that you let them cut into you and mix your blood with theirs."

Cord eyed her with thinly disguised distaste. Blithely Roxanne continued.

"Maybe that ol' Indian thought he'd turn white if he took you into his family."

Vesper winced as Cord's face hardened. She knew the hurt hidden behind his icy words.

"My family matters are private, Miss Lawrence. I'd rather not discuss them."

Petulantly Roxanne bit her lip. She had failed her stepfather and, even worse, had failed to win the attentions of this mysterious, fascinating man.

Vesper yearned to talk to Cord, to reassure him that she, at least, admired and respected Running Wolf. But she had acted too conspicuously already. She felt the raking eyes of Augustus Bledsoe on her.

Bledsoe was pleasantly surprised. The charmless spinster had some spirit after all. She actually had a promising bosom, now that she was sitting up straight. Her skin glowed, as if it would be fine to the touch. The life in those big violet eyes would be fun to tame, he thought. His tongue licked at the corner of his mouth as he imagined her kneeling naked before him, pleasuring him. The fat man's attention was torn from his imaginings by Belle's calling for dessert, a rich praline pie topped with fresh cream. Then, with her charming hostess smile, she announced, "Your attention, everyone. Augustus has a special toast to propose."

With more intensity than he had expected to feel, Bledsoe stood, raised his wineglass, and saluted Vesper.

"To Vesper, my lovely bride-to-be, I declare my lifelong devotion and esteem. Ladies and gentlemen, I give you the future Mrs. Augustus Bledsoe."

Vesper's whole body sagged. Her face turned white. Now she was trapped. Bledsoe, who had only faintly repelled her before, now disgusted her with his heavy, aging body. Her eyes scanned her intended, taking in the beads of sweat on his balding pate and his fleshy fingers clutching the delicate stem of his wineglass. He was looking at her gloatingly, as if he already owned her. Vesper shuddered. Instinctively her eyes sought Cord, but with a sense of shame she looked down quickly.

Cord was stunned by the announcement and the change in Vesper. From a glowing, vibrant girl on the verge of womanhood she suddenly reminded him of a fragile doe, fleeing helplessly from the hunter. The leering face of her fiancé infuriated him. It was the finishing touch to a disastrous evening. To the consternation of his host and hostess, he bade the company an abrupt farewell and departed.

As the cool wind of the Washington spring evening hit his face, he was amazed at his inner turmoil. How could he let the daughter of an unprincipled Washington swindler get under his skin? Yet her imploring eyes haunted him. Part of Cord wanted only to shield Vesper from anything or anyone threatening to harm her, while another part hungered to master her, to make her all his. With her perfection emblazoned in his memory, he made his way back to his hotel.

Back at the dinner table, the remaining members of the party exchanged looks of surprise.

"That's one fish you haven't caught yet, Freddy," Bledsoe said dryly as they all heard the front door slam.

Vesper intercepted an apologetic grimace from her father to the man he insisted she marry.

"Don't worry," her father answered. "Another visit to my Senate chambers and a promise of more beads and firewater should reel him in. I'll see to it first thing in the morning."

No one but Vesper seemed to understand or care about the veiled conversation between the two men. Vesper knew immediately that they were planning to dupe Cord Travers, and she found herself caring deeply what happened to him and his cause. For the rest of the evening, Vesper was silent, and, as usual, no one noticed.

After the men had finished their port and rejoined the ladies, Bledsoe invited Vesper to stroll with him on the verandah. She gave him a reluctant smile.

"Oh, Mr. Bledsoe," Vesper began, hoping to avoid being alone with him, "my head is pounding. Perhaps another—"

Belle interrupted sharply.

"The fresh air will do your little head a world of good, honey. It's time your fiancé and you got to know each other better. Run along, now."

Belle pushed Vesper at Bledsoe, who willingly took her arm and led her away.

"You must learn to call me Augustus," he murmured in her ear, tightening his grip on her bare arm. "After all," he said as his wide thumb rubbed up and down her arm, "we will soon be man and wife."

31

He released her arm for a moment to pull out of his pocket a velvet box. As he handed it to her his voice deepened.

"A reminder of the night when you will belong to me."

Unwillingly Vesper opened the box and removed a huge gold ring. Clawlike settings held a bulky, square-cut emerald of five carats which was surrounded by four single-carat diamonds. The overall effect was gaudy, ostentatious to the extreme. It was the sort of jewel a pirate might present to his favorite concubine.

Impatient with her hesitation, Augustus slid the ring onto her finger, where it hung heavily. He raised her hand to the moonlight, turning it so that the facets gleamed. He seemed to revel in his own generosity. To Vesper, the chunky ring weighing down her hand made her feel as if the marital yoke were already laid across her shoulders.

Vesper's feeling of being trapped increased as her bulky fiancé directed her to the darkened far end of the verandah. He pulled her tightly against him, and his protruding belly knocked the breath from her. His thick lips sucked at her innocent mouth, and he forced his swollen tongue between her lips, almost gagging her. Her fists pounded ineffectually on his shoulders. But he did not release her until he was satisfied.

Still holding her in a viselike grip, Augustus Bledsoe threw back his head and laughed. Roughly he nuzzled her neck and said, "You don't know anything about what I will take from you, do you, innocent virgin? I will have to teach you how to pleasure me."

His little pale blue eyes gleamed with feral hunger. Vesper shrank back until she felt the cold iron of the railing dig into her back. She was nauseated by his

winy breath, his cruel, bruising kiss, his insinuating
fingers kneading her exposed back and shoulders, his
corpulent flesh pressing against her. She forced
herself to reply.

"Mr. Bl— Augustus . . . Please release me, sir.
We are in my father's house and we are not yet
married."

"Your father has already given you to me, foolish
girl. I will begin your education now."

He grabbed her wrist and pulled her hand toward
him.

"Your first lesson is to learn where a man's power
comes from."

He brought her unwilling fingers to his groin and
pressed them against the bulge swelling within his
trousers. With a stifled cry, Vesper wrenched herself
from his grasp and fled down the dark verandah into
the parlor and past the surprised faces of her family.
She rushed up the stairs, sickened by Bledsoe's lewd
suggestions and coarse actions.

She could hear his unctuous voice reassuring her
family that young brides are often skittish. Vesper
slammed her bedroom door to shut out their companionable laughter and threw herself on her bed,
weeping bitterly. Never had she felt so alone.

# Chapter Four

VESPER COULD NOT SLEEP. PERHAPS IT WAS THE SPRING storm raging outside her window. She tossed and turned, throwing off the bedclothes, untwisting her rumpled lawn nightgown. Images hurtled through her mind, keeping her body tense and awake. She pictured the magnificent male presence of Cord Travers, valiantly shielding a fallen Indian boy from a marauding grizzly bear and fearlessly shielding Vesper herself from a raging whip. She remembered his resolute stand against her father's insulting prejudice toward Running Wolf.

She had not been able to keep her eyes from Cord all evening. And then, when his eyes had caught hers . . . Vesper's heart began to pound as she relived the moment when time seemed to stand still, when their eyes locked. She could not tear away from his burning, magnetic stare.

If they only had been alone, she knew, he would have kissed her. What would it have been like to feel his firm, finely etched lips against hers? Vesper blushed furiously at her own boldness. A shiver ran down the length of her taut body, and she pulled the comforter up to her throat.

She had received a kiss that evening, she recalled unwillingly. The unbearable moment when Augustus had forced his attentions on her loomed unwelcome in her mind. She refused to imagine what marriage to him would mean. Belle must be wrong, because Vesper knew she could never learn to love this offensive man. She was not even sure she could learn to endure him.

Restless, Vesper heaved the coverlet to the floor. She wondered what tied her father to Augustus Bledsoe. She supposed it was their mutual love of power. They regarded other people as commodities to be used with no thought of honor. How many naive idealists, and even seasoned politicians, had fallen prey to her father's and Bledsoe's wheelings and dealings?

Vesper sat bolt upright in bed, clutching her pillow to her. They would not use Cord as they had so often used others. She herself would see to it. During a lull in the storm, a whisper of birdsong announced that dawn had arrived. Determined though weary from her sleepless night, Vesper went to her washstand and splashed water on her face from a flowered porcelain bowl. In the mirror above, she saw shadows under her eyes.

She would go to Cord Travers at his hotel and warn him of her father's intentions. How she looked did not matter, she insisted to herself as she put on a simple dark green gown and pulled her hooded cloak around her. But she felt for the first time a feminine twinge of vanity and, just for a moment, wished for some of Roxanne's allure.

By the time Vesper reached Cord Travers' hotel, she was soaked to the skin. Sending a clerk to fetch Mr. Travers, Vesper stood by the massive stone fireplace, her wet cloak steaming in the heat. When she held her hands out to the fire, she saw them shaking. What would he think of her, coming at dawn to his hotel? She started at the sound of her name.

"Miss Lawrence?" rumbled a dark-timbred voice.

She whirled. It was he, looming over her. His voice sent tremors through Vesper.

"Are you in trouble? Has something happened?"

"N-no. I had to come. It's about my father. I must see you alone."

She watched his face tighten. She thought he was angry, and she could not blame him for despising her whole family after the travesty of last night's dinner party.

"Are you willing to risk your reputation? You'll be alone with me in my rooms. Running Wolf is not here either, to protect the honorable Lawrence name."

His voice was harsh and unwelcoming. The air between them was charged with tension. She had not expected that he would be cold to her, and her resolve wavered.

"I thought I . . ."

She swallowed nervously as his eyes swept over her wet, disheveled form in one assessing glance. She pulled at the skirt clinging to her legs.

"What do you really want, Miss Lawrence?"

He stepped closer to her, pinning her with his emerald-green eyes. With one finger he lifted a wet curl from her temple and smoothed it back. Vesper forced herself to look away from his beckoning stare and summoned up her determination.

"Some things are more important than social reputation, Mr. Travers," she managed to say in a voice that was almost firm. "If we can speak in your rooms, sir . . ."

She gestured toward the stairs. Cord was intrigued by her persistence. As he led her up the stairs he struggled to disguise his strong desire for her, treating her gruffly instead. In his sitting room, Cord offered Vesper a seat on a plush burgundy velvet sofa and stationed himself some distance from her next to the crackling fireplace.

"Well, Miss Lawrence?" he growled, folding his arms across his massive chest.

Unseen in a fold of her skirt, Vesper's hands clenched. Haltingly she began.

"You see, ever since my father became chairman of the Senate Bureau of Indian Affairs, he has often made promises to Indians that he never meant to keep."

She went on to report the conversation she had overheard after Cord had left the dinner table.

"But there is one politician, Senator Dennison, who can be trusted to give you a fair hearing." She paused and murmured, "You and your foster father deserve at least that much."

As Vesper looked up into his eyes Cord was hard-pressed to keep his growing desire for this purple-eyed enchantress concealed. Her every word confirmed his impression that here was a woman who shared his innermost beliefs. Her courage in coming alone to him to expose her own father's deceptions reached deep inside him. She was like a fresh breeze blowing through the stale prejudices so common in her world.

Her whole body trembled with sincerity. The lavender shadows under her eyes only accentuated the powerful appeal of her exquisite face. He found himself staring at her perfect pear-shaped breasts, their nipples clearly outlined by her damp bodice.

Cord heard the tears in Vesper's voice as she said, "I hope you don't think ill of me for revealing my father's secrets."

Cord crossed the room and gently cupped her pearly cheek in his hand for a moment. In a voice warmer than he had intended, he reassured her.

"I will see Dennison tomorrow, and for that I thank you. As for your father, I already knew. Running Wolf and I have met many men like him, and his words did not fool us. But you fooled me. I never expected to find a gallant spirit like yours."

The touch of his hand on her cheek had sent a streak of excitement tingling through her, and his admiring words warmed her like the glowing summer sun. Vesper smiled dazzlingly up into his face. The invitation in her smile drew him to her. Against his better judgment, he sat down at her side.

Vesper shyly murmured, "I've admired you, too, Mr. Travers."

She paused, and their eyes exchanged wordless messages.

Hurriedly she added, "I never even thanked you for rescuing me from that slave driver."

Cord stared into space.

"When I saw you standing up to that worthless scum, it brought back to me the memory of a thirteen-year-old boy who was made to watch a slave his own age take one hundred lashes . . ."

Instinctively Vesper knew he was the youth in the story.

"And what did you do?" she prompted softly.

"I stood between the overseer and poor young

Jonah to stop the whipping. My father locked me in my room and had me fed stale bread and water for a week."

Vesper touched his buckskin sleeve sympathetically. Her eyes were wide.

"Is that when you left your father's plantation?"

"My father and I fought constantly for the next two years. He wanted me to learn to run the plantation his way. But I couldn't. All I saw was that white men wear as many chains as black men do. I was never free to act as I believed, only as I was expected to. I struck out on my own, looking for a place where a man could live by his own rules."

Cord's words sent a thrill of freedom coursing through Vesper's veins. It was as if he were describing her own life. She knew those chains all too well, the ones that now bound her to Augustus Bledsoe.

Quietly she asked, "And did you find that place?"

"When I am in the Indian Woods, I can breathe free."

She saw a muscle in his jaw contract.

"But whenever I come east, I feel myself tighten. I've been angry ever since I came to Washington. . . ."

Cord's eyes swept over her and his face softened.

". . . though I'm not angry now."

He tilted her head back so that she was forced to look directly into his leaf-green eyes.

"You are so beautiful."

Vesper was overwhelmed by the feelings he evoked in her. A sense of joy filled her. He found her beautiful! She pleased him! Her body ached with a longing to be held in Cord's arms. A violent shiver shook her. Cord looked down at her quivering form with consternation.

"You're cold . . . and shivering. You've got to get out of those wet clothes."

He encircled her shoulders firmly with his arm and led her toward the roaring fire.

"Take off your cloak," he directed. "I'll get a robe to warm you."

He disappeared into the bedroom, and reluctantly, knowing he was right, Vesper removed the dripping cape. Though the heat from the fire spread through her body, her teeth chattered uncontrollably. Why couldn't she stop shaking? she asked herself nervously. And then he was there, holding a huge buffalo robe out to her.

"You'll have to take off the rest, too," he insisted gruffly.

He forced his eyes from her quivering body, whose superb lines were almost completely revealed by the sodden dress. Clutching the robe to her bosom as if to shield herself from his penetrating eyes, Vesper stared at him, openmouthed. Did he really expect her to take off all her clothes as he watched?

"I'll wait in the other room," he said in a strangled voice, forcing away the image of Vesper naked in the firelight.

In the bedroom, he closed the door and paced tensely, his own hungry emotions seething. He must not touch her, he warned himself. She was untried, innocent, and he would be gone from her life in a few weeks. Cord fought his clamoring instinct to claim her, to make her his woman.

Running Wolf's words haunted him: "She is the woman whose spirit is equal to yours." Grimly he fought a battle harder than any he had ever waged. Thinking himself under control once again, Cord opened the door and was surprised at the force with which it slammed against the wall.

Vesper started and stared at his glowering form as she gripped the hairy folds of the buffalo robe around her bare body. The sight of her took his breath away. Her magnificent face was flushed and her long silken locks tousled wildly about her shoulders. Again their glances locked. In her eyes, amethyst pools he was drowning in, he read the beguiling combination of desire and bewilderment. Cord's heart pounded like a hammer.

In a rasping voice he said, "I can't fight both of us."

He went to her and she came willingly into his arms. His mouth rained fevered kisses across her face and down the regal column of her pulsing neck. All of Vesper's senses came awake. She was keenly aware of the extraordinary power of his arms, pressing her to him.

She drank in the heady male scent of him, the blend of sun-drenched woods and warm leather that was uniquely his. The caress of his lips as they ranged over her far exceeded Vesper's tumbled imaginings of the night before. Every brush of his mouth added to the flames that flickered to life within her. With a groan, he gripped the shining lengths of her hair in his hand and pulled her head back. His mouth covered hers with searing intensity, branding her his forever.

Any hesitation or fear Vesper might have had was swept away by the utter rightness of his demand. Instinctively her fingers opened and let loose the buffalo robe at her neck. Her arms stole up his broad back, feeling his supple muscles rippling under the warm leather of his deerskin shirt. When her hands reached his neck, her soft fingers found the crisp tendrils of his bronze hair and she could not resist entwining her hands through them.

Aroused by her response, his kisses changed. At first subjugating, they became teasing, erotic. His lips nibbled softly at hers, pulling, nipping, tasting.

41

His tongue licked into the corners of her mouth and traced the line between her lips.

Vesper was dizzied by his deliberate courting of her senses. Her knees buckled and she clung to him as the single solid element in her whirling world. Her lips parted before his expert caresses and his tongue surged into her mouth. She could not stop his sensuous plundering of her secrets. His tongue stroked wholly new sensations from her. She never wanted them to end.

But now his probing tongue moved on, tracing a line along her jaw and then down her neck. The teasing of his tongue against her flushed skin was excruciatingly evocative, causing her to arch instinctively against him. Pressed against his loins, she was engulfed by the heat of his desire.

Cord needed no further encouragement. He leaned her back far enough to allow the hide robe to fall. Sliding his hot fingers beneath the robe at her shoulders, Cord eased it down to her slender waist. Her proud breasts quivered under the hungry gaze of his eyes. Modestly her hands flew to cover her bare bosom, but he caught her fine-boned wrists in his hands and held them away.

"Don't hide yourself from me," he growled. "You are exquisite."

Tenderly his hands cupped the perfect globes of her breasts, his thumbs brushing over her already engorged nipples, sending frighteningly delicious spasms through her. Vesper moaned. When he lowered his mouth to worship one globe and then the other with tongue and teeth, she was overcome by dazzling waves of sensation. Vesper's breath came raggedly.

"I can't breathe," she implored, in the same instant wanting and not wanting him to stop.

His burning mouth traced a path back up to her lips.

"You do the same to me, my darling," he muttered against her mouth. "Let me show you."

Stepping back slightly, he took up her hand and held it against his racing heart. The thudding of his heart against her heated fingers stirred her profoundly. But Cord caught sight of a gaudy ring on Vesper's left fourth finger. With a jolt, he realized he was taking another man's woman. In a single lithe movement, he retrieved the buffalo robe which had fallen to the floor and wrapped it back around Vesper.

Her eyes were dazed pools of wonderment when Cord said, "Forgive me, Vesper. You belong to someone else and are too innocent to know where I was leading you."

He forced his hands away from her shoulders.

"I should be horsewhipped."

He stood before her, dejected. Shame coursed through Vesper as she gripped the robe to her. Her voice was low with bewildered pain.

"What you must think of me! I've never . . ."

Her voice broke.

"I'm so ashamed."

Cord moved to hold her comfortingly. He stopped, forcing himself to keep his distance.

"How could you know?" he began, his voice tender. "How would you know what power you wield over men?"

He stared at her in rapt longing.

"We will never meet again. I could not trust myself."

Inside Vesper, a sobbing voice was pleading, don't go! But her shame at betraying her fiancé, even one she neither loved nor wanted, silenced her.

Mutely she watched Cord Travers walk out of his hotel room and out of her life. Lifelessly she began to pull on her damp chemise and pantaloons. She felt drained, as if Cord had taken her spirit with him. How could she have yielded to Cord Travers what, by rights, belonged to Augustus Bledsoe?

When Cord had kissed her, her body had responded with a will of its own, needing to move closer and closer to him, aching to be completely one with him in some way. Again her body flushed at the very thought of him. Flustered, she hurriedly put on the rest of her clothes. Vesper tried to ignore the tingling sensations each brush of the dress brought to her excited skin. But she could not. She had been awakened to the physical experiences of life and she began to yearn for all the challenges that a woman must face.

Vesper walked along the sprawling city avenues toward her father's fashionable house. She barely noticed the slender beech and dogwood saplings that lined the streets. Ordinarily she would have been delighted to see the fresh new leaves and pale white petals, but her thoughts were on her own burgeoning womanhood.

She was not sure what lovemaking with a husband would be like, but she imagined an intense sharing followed by utter serenity in his arms. There would be a child of their union, and she would nurse and protect the child. She would stand by her husband's side as they built their future together. They would watch their child grow. In her mind, Vesper saw a house solid and true, filled with love and laughter.

Unexpectedly, Vesper was jostled by a fat, balding tradesman setting up his stands of tin pots and pans. He snarled an apology, reminding her of Augustus Bledsoe. She quickly turned away, dismayed, realizing she was not imagining her fiancé as the husband in her vision. When she tried to place him there, her dream shattered. Shamefaced, she admitted to herself that her imagined husband resembled Cord Travers, whom she must forget.

Finally reaching her home, Vesper walked around to the back of the house and crossed the verandah to a set of French doors opening into the drawing room. If she could return to her bedroom unnoticed, no one would know she had made an improper visit to a bachelor's quarters.

Opening the French doors as quietly as she could, Vesper stared down at the vulgar cluster of jewels on her finger that symbolized her bond to Bledsoe. A bulky form rose and confronted her. Vesper froze as her fiancé's furious voice broke the silence.

"Where have you been?" he bellowed. "I have a right to know."

"Augustus, what are you doing here?" Vesper whispered.

"I had planned to take my betrothed for a carriage ride before breakfast," he snapped. "But she, clearly, had other plans."

Bledsoe took a threatening step forward.

"I demand to know where you have been."

He looked like a furious boar to Vesper, who was surprised to find herself offended rather than frightened by his proprietary manner.

"I do not have to answer to you, sir," Vesper said coldly.

She tried to sweep by him, but he grabbed her arm and twisted it, snarling, "You're mine, and don't you forget it."

He dragged her down the central hallway and into her father's still-dark study.

"Maybe you need a lesson."

He forced his wet, rubbery mouth against hers. Vesper backed away until her body met the edge of the marble-topped desk. She tried to escape from him, but his corpulent thighs pinned her to the desk and he tore open her shrouding cloak to crush her full breasts in his hands. Paralyzed with pain, Vesper was forced to endure his bruising fingers.

"You may fight me now, but I'll soon have you begging for my favors. When our wedding night is over, I will be your master and own you body and soul."

His little pig eyes shone with an unholy light.

"I will ride you into submission, my virgin mare," he taunted her. "You will kiss the whip that licks your flesh."

Horrified, she watched as a jagged dueling scar along his cheekbone flared livid. For the first time, Vesper glimpsed the ruthless evil being behind Augustus Bledsoe's mask of civility. Revulsed, she tore herself from his grasp and ran to the door. Her amethyst eyes glared fury at him.

"You will not have me," she vowed. "I will not be shackled to a man such as you!"

Before he could take more than a step toward her, Vesper had torn his betrothal ring from her finger and hurled it at him. He watched, horrified, as five thousand dollars' worth of jewelry flew through the air, hit him on the chest, and bounced off to roll beneath the senator's huge desk. In an instant, he was on his hands and knees, searching frantically for the expensive piece. Momentarily freed by Bledsoe's greed, Vesper whirled through the doorway and rushed up the stairs to her room, vowing she would find a way, with Lucinda's help or on her own, to free herself from this impossible marriage.

# Chapter Five

"VESPER, HONEY, LET ME IN," CAME BELLE'S SUGARY
voice through the closed door of Vesper's bedroom.
"You've lain in bed for the longest time—six days
now—and your father is beginnin' to worry."

She listened expectantly, but there was only silence. Her patience was exhausted. Belle had had all
she could take of Vesper's spinsterish vapors.

"Vesper Lawrence! Open this door right now!"
she demanded, all honey gone. "Tonight is very
important for your father, and we must be by his
side at the White House. Besides," she cooed slyly,
"it's high time you were seen in public with your
fiancé."

Vesper, who had huddled miserably under the
bedclothes, trying to block out Belle's presence as
well as her words, paled at this latest pronounce-
ment. Since the ill-fated night of that unnerving

47

dinner party, followed by Augustus Bledsoe's disgusting overtures, Vesper had feigned illness just to avoid any further exchanges with the whole unconscionable lot of them—Bledsoe, Belle, Roxanne. And, in her own mind, she had felt ill, as if a pervasive virus had crept inside her, weighing her down so that her limbs felt heavy and useless, strangling her so that her brain seemed light and empty.

Now, as she listened to her stepmother retreating in a huff, she realized there was no serenity to be found in avoidance. Vesper would have to face them all. She thought wistfully of the indomitable frontiersman who had swept in and out of her life with such dazzling impact. She had seen the power of his stubborn resistance in fighting for the rights of all people, even honoring her own unwanted commitment to Bledsoe.

An angry, prideful blush spread across her wan cheeks. She would stand up to her father and tell him this marriage could not go forward. Then she would go to the President's ball a free woman. She threw the covers from the bed and got up to survey her wardrobe. As she moved across the floor, the door to her room suddenly swung open and Roxanne flounced in, a triumphant gleam in her small eyes.

"I knew you were only pretendin'. Just wait till I tell Mama. You'll pay this time, Vesper."

With newfound strength, Vesper coolly glanced at her short half sister and yawned.

"I've no time for your childish pranks, Roxanne. Go and fetch your mother back here. Tell her I need a new dress for tonight . . . oh, and one more thing."

Vesper paused before dismissing the blond younger girl.

"It's not ladylike to crouch in hallways and peek through people's keyholes," said Vesper in a voice icily self-possessed.

Roxanne, her mouth open in disbelief, found herself obeying. She backed out of the room and flew toward her mama's rooms. The unfamiliar melodic tinkle of Vesper's laughing followed her down the hall.

A perplexed Belle, for once silenced, listened to Vesper's demands for a dress worthy of the President's ball. Belle pounced on the opportunity to show off and called her seamstress to redesign one of Vesper's newer gowns. Vesper stood proud and still as a queen while Belle and the little black-skinned seamstress measured, pinned, and sewed one of her unadorned white gowns into a sumptuous creation of ribbons, roses, and ruffles. Four hours later, Belle threw back her hands and the seamstress plopped down onto a small mountain of dainty yardage.

"There!" Vesper's stepmother said with a flourish, pushing her own dangling curls back into place. "It's done, and it's beautiful. Now, don't ever tell me I never did anything for you . . . just look at yourself."

"Yes, missy," breathed the exhausted seamstress. "You be pretty as a picture."

Vesper turned slowly to face the full-length looking glass. She recognized her face with its huge amethyst eyes framed by ebony locks, but the body . . . and the dress . . . surely they belonged to someone else. Her reflection revealed a young woman of well-endowed proportions and regal carriage. Where her shoulders and arms had been demurely covered, now the pale skin of her elbows and forearms was bared, her upper arms swathed in a triple tier of fine Chantilly lace. The plain, rather severe neckline had been replaced by a gently flowing, off-the-shoulder décolletage which enhanced the natural pattern of the watered silk and displayed her deep cleavage. The bodice embraced her tightly, dipping to a sharp vee below her waist. A matching ruffle of lace followed the line of the décolletage, giving the dress an air of innocent grace.

With a fuller horsehair petticoat than before, the skirt belled out from the generous fullness of Vesper's hips. The seamstress had artfully added a deeply scalloped row of lace at the base of the gown, caught up at each rise by three roses fashioned out of pink, lavender, and violet satin ribbons. The same three hues in braided floss hung down alongside the delicate roses. With white kid boots, netted gloves, and ribbons and lace for her hair, Vesper seemed a vision, even to herself. She enjoyed the moment, noticing her startling womanliness for the first time.

She was keenly aware of the material clinging about her, hugging her, and a sensuous thrill rippled through her. For an instant she was reminded of the stimulating tingle of Cord Travers' buffalo robe as it had caressed her naked damp body only a week before.

Her conviction deepened at that moment. Perhaps she was not meant to be Cord's wife, but she'd have to be shackled and led to the altar in chains before she would give herself to Augustus Bledsoe . . . and now she was ready to tell her father so. She swept out of her bedroom with a dignity that Belle tried to ignore.

Vesper was sure she could convince her father to break her engagement to Augustus Bledsoe and knocked decisively on his study door.

"Yes?" he grumbled, his head bent over a sheaf of papers.

"Father, I must speak to you . . . about Aug—
Mr. Bledsoe."

The senator glanced up, noting with amazement
his daughter's high color first, then the luxuriant
white gown, finally her poised beauty. Ah, he
thought to himself, either Belle has finally made
good on her threats or the notion of marriage is
beginning to agree with Vesper.

Vesper stepped forward with authority.

"I can't . . . I won't marry him."

Freddy Lawrence frowned, arching an eyebrow,
and put down his pen.

"I don't have time for this girlish nonsense. Augustus Bledsoe is a fine, upstanding man who will do
a lot for you . . . and for me."

"But he . . . he makes me very uncomfortable,"
she stammered. "He doesn't suit me, Father."

Immediately she knew she had said the wrong
thing, for his eyes narrowed.

"How would you possibly know what suits you?"
he demanded hotly. "You wouldn't recognize a good
catch if he bit you!"

His bullying left her tongue-tied. She could only
repeat what she had already told Belle. When Lawrence ignored her, she realized she would have to
tell him about Bledsoe's vile sexual threats, regardless of the two men's long-standing friendship.

Finally Vesper blurted, "He told me he'd make
me his slave."

Her father scoffed and turned his attention to the
papers on his desk. Her eyes grew wide in desperation.

"He threatened to whip me."

Lawrence shot out of his seat.

"Are you trying to tell me there is something
wrong, something so despicable about your father's
closest associate, that you can blithely stand there

and defy my wishes? This is the mindless prattle of a fearful old maid."

"Please, Father, I beg of you, please release me from this engagement," Vesper cried piteously. "I promise I'll marry the first eligible young man who wants me."

But the senator was immovable.

"There will be no other man for you, Vesper. You will marry Augustus Bledsoe, and that is that. I'll brook no scandal. Is that understood?"

To her chagrin, he waved her away as an irritated schoolmarm might dismiss the class dunce.

At eight o'clock that evening, a shiny black carriage drawn by four matching horses pulled up before the Lawrence house. Belle and Roxanne eagerly stepped out toward the footman. They gathered up their gowns and cloaks so as to prevent the ever-present Washington mire from staining their finery. Belle carefully tossed her curls and looked behind her.

"Well, Vesper, are you coming?" she asked acidly. "Washington awaits you."

A firm masculine hand guided Vesper out the massive front door.

"I'm so glad we understand each other, my dear," Senator Lawrence said to his daughter. "We can't keep the President and Mrs. Tyler waiting . . . or Augustus, now can we?"

It was a dejected Vesper who followed her father's lead to the waiting carriage. He handed her up into the enclosed cab, and from the mocking disdain evident in her stepmother's flashing eyes, Vesper knew that her father had revealed her feeble attempt to break the engagement. Of course, Belle would have run with the humiliating tale to Roxanne.

Vesper sat in the carriage, knowing she'd made a

fool of herself before the whole family. Thank heavens Taylor had already left for the evening, Vesper thought, or she'd have received some flippant comment from him, too. As it was, she was sure she would have to endure the rest of this interminable evening. She shifted uncomfortably in her seat and her stiff gown rustled about her.

As the carriage bumped and bounced its way along the uneven pathways toward Pennsylvania Avenue, Vesper's misery increased. Even when the paved road flowed smooth beneath the hooves of the horses and the carriage wheels, Vesper's heart continued to lurch desperately. But the other passengers settled into the easy rolling rhythm of the conveyance.

"Mama," Roxanne whined, "you always promised when Vesper was married, it'd be my turn to pick a husband. And I want a dress like Vesper's. Except can mine be red?"

Belle laughed in a cooing voice, patting her daughter's cheek fondly. But Vesper paled. All this jibber-jabber about weddings and dresses left her sick at heart. Quivers of frustration ran down her back, and the silk and lace of her gown tickled her irritatingly. As she hunched over in her seat the material pulled and tightened and Vesper gasped for air.

She looked down at this monstrous creation fabricated to show off her newfound, hard-won freedom, and laughed inwardly at the irony. Her feminine charms would be on display, all right, and, before the evening was over, all of Washington would know she belonged to Augustus Bledsoe. Bitter tears welled in her eyes, but a newly born stubborn pride refused to let them spill.

Belle leaned toward her dour-faced stepdaughter and pinched her elbow.

"Heavens to Betsy, child," Belle chided, "you

look as though you were goin' to a funeral instead of a ball. Pinch your cheeks, girl . . . and smile, like Roxanne."

Belle beamed benignly in her daughter's direction as the horses began to slow and turn into the circular driveway of the Executive Mansion. The northern facade of the great white structure was lit up from within by the light of a thousand candles. The carriage stopped before a massive yet gracious portico of Ionic columns. Several slave footmen in satin livery helped the guests from their carriages and past the grand doors into the large marbled entrance hall of the White House.

The Lawrences were a popular family among the political elite, and the senator and Belle were hailed repeatedly by friends, associates, and hangers-on. Vesper was used to the attention given the other members of her family and, as was her custom, became as invisible as possible, lowering her eyes, holding her hands quietly behind her, dutifully following the more gregarious Lawrences like a patient shadow.

Senator Lawrence turned to his wife and said, "Madam, I'll meet you in the Blue Room. But first I'll have a cigar with Halley from Louisiana and the new English envoy."

"Come along, girls," Belle prompted in her brightest maternal tone. "We must refresh ourselves before bein' presented to the President and Mrs. Tyler. And, Vesper," she hissed darkly, "don't you dawdle this time."

Mother and daughter stepped briskly forward, their demi-heels clicking like country crickets across the polished floor. Vesper reluctantly trailed after them through the main hall into an antechamber flanking the elliptical Blue Room where the ball was to be held.

Once in the antechamber, the Lawrence ladies removed their velvet cloaks and joined the other female guests in last-minute primping and in a quick preview of the current gossip. Vesper stood off to one side. Most parties she attended were boring chores, but this one, Vesper felt, would be a task worthy of Hercules, a matter of survival between the threat of Bledsoe and her own failing courage.

Had she been privy to the whisperings of any of the little cliques in the antechamber, she would have been surprised to learn that she was the main subject. Despite her usual habits, Vesper could no longer hide within her former passive shell. The revelation of her startling beauty made fragile by her pale skin, her sad, distracted expression, and her poised reserve, all served to color her a beguiling figure of mystery. When the gossip reached Belle's little group, the vivacious woman tittered out loud, her eyes glittering in vicarious pleasure over this unexpected acknowledgment of her stepdaughter.

"Vesper's always been a bit of a mystery to me," she said in a droll voice just loud enough to reach Vesper's ears. "But I must confess, ladies, it only proves that love triumphs over all."

Several of the younger girls simpered at Mrs. Lawrence's clever remark. They had heard enough from Roxanne to understand Belle's cutting thrust. Anger and helplessness caused Vesper's exposed skin to suffuse with a burning glow, only enhancing the deep fiery gleam in her amethyst eyes. Impulsively she tossed her head in disgust and swept from the room.

"She forgot her dance card, Mama," Roxanne simpered.

"That's all right, dear," purred Belle. "Whatever would she need it for?"

Vesper propelled herself from the hot pan into the

open fire. Her father stood outside the antechamber, waiting to escort his ladies into the Blue Room. Instead of avoiding the growing swirl of people, she now faced the ordeal of the reception line.

"My dear, what a pleasant surprise," exclaimed the senator.

He stared at her for a moment, taken aback by her surprising beauty. Extinguishing the stub of his cigar in a sand-filled urn, he unquestioningly took her arm in his.

"I believe I will have the honor of escorting the prettiest woman at the ball."

Vesper was forced to stroll along with her father. She glanced hurriedly from right to left but saw no reasonable means of escape.

"There, there, my dear," soothed Senator Lawrence. "Augustus will be along directly."

Vesper's heart froze within her and her mouth became dry. She thought herself incapable of taking another step, much less responding to the greetings of the President and First Lady. But that same resistant streak that had kept her tears in check in the carriage rose to her defense again. She smiled and spoke politely to the Tylers and the grown children from the President's first marriage.

"Done prettily, Vesper," her father said, patting her on the back. "I begin to think I'm losing an asset I never knew I had."

She darted a nervous glance at him. Had she finally found her lever with the man? Perhaps later in the evening she could ask him to reconsider her engagement once more, suggesting some other way in which she could boost his political career. But now there was no time. Belle and Roxanne had caught up, having made their greetings to the Tyler family, and they demanded the senator find them a pivotal spot along the dance floor.

"And, Freddy," Belle pouted prettily, "we haven't had our dance yet."

"All right, all right, my dear. Let's get our daughters settled first."

The little group made its way through the magnificent salon past a raised dais where the musicians were playing the latest tunes. The main floor was already filled with gaily tripping bodies, and it took a little while before the Lawrences found comfortable seats not too far from the huge fireplace on the east side of the room.

"Perfect!" Belle exclaimed. "Not too drafty, not too warm. Just the place for smart young gentlemen to congregate. Come, Freddy. Mrs. Tyler says this polka is the newest craze."

As the couple moved off to the bouncy rhythm, Roxanne smiled cloyingly at her half sister.

"Best make yourself comfortable, Vesper. You'll be sittin' in the same place till Uncle Augustus comes to claim you."

Vesper ignored her badgering half sister, choosing instead to observe the elegant French style of the Blue Room. The pale marble floor gleamed against the multicandled torchères artfully placed in the oval salon. Both at the garden windows and behind the President still in the receiving line, rich dark curtains hung over arched gilt poles with eagles at their centers.

It was a splendid room, Vesper thought. She relaxed for a moment, and the glow of soft firelight played about her rich dark hair, her jewellike violet eyes, her roseate skin, the rise and fall of her décolletage. The music was gay and lively, breaking through the storm cloud of foreboding Vesper felt.

Roxanne sat poised beside Vesper, eagerly searching the room for her acquaintances and possible dance partners. Her breath quickened as three men in formal attire approached. She lowered her eyes and then raised them quickly, batting her lashes and displaying her dimples.

"Why, boys, I was wonderin' where you've been. Did y'all expect me to sign up my own dance card?" she teased.

"How do, Miss Roxanne."

"Evening, Roxanne."

"Save one for me, but first . . ."

Unexpectedly, the three eligible bachelors turned toward Vesper and, interrupting one another, begged her to choose one of them for the next dance. They tugged gently at her wrist, looking in vain for the little looped card on which they could reserve their places. A startled laugh lilted from her throat, and, before Vesper knew it, the men had her on her feet. After tonight, her life very well might be over, she thought recklessly, if she couldn't elude Bledsoe and his marriage bed. Choosing the one who looked the least stupid, she glided out to the dance floor and placed a tentative hand on her partner's shoulder.

Roxanne stamped her foot in jealousy but managed a brittle smile.

"Well, boys, you've performed your charitable act for the evenin'. I'm certain you've given my elder sister the thrill of her life. But let's start the fun now."

"Sure, Miss Roxanne, in a minute."

"We just want to watch Miss Lawrence."

The man slightly taller turned to the other.

"Never did notice that gal's sweet figure before . . ."

He got no further. The shorter man bristled with chivalrous indignation.

"Suh, that gal is a lady, and I'll thank you to remember that if and when you dance with her."

"I'll dance with her before you do, you little . . ."

Shocked, Roxanne watched the opposing swains march off to settle their disagreement elsewhere. She was disgusted. First Vesper got that new gown. Then she was invited to dance before Roxanne. And now that old mouse had men fighting over her. Just look at her, Roxanne fumed. She must think she's the belle of the ball.

Whirling to the tune of a polka, her skirt swaying like a porcelain bell, Vesper was awakening to the sensuous joys of the dance. When the merry tune first started up, she had felt like a jerky mechanical doll in the arms of her partner. But as she became more familiar with the music's infectious rhythm, a sense of freedom blossomed within her and she took to the rollicking steps as if she had invented them. The firelight glow which had played about her face, bare neck, and chest was quickly supplanted by the natural flush of released energy as she paraded back and forth with her partner.

The gentleman, a frequent admirer of Roxanne's, had barely given a cursory glance to the demure elder sister before tonight's ball. But the magnificent creature before him, who tossed her head proudly, whose neck arched so delicately, whose elegant line was shown to such effect by her tasteful, stylish gown, this Miss Vesper Lawrence was a goddess of a finer mold than any other woman in the Blue Room. As he glanced shrewdly about the grand salon, he knew he was not the only male to have taken notice. Consequently, he smiled twice as much and stretched his brain to create the most elaborate, flattering compliments so that she might grace him with a second dance at least.

Vesper was completely unaware of the effect she was having on the presidential guests, let alone her callow partner. All eyes turned upon her. Fellow senators saluted Freddy Lawrence, and Mrs. Tyler took Belle aside. Soon a buzz of gossip passed from matron to matron. What had come over the elder Lawrence girl?

In truth, the answer was Cord Travers. He had unloosed the passionate woman inside Vesper's choked shell. The music, her desperation about Augustus Bledsoe, and a new, undefined pride in herself brought out her real spirit, splendid and unconfined. She abandoned herself to her emotions, just as she had abandoned herself within the tumultuous harbor of Cord's arms. The force of her feelings had finally prompted her devastating beauty to shine out, and all of young male Washington gloried willingly at her feet.

As the polka ended, a host of men swarmed about her, begging and pleading most gallantly to be included on her dance card. Vesper was overwhelmed by their attentions and allowed herself to be swept into dance after dance. Roxanne fumed as she was all but ignored in the unceasing rush of Vesper's would-be partners. Envious beyond endurance, she flounced out of the Blue Room, intent on calling for the family carriage and going home. In the adjoining room, she caught a glimpse of Augustus Bledsoe, and her lips curled.

"Uncle Augustus," she cried.

The paunchy, balding man turned from his fellows and lumbered toward Freddy's stepdaughter.

"Ah, little Roxanne," Bledsoe began, swinging her around. "Aren't you the belle of the ball!"

She grimaced. Placing her arm through his, she guided him into the Blue Room.

"That's just what I wanted to talk to you about. Just look, Uncle Augustus. Isn't that the most disgustin' spectacle?"

Roxanne pointed to Vesper, and Augustus Bledsoe saw the woman he meant to marry, her opalescent skin glowing with sensuous life, her blue-violet eyes smoldering with vibrant passion. Instinctively his tongue flicked to the corner of his mouth in memory of the sweet taste he had forced from her lips.

"It's shameful, downright shameful," Roxanne fidgeted, playing the distressed niece to the hilt. "Whatever can she be thinkin' of, throwin' herself at those gallant boys? I think she's taken total leave of her senses. Has she forgotten she's an affianced woman now?"

Bledsoe was not blind to Roxanne's jealous motives in running to him. But as he took in the dance scene more carefully, he realized the girl was right. Beyond her jealous snit, there was a sharp jabbing fact to consider. Freddy, Belle, Augustus himself, clearly considered Vesper to be removed from the marriage market. Vesper apparently meant to place herself on the block, and she was suddenly proving to be a desirable commodity. He had to strike now, before Freddy got any ideas of bigger fish in the sea. Nervously his hand stole into his waistcoat pocket and fingered the engagement ring Vesper had rejected.

"Thank'ee, little girl," Bledsoe offered in the most gentlemanly tone he could muster. "My betrothed just needs a gentle reminder of her new position and you'll yet be belle of the ball."

He patted her avuncularly on the top of her curls and insinuated his way through the milling crowds.

"Come along, Roxanne. I have a little job for you."

Roxanne's eyes narrowed and she swept forward with gleeful triumph lurking behind the delight in her eyes.

Away to the far south end of the oval Blue Room, Cord Travers, dressed in his buckskins, kept a vigil among the shadows of the great draperies. His eyes had never moved from Vesper, from the moment she entered the Blue Room on the arm of her father to the brief time she sat by the fireplace till now as she flew about the ballroom in other men's arms. He was the only man present who was not surprised by her incandescent beauty, but he was mesmerized all the same.

Why had he bothered to come? he asked himself over and over. He knew it was impossible to make any political gains for the Santee Sioux here. He had expended his last effort talking to the senator whom Vesper had recommended, and the sad truth had become crystal clear. It was not to any politician's advantage to stand for an Indian cause. Cord would return home to the woods empty-handed.

In truth, he had been driven by an insatiable impulse for one last glimpse of the daring innocent, the sweet tempest, that was Vesper Lawrence. And the sight of her was exquisite agony. She was everything he had bound to his memory, and more—the supple curve of her breast, the trim daintiness of her ankle, her kissable, long swan's neck, those amethyst eyes he could drown in. He ached to hold her in his arms and fought to contain himself from tearing her out of the arms of each of her partners. Yet Cord still exhibited some rational control. He would not approach her, he had promised himself, but be content to watch from afar.

There had been one intriguing development which at first fascinated him but then tore at his heartstrings, the longer he saw Vesper. With his hawk eye for detail, he had noticed she was not wearing Bledsoe's hideous engagement ring. With Bledsoe apparently nowhere to be seen and Vesper accepting the attentions of what seemed like every eligible man in the room, Cord had dared to raise his hopes.

Was it even remotely possible that she had broken the shackles that tied her to her infamous father and his powermongering associate?

Vesper whirled past him again, her dazzling smile setting his heart on fire. He stepped out from the shadow of the rich long curtains, breaking cover, moving to keep her in sight. What he saw made him quail. Part of him wanted to steal back into the darkness, to watch and wait, to reconnoiter the enemy, while another, stronger force wanted to step forward and claim what was his.

Gliding clumsily across the dance floor in an unexpected duo were Vesper's gaudy spoiled sister and that unscrupulous Bledsoe. They circled the floor once, twice, as if searching for prey. Cord's hackles rose, knowing instinctively that Vesper was the object of their hunt. With the sound of his pulse beginning to hammer at his ears, he edged closer to the dance floor, his leaf-green eyes narrowed to wary slits, unaware and uncaring of the stares his presence was eliciting.

The gay waltz came to an end. While Roxanne clapped her hands, delighted to be a part of the ball at last, Augustus Bledsoe wiped his sweaty face, breathing heavily.

"Uncle Augustus, you're so kind to me," minced Roxanne. "Vesper doesn't deserve you."

"All right, Roxanne, we understand each other," he said pointedly. "Now go tell my bride-to-be her stepmother needs her out in the garden. You'll think of something bright to add."

For a moment, the little blonde frowned in puzzlement. Then she brightened. Here was her chance to steal Vesper's thunder, with Augustus's approval no less.

"Why, Augustus Bledsoe, you say the sweetest things to a girl," she remarked coyly. "I just know that if you wait beyond those French doors, Vesper's bound to be lookin' for Belle's lost shawl.''

"That'll do nicely." Bledsoe smiled, gripping Roxanne's upper arm tightly for a brief moment.

His face reddened and the curious jagged scar stood out boldly on his cheek. Then, with surprising speed for a man of his girth, he headed toward the southern windows. Watching him go, Roxanne shivered slightly and gingerly coddled her arm where Bledsoe had squeezed it. A tiny bruise was already beginning to emerge. But her sky-blue eyes lit up in premature glee over the little deceit Bledsoe and she planned for her selfish sister.

Vesper slipped past the French doors and went out into the garden beyond the Blue Room, known as the President's Park. It was just like Belle to ask her stepdaughter to locate a missing piece of lace. Roxanne was useless as usual, refusing to help because her eyes hurt in the dark. Really, Vesper thought, that girl was a walking encyclopedia of concocted excuses.

Dutifully Vesper had obeyed. But now that she looked about the poorly lit park, she began to wonder whether it was merely a ruse to separate Vesper from her dancing partners. For once, she was enjoying herself, and Belle and Roxanne couldn't bear it. Impulsively Vesper whirled about and dipped her full skirt to and fro, reveling in the unexpected magic of the evening. She had never felt so completely alive . . . except for a past Saturday morning when she had first felt the rise of physical passion with Cord Travers. Abruptly she stopped and turned, instinctively sensing she was not alone.

"Belle?" she called out. "Is that you?"

A male figure of undeniable girth and a forbidding aura of power stepped from behind a magnolia tree.

Vesper gasped and stumbled. Augustus Bledsoe nimbly caught her and pulled her to him.

"Au— Augustus, you frightened me. I didn't expect you."

"Apparently not," he said, continuing to hold her in a viselike grip. "Did you expect to hide yourself from me all evening, dallying in the company of those young louts? Have you forgotten you are betrothed to me, shameless hussy?"

His pent-up frustration glowed like embers of blue fire in his beady eyes. Vesper stared back, caught between fear and disgust for this man. She realized if she showed the slightest sign of hesitation or vulnerability, she would lose this important battle. Brashly she wrenched out of his cruel grasp.

"You have forgotten, Mr. Bledsoe, that I returned your engagement ring to you. Neither my father nor you may dictate to me. I am free to make my own choices, and I will."

A diabolical laugh, such as Vesper had never heard, emerged from the coiled depths of the man.

"You will marry me, Vesper Lawrence, and you will wear my ring now," he declared in a rough, rasping voice. "Hasn't your father informed you you have no choice? Don't you know you're part of the bargain I struck with Freddy when you were only a child?"

A paralyzing chill overtook Vesper.

"You're mad," she cried. "What are you saying?"

"On the contrary, my dear, I'm quite sane and very much in control. You see, it's been simple. In exchange for financing your father's political career, I . . . shall we say . . . purchased his vote and influence in the halls of Congress. Whatever I want, I get. Now it has become convenient for me to make Freddy's personal decisions for him as well."

Bledsoe moved toward Vesper, oozing confidence.

"And so, you see, ripe virgin, you are at my beck and call."

Lightning fast, he seized her left wrist and from his pocket withdrew the cursed ring, symbolic of his ownership. Vesper was trapped, and they both knew it. Helpless, hopeless, she felt the heavy web of deceit and despair close over her. She swayed, her violet eyes rolling skyward, dangerously near to fainting into the loathsome grip of Augustus Bledsoe, when she heard a deep rumbling voice barrel out of the dark. Her eyes flew open and her heart sang with hope.

"Take your dirty hands off the lady, you bastard. You may have bought the father, but the daughter is not for sale."

Bledsoe turned swiftly about, looking for the unwelcome intruder. A howl of rage emitted from his throat when Cord Travers, sure and calm, strode out of the blackness.

"You!" the fleshy man snarled. "No man hears my secrets and lives."

Violently thrusting Vesper to the ground, Bledsoe tore out a pistol from his vest and pointed the deadly weapon at the stalwart bronze giant.

"You've made a lot of mistakes, Travers," blustered the burly man. "You should never have come to Washington. Did you honestly think you could make your voice heard in the corrupt halls of Congress?"

Bledsoe laughed hoarsely and the pistol shook unsteadily.

"But your worst mistake was laying claim to what belongs to me. You're no smarter than those redskin friends of yours."

Before the sentence was out of his mouth, Travers

had sprung forward, grabbed the pistol-holding arm, twisted it behind Bledsoe's back, and yanked hard. In a moment, the small gun dropped harmlessly to the ground. Vesper reached for it and impulsively threw it deep into the far reaches of the President's Park.

"Go back, Vesper, where it's safe," Cord warned. Then he released the squirming fat man.

"Another display of your Washington manners, Bledsoe? I think a lesson in Indian fighting might be in order," Travers said with cool assurance.

Slowly and deliberately he unsheathed his hunting knife. He took one step forward and then another. Like a frightened rabbit rooted to one spot, Bledsoe eyed his adversary and thought he saw death in those relentless green eyes. He screamed shrilly at the top of his lungs, and Vesper cupped her hands to her ears to blot out the piercing squeals.

Almost immediately guards carrying lanterns and rifles erupted on the scene, quickly surrounding the bizarre trio. Astounded guests rushed from the Blue Room to encounter a tall, armed backwoodsman apparently about to savage a well-respected Washingtonian whose eyes were popping out of his head and his brand-new fiancée whose dress and face were smudged with dirt. Six guards overpowered Cord and he was forced to relinquish his knife. He was held down while another guard aimed a rifle point-blank at him. Cord froze. Bledsoe saw his chance and took advantage of appearances.

"Arrest that madman," he demanded, pointing a meaty finger at the besieged frontiersman.

Bledsoe lurched toward Vesper and, in a show of protection to the assembled throng, hugged her roughly. She struggled fruitlessly in his grasp.

"My poor dearest one," he said loudly enough for all to hear. "What you have been through!"

He turned, peering into the crowd.

"Freddy? Freddy Lawrence! Your daughter should be taken home immediately."

"No," Vesper cried. "I'm not leaving with him . . . or anybody. Mr. Travers was just trying to—"

". . . avenge his political disappointment on the family of one of our city's most influential men," interrupted Bledsoe, his voice ringing. "You'll be sorry you ever set foot out of the wilderness, boy." To the captain of the White House guards, he enjoined, "Take him away."

Senator Lawrence pushed his way through the crowd, a look of consternation and shock on his face.

"Augustus, old chap, are you all right?"

The bulky man took a deep breath and smoothed his vest down over his belly.

"Attend to your daughter, sir," he whispered harshly.

"Father, you must believe me," Vesper implored. "It wasn't that way at all. Mr. Bledsoe was taking advantage of my . . . situation . . . and Mr. Travers only tried to protect me."

"From your fiancé?" Lawrence asked incredulously. "A man I trust with my own life?"

Vesper stared hard at her father, sickened by the knowledge that, indeed, his life was in the corrupt hands of Augustus Bledsoe.

"Please listen, Father. Mr. Bledsoe pulled out his pistol—"

"Of course he did, my dear," Lawrence said smoothly, "just as any self-respecting man would to protect his claim." Eyeing his friend boldly, he said, "Let's see this horrible weapon, Augustus."

With an odd look of triumph, Bledsoe shrugged his shoulders, shook his head, and looked sadly at Vesper as though she were a demented doll.

"I'm sorry to say, Freddy, that, in her fright, my tormented sweetheart took my gun and threw it somewhere out there."

He pointed to the darkness far into the garden. All eyes flew to Vesper in even greater surprise.

The senator faced the crowd of guests. In his finest oratorical voice, he said, "Please make my profound apologies to President and Mrs. Tyler. I promise that such a foul crime as this shall never be repeated as long as I am in office. I am saddened by this proof of savagery committed by a self-professed Indian lover. May we learn the proper lesson from this tragedy and guide our federal policies accordingly." He bowed his head as if overcome by his emotions.

Vesper raged within. Was there nothing she could say or do to shed the light of truth on this foul deception? She looked at Cord, pinned down in the dirt. His green eyes flickered with an undaunted spirit, suffusing her with courage.

"Let him speak," she begged her father. "Let him defend himself."

"Yes," the senator suddenly obliged, assuming that the backwoodsman would make a fool of himself. "Let's hear what the savage has to say for himself."

Cord was brought to his feet and shoved forward for all to see. With quiet dignity, he brushed off his dusty buckskins and looked at the guests one by one in their Washington finery. He stared long and hard at Frederick Lawrence and Augustus Bledsoe.

"I live by the principles on which our government was founded—that all men are free and equal, that all men may pursue a life of liberty, and that a man is innocent until proven guilty."

"The man's crazy," mumbled Bledsoe before yelling, "I demand justice. Take this wild man away!"

The guards sprang into action. Cord was quickly

manacled in iron chains, to be led away to a jail cell in the federal courthouse. As Cord passed by Vesper their eyes locked in bonded fury, pain, and love.

"I'd do it again to keep you safe," he whispered.

Then he was gone. The crowd dispersed slowly back into the White House, and Vesper was turned over to a white-faced Belle as Lawrence and Bledsoe went off, their heads bent together.

During the bumpy ride home, Vesper sat in outraged silence, ignoring Belle's ineffectual ministrations and Roxanne's pouting. Something in Vesper had hardened. She realized she could no longer tolerate living in Washington, where the practice of deceit had been honed to a fine art. She would be bidden by no one, she resolved.

Instead of floundering about helplessly between her family and that loathsome beast, Augustus Bledsoe, she would start a new life elsewhere. The undaunted spirit of the golden man, with his iron-hard determination and his molten jade eyes locked onto the future, burned brightly in her imagination and filled her with inspiration. And her first order of business, she decided, was to make Cord Travers free again.

# Chapter Six

EARLY THE NEXT MORNING, A RESOLUTE VESPER climbed the three worn wooden stairs of her Aunt Lucinda's boardinghouse and rapped on the simple door. The plump, peach-cheeked servant, who had been with Lucinda Moore for as long as Vesper could remember, welcomed her in and announced the girl's presence to her aunt. Vesper entered the dark, sparsely furnished, but fiercely clean little parlor where Lucinda sat, ramrod straight, in a threadbare armchair, her feet resting on a round rug made of braided rags.

Her niece was struck, as always, by the manner in which Lucinda seemed to preside over her tiny kingdom of genteel poverty with the iron pride of a queen. The older woman's bony, angular face, with its strong nose and determined chin, was revealed unflinchingly to the world by her salt-and-pepper hair, drawn tautly back into a bun, with no curls or bangs to soften her aspect.

Her aunt gave Vesper a sharp look and gestured her niece to a nearby chair. Lucinda, with her canny clear-sightedness, immediately noticed a startling change in Vesper. The reports in this morning's rag sheets must be true for once, she mused. Normally Lucinda disdained to read the empty, gossipy newspapers that so many of her boarders gobbled up eagerly every morning with their breakfasts. But today the vulgar inch-high headlines had blared her niece's name, and she had been forced to study the sensational story in all its flowery, exaggerated verbosity.

Referring to Vesper as the Cinderella of last night's presidential ball, the article went on to report how the city owed another debt of gratitude to Mr. Augustus Bledsoe. Besides the many civic improvements he had sponsored, Mr. Bledsoe, popular bachelor-about-town, had now presented Washington with his finest gift: the shimmering glory of Miss Vesper Lawrence, whom his love had transformed from a quiet wallflower into a society beauty.

The story went on to enumerate, at nauseating length, the dances Miss Lawrence had dominated. Finally the rag had described, in effusive and gloating detail, the scandal that had prematurely ended the ball. The triumphant Miss Lawrence had been basely attacked with a hunting knife by a hulking, savage frontiersman and had barely escaped with her life. Finishing the article with a snort of derision, Lucinda had been sure that most, if not all, of the lurid tale was fabricated.

But here before her very eyes was evidence to the contrary. Gone was the meek, withdrawn little girl with perennially downcast eyes. In her place was a grown woman with back held proudly straight and fine, flashing eyes. This new Vesper looked capable of grappling wholeheartedly with whatever her destiny might lead her to. There was a keen, hard edge to the girl that had never been there before. Something had made her dreamy, idealistic niece decide to take the world by storm, and Lucinda could not help but be grateful to whoever was responsible.

In her no-nonsense voice, Lucinda asked, "What's this I hear about you being attacked by a madman?"

Vesper colored but met her aunt's penetrating look with one of her own. She described the actual events, explaining that the "savage" was an innocent man who had been framed.

She concluded, "Augustus Bledsoe is an unprincipled scoundrel, and he'll not get away with this."

"And how do you propose to stop him?" her aunt inquired tartly.

"I'm going to free Cord Travers from jail, and you're going to help me, Aunt Lucinda," Vesper declared.

Lucinda's nut-brown eyes widened in shock as she sat bolt upright in her chair. What had happened to helpless little Vesper? She did not protest as her niece told the whole story of the last week, including the revelation of her father's betrayal and Cord Travers' fiery sense of honor. Lucinda interrupted only once.

"You're in love with him, child, aren't you?"

The direct question flustered Vesper for a moment.

"That's not the point. No matter how I feel about him, the real issue is that an injustice has been done and I will not stand for it."

Lucinda gave Vesper a warm smile and leaned forward to press her arm quickly. Her niece had finally found her match, and Lucinda was very glad indeed. For many years the older woman had watched helplessly as Vesper perished by inches in the unhealthy air of the Lawrence mansion.

The girl was smart—there was no denying that. But her intelligence only seemed to work against her, for it was of a bookish, wishful sort. She was easily demoralized by pettiness, hypocrisy, or self-ishness masquerading in gracious dress. And those qualities flowed without stint in her father's house. Lucinda had tried in vain to imbue the girl with some of her own starch.

And now look at her! The elder woman found herself wanting to meet the man who could work this transformation on her niece. Honor, Lucinda thought. He would have strength, honor, and cour-age. She was swept by a wave of gratitude toward the unknown Cord Travers. None of this showed on her austere face, however, as she sat back straight in her chair and waved a bony admonishing finger.

"Just suppose we actually free your young man. You won't be able to stay in Washington after that."

"Oh, Auntie, couldn't I stay with you?"

"Impossible. They'd find you. I'll send you to a utopian commune I know in New England. Martha Fellowes is an old friend of mine there. I'll prepare a letter of introduction for you."

"I like that, Auntie. A community run on princi-ples. But first we must rescue Cord."

The two women brought their chairs closer togeth-er as they began to sketch out a workable plan. Gray head leaned toward glistening black one, watched only by the walls of books in Lucinda Moore's simple parlor.

It was a chill, damp midnight. Vesper forced her hands to hold the reins steady as she guided her horse-drawn carriage down the shadowed streets. Between the pools of amber light cast by infrequent candlelit street lamps, the avenues were dark and silent. Running Wolf's quiet voice sounded in the darkness from the floor where he had crouched down to conceal himself from all eyes.

"We are near."

Involuntarily Vesper shivered. It would never work. She had been a fool to suggest this wild scheme. Her throat closed up, stilling any answer she might have given Running Wolf. In her feverish imagination, the eyes of Augustus Bledsoe seemed to watch her, sneering at her feeble plan, telling her she would never escape his clutches. The calm, even voice of her Indian companion interrupted her building panic.

"When you are inside, make no unnecessary sound. More soldiers guard the back, and they must not know what we do."

Running Wolf's practical words strengthened her. He believed the plan could work.

"I will remember," Vesper whispered as she pulled the carriage to a halt in front of the heavy brick and iron jail that dominated the dark street corner.

Deliberately she tugged hard on the reins so that the horses half reared. Her heart gave a lurch as the two armed men pacing at the entrance looked up curiously at a lone woman highlighted by harsh lamplight. The moment had come. Now everything depended on her. If she failed, Cord Travers' life was forfeit. Vesper's mouth felt dry as ashes.

"Oh, gentlemen," she forced herself to carol out in sugary tones. "I do hope you'll forgive me for interruptin' your important duties, but I so desperately need your help."

In the little pause that followed, Vesper's heart leaped into her throat. They weren't going to fall for it. She couldn't use the feminine wiles she had seen being practiced all around her. But wait. It was working. The two soldiers, helpful expressions on their faces, had cautiously lowered their rifles and were approaching the carriage. Heartened, Vesper launched into the next phase of her act.

"I was foolish enough to take my daddy's grays for a drive, all alone. I just don't know what I was thinkin' of. They're just too much for my poor little hands."

Vesper paused, batting her sooty eyelashes furiously and sending the two men helpless little looks from under her fluttering lids. Perfect. They were responding right on cue. Both men doffed their hats respectfully, sharing an amused glance at this adorable little fool. Why should I be surprised? Vesper asked herself. She'd seen Belle and Roxanne use helplessness to advantage countless times. It was easy.

"Now, don't you know better than to travel alone at night, little lady?" one of the men admonished.

"Oh, I do know better, of course," Vesper interrupted, slapping at his shoulder playfully with the ends of the reins. "But sometimes I just feel so . . . restless."

She sent the man a soulful look from her deep amethyst eyes. He swallowed audibly, moving closer to her.

"Why don't you come inside for a little while and rest those dainty hands," he invited.

Vesper looked down, her blush only half feigned. Was it working too well? How would she fight off two burly soldiers if they accosted her once she was inside the ironbound walls? It was a knife's edge she had to walk between invitation and distance.

"It's so kind of you to offer me shelter after I've been such a thoughtless ninny."

She hesitated, drawing out their suspense with a

skill that surprised her. Her seemingly shy gaze swept over the two bemused men.

"If one of you will tie up these fractious old horses, I would be happy to accompany you inside."

Her request was eagerly obeyed, and Vesper, letting her trim ankle flash provocatively as she climbed down, allowed the soldiers to escort her into the forbidden interior of the building. She noted with satisfaction that their guns hung negligently over their shoulders.

They had hastily dusted off a table and poured her a cup of tepid tea when Running Wolf entered the guardroom, his rifle aimed directly at the two men.

"Put your guns on the floor," the chief ordered in a calm voice that knew it would be obeyed.

Reluctantly the guards disarmed themselves, shooting their fair guest apologetic glances. They were staggered when she pulled several lengths of rope from inside her cloak and proceeded to tie them to their chairs.

"Why, you tricky little baggage," began one of the men, but a gesture from Running Wolf's rifle quieted him.

"Use their neckcloths to silence their words," the tall Indian directed Vesper.

Gingerly she untied the small yellow bandannas and gagged her two former admirers, trying not to bind their mouths too tightly. Running Wolf reached up with his rifle and hooked the ring of keys that was hanging on a nail in the wall.

"Come now," he said to Vesper.

She hurried after him down the dank corridor of cells, a fierce drumbeat of gladness beating in her chest. In a moment, Cord Travers would once again taste the air of freedom. In a moment, she would see him again.

The last twenty-four hours had been a nightmare

for Cord. He could master his own hatred of being jailed. He could subdue his fear of coming death. But what tore his fortitude to shreds was the thought of Vesper left to the mercy of that filthy animal, Bledsoe. An ugly vision kept flashing through his mind of Bledsoe's thick, cruel fingers circling, clamping down, bruising Vesper's slender neck.

Cord had taken his measure of the man and knew instinctively that Bledsoe's only principle was to please himself. He would walk over corpses, breaking anyone in his way, to gain his pandering ends. Power—political, financial, sexual—was his mistress and it drove him, goaded him deeper and deeper into evil. Cord was certain that Bledsoe's most intense feeling of power came from inflicting pain on others. He had perverted his own humanity until he had become a twisted, misshapen creature.

Cord's huge fists had bent the iron bars of his cell as he was assailed by the picture of Vesper, with her fine, unstained honor, her giving, innocent eyes, her sweetly evocative discovery of her own womanhood, trampled by Bledsoe's uncaring hungers, mauled by Bledsoe's voracious fingers. But even the mountain man's enormous strength, fueled by desperate fury, was not enough to tear apart the iron cage that held him. He had beaten the walls in frustration, prayed to gods Christian and Sioux.

Now it seemed his prayers were being answered. Stealthily making his way toward Cord's cell was Running Wolf, followed by Vesper herself. Cord's heart leaped in joy. She walked unbroken, her spirit pouring unquenched from her eyes. Their gazes met, locked, as if never to look away again. Cord felt his massive strength tremble at her nearness. He was undone, he who had believed himself to be invulnerable.

His huge hands trembled on the bars as Running

Wolf tried key after key on the lock. Cord tore his eyes from Vesper, shaken by the intensity of his need for her.

"It's the crooked iron one on the end of the ring," he directed in a harsh whisper.

When the huge door flew open, giving a long rusty creak, all three froze, throwing agonized looks toward the back entrance. But their luck held. There was no response from the guards.

"How did you manage to get inside the building?" he growled at his longtime Indian companion. "Both entrances are guarded."

The old man's eyes crinkled in a rare smile.

"It was not I who managed it, my son, but the woman. It is her plan and by her invitation that I stand here before you."

Cord turned back to Vesper. The astonished admiration in his eyes made her heart leap like a freed bird. He reached out and cupped her face in his massive hands with a gentle, worshipful touch.

"I'm never quite sure who's rescuing whom when we're together," he growled softly.

A hoarse shout from the front room broke through their preoccupation. One of the guards had managed to loosen his gag, and was yelling for his fellows.

"We've got to get out of here before reinforcements arrive," Cord said, directing his rescuers back down the hall and out to the front office.

Outside, taking in the situation with one resourceful glance, Cord rushed to the two horses and began freeing them from the carriage traces. Running Wolf cocked his rifle, covering their retreat.

"Hurry," Vesper urged Cord. "You should be safe if you ride from the city immediately."

"And you?" Cord demanded, untangling the second horse.

"Don't worry about me," she insisted.

Breathlessly, looking over her shoulder every second, she told him of Lucinda's letter. Holding the reins of the freed horses, Cord stared down at his plucky darling with a disbelieving glance.

"That's the first foolish thing you've said since I met you, Vesper Lawrence," he grated.

He pulled her against him, forced her head back, and masterfully covered her mouth with his. All plans, all pride, lay shattered at the onslaught of his fiery kiss. It was all she could do to cling weakly to him as her knees wobbled dangerously and her breath stopped altogether. Shots rang out behind them, splitting the velvet night.

Running Wolf, already on horseback, fired a warning salvo. Cord swept Vesper onto the remaining horse, leaped up behind her, and urged his mount down the cobbled streets. He held Vesper against him, cradling her against his body like the precious treasure she was to him. They galloped down the long avenues of the capital, the night air whistling behind them, their pursuers losing ground steadily.

He was leaving intolerable civilization behind, Cord thought. And once again its ways had defeated him. But this time he was carrying away with him a prize greater than any he had ever sought or imagined, a woman so beautiful it took his breath away to look at her. Her spirit was as lovely as her appearance: open, upright, giving, possessed of a deep strength that she did not yet know she had.

Perhaps this last trip to Washington had been preordained. They had been meant to meet. With satisfaction, Cord noted that the pursuing hoofbeats had died down. They were free.

Imprisoned in his arms, Vesper felt real freedom for the first time in her life. All of her senses were tinglingly alive as his scent, his touch, the thudding of his heart, coursed through her. She felt the fetters of self-doubt and fear fly from her in the night wind that rushed by the hurrying horses.

They sped past the last houses of the city, but she was not thinking of Washington, of Bledsoe, or of anything else she was leaving behind. Instead she leaned forward eagerly, intent on her future, rejoicing that fate had bound her to the one man she wanted.

# Chapter Seven

THE LONG NIGHT HOURS PASSED IN A SUBLIME BLUR FOR Vesper. In the cleansing wind, her hair was loosened from its confining pins and streamed about her, sweeping her face, whipping past her shoulders, brushing against Cord's broad chest. She should have felt saddle-sore, but she was only aware of the careful strength with which he held her to him as their straining horse loped along the dark paths.

She felt somehow transformed. No longer did she have to hide behind her demure, unhappy facade, bound by the dictates of her exacting family. For the first time she felt free to stake claim to her own life.

Vesper became slowly aware of the rasping, frantic rhythm of the horse's tortured breathing. In the graying light of dawn, she realized just how exhausted both mounts were. Only city carriage horses, they were unaccustomed to the unceasing run all night long. Sweat poured off their sides and foam churned about their mouths.

"The horses can go no further," cautioned Running Wolf.

"I know. We'll have to stop," agreed Cord. "If we swing up onto the National Road, we're bound to find an inn and stables."

". . . where there are white men's wagons, my son." The old Indian frowned, his weathered brow furrowing deeply.

"True enough," Cord warranted, "but if we want to get fresh horses, we must stop where the stagecoach offices are. You worry too much, my father. No message from Washington will have preceded us."

Vesper came alert at Cord's words and stiffened. They couldn't be caught, not after coming this far. She'd never go back. She had made that vow when Aunt Lucinda and she first discussed an escape plan. She'd stop at nothing to have a life of her own now . . . with the man of her dreams.

Cord felt Vesper's startled reaction. He leaned into her, closer, to reassure her and explain their planned route.

"The worst is behind us, my brave one. From this point on, our adversary is Mother Nature. Running Wolf and I have contended with her many times and she's never beaten us yet."

He was aware of the minute uncoiling of her tension as she slowly relaxed against him again. He breathed in the perfume of her tangled black tresses and felt with surprising satisfaction how the supple softness of her back found a home against his hard chest. He glimpsed the pale, almost translucent skin at the nape of her neck and was struck by Vesper's vulnerability. With an impulse brought on by an overwhelming need to protect this daring yet innocent girl, he bent nearer to the exposed spot and tenderly brushed his lips upon it. A gentle sigh escaped from Vesper, and she wondered if every morning were as perfect and lovely as this one.

Shafts of morning sunlight filtered between the thick spread of trees as the exhausted horses slowly ambled toward the main road. Signs of spring were everywhere. Hardy little daisies bloomed in nestling clumps of bright color along the leaf-strewn path. Chipmunks dashed from tree to tree, chattering constantly, and the occasional flash of a fleet deer's hoof could be seen among the mighty hemlocks. Birdsong filled the air with lilting joyful music that charmed Vesper.

She felt totally at ease and in harmony with this new world about her. She knew without a moment's hesitation she could trust Cord and his Indian father with her life. But a glimmer of worry crept over her. She twisted slightly so that she faced Cord for the first time since he had kissed her at the jailhouse.

Timidly she said, "I don't want to hold you back. I'm afraid I'd only be a burden to you . . . make it difficult for you and Running Wolf to get home quickly and safe, to get on with guarding your lands and people."

Her eyes grew rounder and deepened in intensity. Cord took one look at her and knew he was lost forever. He'd never been afraid of anything in his life, but the thought of losing this raven-haired beauty, whose soul matched his own, tore at his guts. He chose his words carefully.

"There's no denying it. I'd be lying to you if I did. It'll be hard for you at first, Vesper. But," he added with a glint of teasing humor in his voice, "any gal who can bamboozle federal guards and rescue a dangerous prisoner from under their noses won't let a little thing like a cross-country trek get her down!"

It was just the right touch of levity, and he could see the despair drain from her luminous face. He continued, fed by the promise of their first journey together.

"Of course, we'll be sleeping on the ground at night with only a bedroll and a campfire for comfort. But then there's the view of the stars . . . millions of twinkling lights flickering like tiny white flames against the black sky. There's nothing else like it."

Vesper was enthralled. She smiled, dazzling Cord with her vibrant beauty. She was happy. She nestled cozily into his arms again, freed from her momentary worry.

"Tell me more, Cord," she demanded, secretly hoping this glorious adventure would never end.

"Well, it'll take us three or four weeks to get to Santee Sioux territory, passing through forests and grasslands. We'll ford rivers where we can and cross the Mississippi on a flatboat. We'll hunt and fish for our food. We'll probably get soaked to the gills by a cloudburst or two—"

"Enough, enough," Vesper interrupted, laughing. "All this in a month? It sounds like it could take a lifetime."

Suddenly, all was silent. Running Wolf, always slightly ahead of Cord and Vesper's horse, scouting their course, rode on in patient vigilance, as if nothing had changed. But it had. They had been jovial, teasing each other, content in the dream of their future. Now the reality, the finality of their past actions and idle words, caught up with both of them.

In a voice lower than she had ever heard him use before, Cord rumbled, "Our paths seem to be entwined . . ."

". . . as if it were meant," Vesper heard herself echo softly.

He recognized in Vesper a current of underlying

strength and a kindled fire to commitment for which he cherished her. She might not know she possessed these sterling qualities, but she would come to know with him.

"I want you with me," he said, making himself more vulnerable to her than he ever had to anyone in his life.

"I want to be with you," she murmured, never more certain of anything in her life.

Up ahead, Running Wolf stopped, shielded his eyes, and peered into the distance.

"Fierce Bear," he called, "white man's roofs lie beyond the next bend."

Vesper saw Cord's face harden into the grim mask she realized he always affected in the white man's world. The lines of his chiseled jaw became more angular and a veil of implacable caution slid over his leaf-green eyes. All that remained of the vulnerable, trusting man she had just witnessed was the gentle pressure of one arm holding her against him.

Cord urged the tired horse forward, and the beast painfully trotted, catching up to the vigilant Indian. Running Wolf pointed, and Cord silently nodded.

"Where?" Vesper demanded. "I can't see anything."

"Your first lesson, my daughter," cautioned Running Wolf. "If you will be one with the land, you must heed your instincts and sharpen all your senses."

Her eyes wide, Vesper nodded, promising herself she would live by this lesson. Running Wolf seemed to study her and then smiled.

"Cord Travers has chosen you and you have chosen him. So it shall be," he said.

It sounded like a blessing to Cord.

They rode up to a two-story inn amidst a small clearing along the dusty wide road. To Cord and Running Wolf, the inn was ordinary and what they had expected to find—simple and serviceable—with a barn and shed behind to house horses, supplies, and equipment. But to Vesper, the inn was quaint and lovely. There were vines of wisteria trailing about the doorway and entwined along the second-floor railings. She noted the well in front of the inn with its weathered wooden handle and bucket and the rich dewy moss clinging to the moist masonry.

While Running Wolf led the horses to the stable for a well-earned rest, Cord took Vesper into the public room of the inn, deserted except for the innkeeper bustling about behind the bar. Cord frowned, knowing he must leave Vesper for a while. There was still business to attend to.

"Stay here and talk to no one, Vesper," he reminded her, with caution in his voice. "We're not home free yet. There are possible dangers lurking in every corner. We can't take any chances."

She gazed at him steadily.

"I won't risk our freedom, Cord. It means too much to me."

There were those fiery violet eyes again, their depths shimmering with ardent emotion. Whenever he stared into them, the light of truth shone clear to him. She could never lie to him, he realized. Her soul was open to him through those dazzling orbs.

"I must leave for a little while . . . the horses, Running Wolf, supplies . . . and other things," he said, trying to maintain his composure. "I'll speak to the innkeeper about rooms upstairs for us. You can rest until I return."

She nodded. She would wait for him, even patiently. But rest? That was impossible. She was too keyed up from the escape, the ride, Cord's nearness.

"Hurry, Cord," she said eagerly and then blushed.

Cord smiled widely and was gone. Vesper sat on a rough-hewn bench, leaning against the unpainted plank wall, and closed her eyes. Maybe Cord was right. All of a sudden she felt as though she could sleep for a week. Her mind wandered over the jumble of faces and events of the last week which had changed her life forever.

"Missus, you come vid me now."

Vesper's eyes flew open. There before her stood a bristly-mustachioed man who wiped his hands on a stained and smelly apron.

"I take you to your room. Your husband, he pay me already for best room in inn."

As if to demonstrate the veracity of his words, the innkeeper jiggled a pocket from the apron's depths so that Vesper could hear the familiar clink of coin upon coin. He smiled, exposing a crisscross of uneven yellowed teeth. She was touched by Cord's care of her. Once again he had thought of her reputation, even here in the wilds. He must have asked the innkeeper for a room for his wife so as not to embarrass her.

Vesper rose stiffly and followed the man up a flight of rickety stairs to a door at the top of the landing. He unlocked the door, handed Vesper the key, stood aside, and bowed.

"I hope you ant your husband vill be very heppy on your honeymoon," said the funny little man.

"Thank you," Vesper had to respond.

She entered the room and closed the door. Taking a deep breath and remembering Cord's words, she decided to relax. She looked about the room. An imposing dark and heavy wardrobe took up most of one wall. Next to it was a rather precarious three-legged table on which sat a chipped porcelain bowl filled with water. Above it was a window covered by faded chintz curtains. Through the window she could just see the forest beyond.

Then she sucked in her breath and stared at the one single bed along the length of the remaining wall. She paled, then reddened. The little innkeeper had been serious, having no reason to doubt that Cord and Vesper were married. But Cord knew better, she told herself. She felt confused and angry.

It was one thing to find a place to refresh themselves. But it was quite another to pass pretense off as reality. Was her virginity to be his reward? Was that what he had expected, even planned, all along? Had her judgment been so awry?

Gingerly she approached the bed with its iron-railed headboard and footboard. She touched the rough wool blanket with her fingertips, then pushed up and down on the mattress to test its firmness. Would such a scrawny bed support both their bodies? Aghast at herself, she sat down abruptly on the bed. What was she thinking of?

Of course, there was only one answer, and they had made their choice. But when was it? she wondered. Back at the jail? At the ball? Was it that morning in Cord's hotel room, or at the dinner party the previous night? Perhaps the inevitable moment came when they first laid eyes on each other, trying to save that poor slave from a miserable beating.

Whenever it had been, they were together now, wanting to be together, wanting each other. They had said as much on the magic morning ride out of the forest.

"Conventions be damned," Vesper said out loud.

If it was her body he desired foremost, it was her body he would have. She stared at the bed for a moment, then stood and walked toward the wash-stand. She would take Cord Travers on any terms he offered, with or without benefit of clergy. He had made her come alive, and she would live for him now. She felt a closeness with him and she wanted to revel in the sensation of belonging to him, belonging with him in the home they would build together.

She tore off her clothes and doused her face and hands in the tepid water. She sluiced off the layers of dirt and dust accumulated along the trail before dressing again. Her long hair was a tangle of knots, but she worked painstakingly at each snarl with her fingers until her tresses hung softly about her shoulders and back.

She heard footsteps coming up the stairs and knew without a doubt they were Cord's. There was a brief knock at the door and the sound of it opening.

"Vesper?" he called, his back to her as he secured the door. "Are you awake, honey? I have something important to ask you."

"I'm ready, Cord," she answered huskily, mumbling to herself, "ready as I'll ever be."

He turned to face his beloved, a tender smile on his face which quickly froze when he saw the half-uncertain, half-sultry expression in Vesper's eyes. What was she up to? In a second he knew the answer.

"Vesper, what does this mean?" Cord asked in mock innocence.

In her nervousness, she was unsure what to say and she missed his ironic tone.

"Well," she began hesitantly, "when a man and woman . . . I mean when you and I . . . you kissed me . . . the ride . . . this room . . ."

She looked about helplessly as her few womanly wiles deserted her completely. No, she told herself firmly. She couldn't lose him now. With a kind of impulsive grace, Vesper drew herself up and propelled herself toward Cord. She threw her arms around his neck, and the renewed contact of skin against skin rekindled her urgency. She pressed her body to him and swayed back and forth, sending waves of vibrant desire through her.

Afraid to look at him, she buried her head against his well-muscled shoulder, her sensitive face feeling the long, hard tendons of his neck. Instinctively she nuzzled closer and brushed soft, feather-light kisses along the hollows of his throat and the underside of his chin. She expected him to pull her roughly to him, until neither one of them could catch their breaths, then lift her up, cradling her in his arms, and lay her on the bed.

Cord did nothing of the sort. Half amused, half curious to see just how far Vesper would go, he had remained still as a poised cat. He knew that if he laughed she would be mortified, although a part of him found her overt, awkward flirtation endearing. He loved her even more, for it showed how much she wanted him and how much she was willing to give up to have him.

But the charade was over, and it was about time Vesper found out. Cord raised his arms to hers, still entwined about his neck, and gently disengaged them. He stepped back and looked seriously at the girl's face, which became more scarlet by the minute.

Vesper was aghast. If she had seen a way out, she would have dashed from the room.

"You . . . you don't want me?" Vesper whispered in a broken voice.

The stern set of his features dissolved into a lopsided grin.

"Can't you tell how much, little wildcat?"

"Oh, Cord, I'm so ashamed. I thought . . ."

"You thought right."

He glanced briefly at the single bed, and her eyes trailed after his.

"But I thought we might wait until after the wedding."

His green eyes sparkled with revealed love, and Vesper was flooded in the wake of it.

"I love you, Vesper Lawrence, now and forever. Can you be happy as a frontier horse breeder's wife?" he rumbled.

"Oh, Cord, I'd beg for pennies if it meant we could be together. I love you."

For a timeless moment of rapture they stood wrapped in each other's arms, each a safe harbor for the other, each stronger for the other's love. They kissed, and the depth of their commitment was branded on their lips.

"I only left you to find a preacher," Cord confessed. "I had to do some fast talking to convince Reverend Dooley I wanted to get married, not rob him. He's waiting for us downstairs, Vesper. So if you don't mind exchanging vows in the middle of nowhere . . ."

"I'm ready, Cord," she answered with a quiet pride, her heart brimming with love and hope.

She seemed to float down the stairs at Cord's side, a smile of pure happiness dancing across her face. This is it, she told herself, the beginning of paradise.

The marriage vows took only a moment to repeat. When Reverend Dooley asked for the exchange of rings, Vesper threw Cord a panicked glance. But from a soft leather pouch which hung at his waist Cord lovingly extricated a thin band of gold and placed it on the fourth finger of her left hand. The ring fit perfectly. Cord lifted her hand and kissed it in token of tender possession.

Eyes shining, gazing at each other alone, the

couple retraced their steps upstairs and back to their room. In the back of the public room, Running Wolf nodded solemnly and silently mouthed a Santee Sioux blessing upon the newlyweds.

Once within the privacy of their room, Cord enfolded Vesper in his massive embrace, holding her to him as though he would weld their bodies together. Vesper relaxed completely, reveling in the knowledge that no one could tear them asunder. The strong, sure beat of his heart echoed hers. She fit perfectly within his clasp, her contours matching his as if they had been cut from the same mold.

Slowly they drew apart. Cord bent his head and fit his mouth over her lips. At first gently and then with increased intensity, he kissed her, finding her lips unbelievably responsive to his pressure. He ran the tip of his tongue along the yielding, trembling flesh. He sought the velvety warmth of her cheek, the smooth skin of her neck, the pulsing hollow of her throat. He found her tender earlobe and softly blew his hot breath into her ear.

"You are my wife," he murmured. "Now be my lover."

Cord lifted Vesper effortlessly and carried her across the room to the bed. Bending low, he laid her down, slowly withdrawing his arms from about her, savoring the last lingering touch of her soft, supple back. Through the smooth buckskin he still wore, his skin tingled from the feel of her.

Eyes blazing with fire at the wonderment of discovering her husband, Vesper raised her hand to his forearm, gliding her fingers past the golden hair encircling his wrist down to the tapering tips of his fingers that were squared off by flat, blunt nails. She lifted her eyes to his, wanting to tell him that she felt more alive, more herself, more purposeful, than she ever had before, and that it was all due to him.

"Cord, beloved," she began in a voice thick with emotion.

"Hush, my love," he quieted her. "Now is a time for the senses and instinct to lead. There will be a time for words afterward. But for now let me take you on this first journey together."

She gazed deeply into his leaf-green eyes, seeing the care, the gentleness, the love, he bore for her. Any hesitation or fear she might have secretly harbored evaporated, and she wanted to open to him, giving him her love, herself, freely.

"Yes, Cord. Love me," she said simply.

It was all he needed to hear. Deftly he unbuttoned her blouse, trailing a line of soft kisses from his sensitive lips. Beneath her thin camisole, her breasts began their first delicious ache of desire and her nipples started to swell in response to his feather-light touch. Vesper closed her eyes and breathed deeply, a soft moan escaping her lips.

Cord covered her quivering mouth with his and drank in her warm sweetness. Of her own accord, Vesper parted her lips, inviting him to delve into the secret delights of her tongue and teeth. Artlessly she pulled at his lips with hers, pressing and demanding, biting and begging for satisfaction. He answered her innocent fervor with his own passion.

His tongue lashed at Vesper's, leaving her dazed and exhilarated. Hungrily she thrust her tongue about his, driven to battle, unsure whether she wanted to dominate or be conquered. But Cord withdrew his mouth from her onslaught.

"Wait, my darling," he chuckled. "There is so much more to discover."

He removed the remains of her city clothing and dropped them to the floor. She lay naked before him, his to touch, to possess, to cherish. Carefully, as if committing her body to his memory, his long fingers traced a sensuous path from her now-familiar lips down the swan's neck, through the tantalizing cleavage and around both breasts, past her taut, smooth belly to the slim line of her hips, and finally to the silky skin of her thighs.

Vesper kept her eyes on Cord as he explored her body, surrendering to his thrilling touch, opening herself to his quest. Unable to stay still, her hands stole up to his chest and she began to pull at the lacings of his buckskin shirt.

"I want to know you, too, Cord," she said and then blushed. "Or am I not supposed to admit that?"

He hugged her tightly to him, rejoicing in her artless response to his lovemaking.

"Always tell me what you want, my love, so that it will be sweeter for us."

He tore off his buckskins and lay beside her so that they touched for the first time in complete naked harmony. A sharp intake of breath escaped from Vesper and she stared at Cord, frightened.

"I feel it too," he answered in response to her unspoken alarm. "It is only our need for each other, impatient to be satisfied."

Her fear soon gave way to the heated sensations of lip upon lip, tongue upon tongue, and Cord's fingers expertly kneading her nipples. The tempo of her breathing increased and her breasts ached against his steady onslaught. Her nipples peaked hard. She twisted under him, thrusting her breasts at him for more of this exquisite torture.

But his hand brushed down to that most secret part of her, past the silky black triangle and into the tender flesh. An instantaneous thrill of icy fire jolted through her, igniting her core. Her eyes closed and an instinctive arch of her hips brought him closer, deeper, inside her. Cord lowered his head, raining hot kisses down the inner curves of her belly and below. He was fast losing control over his own demands, but Vesper's pleasure came first.

She whimpered, yearning to be full of him, to fill him with her overwhelming love. Finally he stretched over her and she felt the pulsing swell of his hunger for her. She parted her legs beneath him and he came to her, thrusting with careful relentlessness into her.

For a brief moment Vesper felt a tightness tearing, giving way with a searing intensity, and then a feeling of ecstatic wholeness cascaded over her. He lay still for a moment until she arched against him. Gradually he increased the pace of their passion, building ever higher.

The passion, long constrained in Vesper, was finally freed, and her unrestrained responsiveness finally wrested his control from him. He took her with a branding ferocity, shattering her into a million golden fragments of ecstasy. Damp, exhausted, completely fulfilled, they lay in each other's arms.

"There has never been anyone like you, Vesper Travers," her husband murmured, nibbling at her earlobe.

"Oh, Cord, will it always be like this?"

"Always, my love. For as long as you look at me with those violet eyes."

She snuggled happily in his grasp. She closed her eyes, enjoying the teasing tickle of Cord's golden chest hair against her breasts. Lifting her left hand, she examined her wedding band as it caught the glints of sunlight.

"It's beautiful, Cord. But where did this ring come from?"

Deep pain flitted briefly over Cord's face and then was gone.

"It belonged to my mother," he said in strained

harshness. "She gave it to me the night she left my father."

He stared out, away from Vesper, as though the memory were fresh before his eyes.

"She came into my room, late one night. Her eyes were swollen and red. She hugged me and pulled the ring from her finger. 'Save it for the girl you love,' she said. She started to cry, and when she kissed me, I tasted the salt of her tears. I closed my eyes and she was gone."

Vesper clung sympathetically to her husband.

"The next day, my father told me she was dead. I was only a child and didn't know what to do but cry. My father sent me to my room, and there, on my pillow, was her ring. I've kept it with me ever since."

Vesper's eyes filled with tears.

"Oh, Cord, we've both been hurt by life," she cried.

She clasped him to her bosom and rocked him gently.

"Never again, Vesper," Cord said firmly. "Not as long as we're together."

"Didn't I just promise that?" she murmured. " 'Till death do us part?' "

"And that," he stated with conviction, "is an eternity away."

A lazy grin returned to Cord's face.

"Enough of the past. We've got a future to build. As for now . . . come here, woman. Let's see what you've learned so far."

Bending toward her, he began kissing, caressing, forcing away the old hurtful memories. Vesper opened to him, her heart brimming over with loving trust. She vowed to ease his pain and matched his every adoring touch. Freely they gave their love to each other, and the past was washed away in the fire of their passion.

# Chapter Eight

SEVERAL WEEKS LATER, THE THREE COMPANIONS RODE past majestic avenues of tall wind-tossed red maples, white elms, and basswoods. The hooves of Vesper's horse sank into the rich black loam and layers of leaf litter as the trail wound in and out along the edge of the Indian Woods. Whenever the path emerged from the fresh-scented, thick green gloom of the forest, Vesper feasted her eyes on the rippling golden expanses of prairie. The land was dotted with lakes that gleamed like jewels, reflecting back to the sky its own cerulean gaze.

The late-morning sun cast a blanket of warmth on Vesper. Whenever the trail plunged the travelers back into the trees, the sudden cool shade with its eddies of moist breeze made Vesper shiver deliciously. A turn in the path revealed white and crimson wild roses just beginning to open, sending sweet beguiling clouds of scent to the early bees.

Vesper almost laughed aloud when the tawny head of a rodent popped out, three long green grass stems emerging on either side of his mouth like an extra set of elegant whiskers.

"What is it, Vesper?" asked Cord, riding up to her side. He took great pleasure in the delightful play of expressions on her face as she discovered the beauties of his world.

"That little creature . . ." she began.

But even as she pointed, the animal turned with a swift flip of his tiny white tail and disappeared.

"He's a late one," came Cord's deep rumble. "Most striped gophers have already lined their burrows and are out advertising for a mate."

How did he know all that? Vesper wondered in amazement. Accurately reading her surprise, Cord laughed.

"This is where I live, honey," he explained. "If you don't learn, you don't last very long out here. The animals teach you how to survive."

He watched as Vesper took in deep drafts of the wild heady air, shaking her wind-tousled ebony mane of hair. She had blossomed in these weeks on the trail, and he swelled with pride at how far she had come from the pale, weak girl of her father's house to this eager, rose-cheeked horsewoman.

The wilderness either made you or broke you, Cord mused, depending on the strength you had inside. Gazing at his precious new wife's flushed face, he was struck by a sudden disquieting fear.

"Vesper, did I mention that my farm is a full day's ride to the nearest trading post?"

"It's truly in the wilderness," she agreed dreamily.

"You'll be far away from other white people," Cord said with a frown. "I'm asking you to give up everything you've ever known. When I left my father's plantation, I wanted to run from a way of life. I went as far as a young man could go. But am I asking too much of you?" he worried.

Cord was shocked to find an infinitely luminous smile on his young wife's face.

"You're forgetting one important thing," she told him, her eyes deep purple pools. "I have something that fifteen-year-old boy never had. I'm leaving that world back there because now I have everything I want, my darling. I have you. And every day I am with you, I feel myself unfolding, growing more."

She paused, trying to find the words to explain the joy he gave her and how much an essential part of her he had become in these few short weeks.

"I discover myself through you."

Cord drank in the eager, giving quality that seemed to emanate from every pore of her body, reaching toward him across the space between their two horses.

His disquiet stilled by the force of Vesper's caring, he said simply, "I love you."

The first days of their cross-country ride had been torturous for Vesper, whose only experience with horseback riding had been decorous hour-long canters on a gentle filly around the softly rolling countryside of Virginia. The horses Cord had purchased were of quite another ilk, bred for stamina and independence. As they had climbed rocky files and splashed through swiftly rushing streams, Vesper's unaccustomed muscles had ached, clenched, and finally cramped.

The three companions had eaten in the saddle, chewing jerked beef and gulping down lukewarm water from a canteen, because the men knew they must put as much distance as possible between themselves and Augustus Bledsoe. Covered with dust and sweat, scored by branches she had been too fatigued to avoid, Vesper found her only comfort in Cord's warm, welcoming arms at the end of the day.

"You'll get used to it, honey," he assured her again and again as he massaged her tense muscles back to suppleness. "In a few days, a week maybe, you'll toughen."

His eyes had pierced into hers, filling her with his belief in her strength. She had needed all of his faith, clinging to him in limp exhaustion, sleep falling upon her like a heavy cloak.

But he had been right, Vesper realized. Now she found the riding exhilarating. She was in easy command of her spirited horse, and had led him across a wide variety of challenging terrain. The dust, the odd food, the ground at night, none of these bothered her any longer. Her body was growing strong and disciplined, healthier than she had ever imagined. Even the air seemed sweeter, the colors more vivid.

Vesper gazed at her hands, brown and hardy as they clasped the reins, and a rush of innocent pride filled her. Her body was becoming a source of great enjoyment to her, she who had only concerned herself with matters of the mind. Vesper blushed, remembering the previous night when she had turned to Cord and begged him to pleasure her again. He had taken her with great slowness, seeming to drink in her uncontrollable moans of delight as a thirsty man gulps water in the desert.

Running Wolf, tactful as ever, had set his blankets a good distance away. Though no one but her husband witnessed her sensual abandonment, Vesper had felt apologetic after their lovemaking, worried that Cord would consider her wanton. Vesper smiled, recalling his words.

"My darling girl, the happier I make you, the more you trust me, then the deeper our love becomes. It is all one—the words, the caring, the pleasure—all make us grow closer."

He had cupped her wondering face in his hands, looking deep into her starlit eyes.

"Nature has given you great gifts, my darling. Only let me show you."

Effortlessly guiding her horse through the rustling trees, Vesper threw her husband an evocative look.

He read the memories on her face and rumbled, "Tonight we'll be together in a real bed. The village is just ahead."

An Indian, dressed only in breechclout and moccasins, appeared for a moment to their left and then melted back into the woods so completely that Vesper couldn't be sure where he had gone.

"Was that one of the tribe?" she asked eagerly. Turning back, she called to Running Wolf, "I think I saw one of your people."

He brought his horse forward until the three were riding abreast. His eyes rested on her kindly, with a glimmer of amusement in their black depths.

"He was a scout, our Santee version of a welcoming committee. That is why you could see him. If we were the enemy, he would never have permitted us to see him. When we reach the village, my people will be waiting for us."

Soon afterward, Vesper began to see curls of smoke rising through the trees and to hear a faint sound of barking dogs. They had reached the outskirts of the Indian camp. Among the bark lodges, black-haired women in tunics, almost-naked children, and stalwart adolescent braves converged on the center of the camp. There was no hurry to their movements, yet they arrived swiftly at the bark lodge house where the elders of the tribe stood.

Vesper was struck by the quiet impassivity of the people. Their faces looked like handsomely carved red stone. Surrounding her horse like so many cinnamon-colored sentinels, they showed no welcome, no dislike, not even curiosity in their deep black eyes.

There were two exceptions. One was the young brave whose honor it was to lead away the horses of the travelers. His hands shook slightly as he took the reins from their hands. The other was the distinguished older woman who exchanged a long, speaking look with Running Wolf.

A wizened tribal elder, magnificent in his finery and proud in posture, handed a long carved rod tied with white coup feathers to the chief.

"We have missed our brother's voice in the council halls. Without his wisdom, our way has been dark. Take back the staff of leadership from my hands."

Accepting the rod, Running Wolf gestured with it toward Vesper.

"The woman is Vesper Travers, mate to our friend of many winters. She is daughter to a man of power, counselor to the Great White Father himself. She has shown great spirit on our journey. I judge her heart to be as the eagle's, and she shall be accorded all honor."

Vesper was greatly surprised at what she could understand of the chief's complimentary words. She had no idea that he had come to value her so highly. She stood proudly before the people as their leader gestured to the older woman he had looked to earlier.

"My own wife, Spring Willow, shall lead her to our lodge."

The woman who approached Vesper, exuding calm authority, could have been nothing else but a chief's wife. She was slender and graceful, though her forty years had lightly frosted her thick braids and weathered her strong face. There was so great an air of self-possession and sureness about her that Vesper, gazing into her quiet eyes, was reminded of a noble forest animal, looking at the world from out of an unconscious eternal present.

Spring Willow's voice was low and melodious.

"Come with me, wife of our white brother. Come wash the dust of the journey from your throat and the ache of travel from your bones."

Smiling, Vesper followed her, leaving the men to their deliberations. From the back, Spring Willow's supple deerskin tunic, with its beaded, fringed margins waving at the knee, undulated with the older woman's every step, revealing a strong, subtle play of muscles accustomed to demanding work. The chief's wife led Vesper to the largest family lodging in the encampment and graciously nodded for Vesper to enter. Inside, around the central firepit, crouched several middle-aged Indian women, who all looked up at the guest's appearance.

The chief's wife introduced her, repeating many of her husband's words. This second time, Vesper was able to follow almost all of the words, thanks to Cord's language lessons on the journey. When the women welcomed her, Vesper was able to answer them, albeit brokenly, in their own tongue. She was pleased to see a warming in their eyes at her attempt, and several women chattered out comments to one another too quick for Vesper to catch.

Spring Willow gestured toward a pile of rabbit skins, speaking slowly.

"Please find comfort in this house."

As Vesper obeyed, lowering herself gratefully onto the soft pelts, Spring Willow brought her a birchbark cup of water sweetened with honey and an upturned tortoiseshell heaped with roasted corn cakes. Vesper savored the flavor of fresh food, smiling shyly at the curious glances of the women as she ate.

"It's delicious," Vesper offered politely to her hostess.

Spring Willow gave her an approving maternal glance, smiling to see how quickly the food was disappearing. Replenishing Vesper's snack, the older woman returned to the task she had been working on earlier—affixing porcupine quills to a half-finished tobacco pouch. Following suit, the other women continued their tasks: pounding berries into dried meat to prepare pemmican, scraping hides, and sewing clothing with bone awls and thread of buffalo sinew.

Vesper watched their skilled fingers with envy. How she longed to become as resourceful as they, to be of use to her husband instead of merely baggage. Spring Willow easily read Vesper's wish to be included.

"Come sit by my side, child," she said.

When Vesper eagerly obeyed, the chief's wife placed a plain buffalo-skin pouch and a threaded bone needle in her hands. Gesturing toward the large pile of quills before them, she picked up a single sharply pointed one and showed the white woman how it must be attached to the material. Then she searched through the pile for another quill that matched the first in length and color. Laying it alongside the earlier one, she sewed it on, piercing the tough hide effortlessly with decisive stabs. Spring Willow waved to Vesper to start her own band of quills.

Gingerly Vesper copied the older woman's graceful movements, and managed to attach her first quill amid a cloud of kindly chuckles from the watching women. Her second attempt was less awkward, and as she found the working rhythm the band of quills began to grow. Satisfaction lit her eyes as she ran her fingernail across the polished rippled surface of her work.

Vesper would have been gratified by the women's words had she been able to follow Sioux fluently. Her beauty, her air of confidence, and her eagerness to learn Indian ways were all touted. She would be good for their white brother, walk by his side in the daylight and assuage his loneliness in the dark of the night. The squaws were well pleased, and kept shooting approving looks at the slender, violet-eyed guest bent so industriously over her unfamiliar task.

Inside the shadowy bark lodge, the tribal council sat in a somber circle, ceremonial firelight flickering over the wrinkled faces of the elders and the smooth-skinned countenances of the younger braves. After a solemn sharing of the peace pipe, Cord reported the disappointing results of the trip to Washington. His words were met with little surprise. The Santee Sioux had found little reason to trust the new white settlers. Why should white councils of power be any different?

"The woods are filled with their fences," reported Climbing Elk, a venerable elder seated at Running Wolf's right. "They would have all the nut groves for their own. It is said that these men would wall out the buck from his doe, the beaver from his dam.

How can this be allowed? Shall barriers be erected by any but the Great Spirit himself?"

There was a stir of agreement at his words. Encouraged, Climbing Elk suggested, "Our young men will pull the fences from the earth. In this way we will not war against the white man, but only against his wrongdoing."

Hawk-of-the-Forest, an older brave, raised a cautioning palm.

"Our way is dark before my eyes, my brothers. My heart cries out in gladness to do this thing, yet I know also that it will bring more forays. Only yesterday, three more of our young braves lay broken on the ground—"

"And seven of theirs have answered with their blood," interrupted a fierce young warrior. "Our brothers did not go unavenged."

Another young man, his eyes glittering with anger, joined in. "Why must we run like frightened mice from the white man? It is our land on which he trespasses. If his actions offend our hearts, let us drive him from it. Only command us, my fathers. We stand ready to fight."

A chorus of cheers erupted among the young braves, to be instantly quelled as Running Wolf raised his hand, facing the eager youths.

"The fires of courage run fierce and true in a young man's veins. In truth, I am made proud by your willingness to die for our people. But the wolf cub, though brave, may bite at the turtle safe inside his shell, or the grizzly who could kill him with one batting paw. We invite you to our councils to learn wisdom. Do so now in silence."

The young braves sat in abashed quiet at their chief's admonishing words. He turned back to the assembled elders, who were nodding approvingly.

"I have walked among the tents of the white man,

my brothers, and they are mighty and without number. It is in my mind that to meet them in full war would crush our people. So we must take the path of the fox, who holds his territory, yet fights not to the death against those who trespass."

Cord watched the young men who had been guarding the tribal boundaries swallow their disappointment as the elders replaced them with calmer, more seasoned warriors. It was all the Santee Sioux could do, he realized. Provoking war would be racial suicide. Yet part of the mountain man reared up in even hotter anger than the young braves, because he knew something they did not.

No matter what tactics the Indians used, in time they would be overcome. The wild, proud land of their ancestors would fall under the white man's plow and be cut to bleeding pieces by the white man's walls and fences and legal deeds. A noble way of life was coming to an end, and Cord had only to look at the depth of sadness in his foster father's eyes to know that Running Wolf saw it too.

Yet once again Cord Travers took a lesson from his Indian brothers. If they could meet the daunting future with such dignity, then so would he. There might be many years left before the inevitable end. He would live each day as fully as he could, with his violet-eyed, inky-tressed lady at his side. He could do no less.

# Chapter Nine

VESPER CAME AWAKE WITH A SNAP. LAST NIGHT, HER first in Cord's . . . no, in their log and sod house, she had viewed the long, narrow bed with a rush of misgivings. After countless nights on the open trail with the hard earth digging into her back, she had consoled herself by imagining the soft comfort of the feather bed to come, not this rough-hewn frame with its unfamiliar underpinning of crisscrossed ropes topped only by a thin mattress barely thicker than a summer quilt. But when Cord lifted her into his strong arms and took her to the bed, his wonderful lovemaking had swiftly dispelled any doubts she felt.

When morning came with the sun streaming into their little alcove, Vesper stretched like a satisfied cat luxuriating in the warmth of its cozy nest. Yes, she thought to herself, a smile escaping from her lips, this bed would do nicely. She turned toward

Cord, only to find him already awake, with one arm wedged under his chin.

"You're studying me," Vesper said in a mock tone of exasperation.

"M-m-m-m-m."

She arched her back, bringing her breasts tantalizingly close to his golden chest.

"Do I pass?" she murmured.

The light behind her sent dazzling sapphire highlights through her lush black mane. Cord grabbed at the long tresses and caught Vesper's lips in a slow, hard kiss. She was breathless and closed her eyes, giving herself up to the exciting dominance of her husband. When the kiss ended, she looked expectantly at Cord, only to find him observing her with an amused glint in his eyes and a wry smile on his mouth.

"Cord?" she asked in confusion.

His smile broke into a wide grin. With one word, she had communicated the wealth of her feelings to him.

"The honeymoon is over, my girl," he said lightly. But when he saw dismay on Vesper's beautiful face, he was quick to add, "I want to be with you too, honey, but on a farm, the work never stops."

"Oh, Cord," Vesper asked excitedly. "Is there work for me, too? Now that I am your wife, I want to do my share."

He wasn't sure which his plucky wife possessed more of: sweet eagerness or lack of knowledge. But he was touched by her readiness to take her place by his side.

"Up and at 'em, Vesper. We'll start with the cabin."

Hours later, Vesper sat by the edge of a small lake which clearly reflected the tall maples surrounding it. But she was unaware of the serene vista about her. She found herself physically exhausted and, she had to admit to herself, totally unprepared for the kind of life she would be leading as Cord's wife. And, so far, he had only shown her the indoor tasks she was to do. True, he had stressed that she would do them with ease . . . eventually. But she was staggered by the work load and her alarming ineptitude.

The cabin was small, she mused, in actuality no bigger than her old bedchamber. But it functioned as a complete house, including within its four walls bedroom, kitchen, larder, laundry, parlor, and library. Cord had promised her he would add a second story to the modest homestead and purchase all the modern conveniences the local trading post could deliver.

At first Vesper had been delighted, but now, as she nursed her sore muscles, all she could think of was how much more work a larger house would entail. She sighed, suddenly aware of the hot sun bearing down on her aching shoulders. She leaned closer to the lake and wet her face, letting the cool water wash away the sudden tears that coursed down her cheeks.

Cord padded up behind her, silent in his moccasins.

"Ready for your next lesson, sweetheart?" he asked lightheartedly.

She jumped up, giving him a quick hug and burying her face in his shoulder. She choked back her tears, not wanting her stalwart frontier husband to know how weak and silly she was. He held her to him tightly, amazed that this woman of beauty and courage was his, yet gently too, afraid that he had overwhelmed her with his demanding expectations.

"Never mind, my love. That's enough for today," he said soothingly.

"No," she answered. "I want to know it all."

He stared into the deep amethyst pools of her eyes, glistening like purple crystal in the light. He saw the fierce determination she was feeling and he resolved not to dampen her tremendous spirit.

"Have you ever been fishing?" he asked in a coaxing voice.

Together, with his arms around her, demonstrating each step of the way, Cord and Vesper caught a slew of buffalofish. Her feelings of ineptitude faded in his sunny enthusiasm. It all seemed so easy when Cord was there to show her. He was pampering her and she knew it. But soon, she promised herself, she would take up the reins of her new role. Life in the Indian Woods would suit her fine. She'd prove it to Cord.

It was another morning, toward the end of the first few weeks of Vesper's new life, and she woke to the familiar call of the Indian braves who came to work the horses with Cord. The Indians never entered the cabin in the dawn hours, respecting Cord and Vesper's privacy. Instead they waited by the door, the younger ones boldly engaged in verbal competition over which one would break more horses that day. The older, wiser men observed the weather, standing motionless as statues until their white brother joined them.

In the alcove, Cord threw on his heavy dungarees and shirt and tied a bandanna carelessly around his neck. Vesper eyed him from bed, hoping to squeeze one last minute from the heat their bodies had generated under the homespun sheets and blankets. Watching him dress and waiting for his good-bye kiss had become a pleasurable ritual for her. But as she shifted her body she felt the first wince of pain shoot through her, reminding her of the backbreaking day ahead.

"Oh," she sighed, stretching her limbs with deliberate care.

"Missing me already?" Cord teased lightly as he sat on a straight-backed wooden chair and pulled on his leather boots.

"I was afraid you'd leave without giving me a kiss."

She winced again, this time not from her deeply aching muscles but because she had lied to Cord. It was a necessary lie, she told herself. She would never let her adored husband know how difficult this way of life was proving to be. Each new day brought her fresh worries about accomplishing even the simplest task Cord expected her to do. She was afraid she'd never adjust to pioneer life, and she couldn't fail Cord. She just couldn't.

Her towering husband smiled and came back to the long bed. He was bending to kiss her when he glanced at her eyes. There was a wealth of misery in her innocent, appealing gaze. He brushed each eye closed with a kiss and sat down beside her.

"What is it, darling? Is it all too much, too soon?"

He weaved his fingers into her raven tresses, stroking the hair he loved to wind about him.

"No, no," she cried vehemently, then broke into sobs. "It's . . . it's just those damned chickens, Cord. They don't like me."

Her tears came thick and fast now. Biting his cheek to hold back the laughter, he cradled his poor befuddled wife in his arms.

"Now, Vesper, I don't see how you can say that. The chickens think you're a very fine woman. They told me so themselves just last night."

She sat bolt upright, tearing herself from his arms. Fire flashed in her amethyst eyes.

**113**

"Don't treat me like a silly child, Cord Travers. I won't stand for it," she insisted.

Cord applauded her.

"There's the woman I love, the woman who stands up for herself, regardless of her adversaries, be they armed guards, raging torrents . . ."

"Or chickens?" Vesper finished softly.

"Most emphatically chickens," Cord echoed solemnly. "Now tell me what is really bothering you."

She reclined again in his arms, grateful to have this stalwart man at her side. But she did not look at him when she spoke to him.

"Really," she said in a high, tiny voice, "I can't manage to get the eggs from the hens. They peck at me, and no matter where I try to slip my hand into their nests, they're there, squawking and biting. I can't keep feeding you biscuits and coffee forever." With more determination she added fiercely, "And you shouldn't have to show me how to do it again."

Above her, Cord smiled, proud of this streak of stubborn pride in his wife. He was certain she would resolve all these minor difficulties. Unceremoniously he stood up and dumped Vesper on the bed, patting her soundly on the rump. A howl came from under the pillows.

"Well said, wife. And now I'll be off to the stables. Oh, and by the way, Vesper," Cord added, his mind on breakfast to come in a few hours, "a steaming-hot plate of scrambled eggs would sure be a sight for these sore eyes."

Another howl, this time of indignation, rose from the bed and Vesper heaved a pillow at Cord's departing figure. But the rich sound of his laughter caught her up and her mood changed to buoyant optimism. If Cord believed in her, then Vesper would believe in herself too.

She dressed hurriedly before the brisk spring air

could chill her heated body. Gone were the fashionable clothes of society. Gone even were the plain but tailored gowns Vesper was used to wearing. Now her wardrobe consisted of a few hastily purchased cotton work blouses and heavy woven long skirts and a few light calico dresses for summer. A simple muslin petticoat underneath, simple dark stockings, and leather boots completed Vesper's daily garb.

As she tied an old yellow bandanna of Cord's around her neck, she looked out the window and saw her husband stride off with his Indian friends. She experienced the sweet ache of longing to hold him once more before he left her sight. There was an ease about this man of hers which she saw only here among the Indians and the horses. Cord was a man of nature, at home in the wilderness. His great height fit among the towering trees; his great strength challenged by the powerful rush of the river current.

Frowning, she wondered whether she could justify Cord's expectations of her. Was she a woman of nature? There was only one way to find out. Her jaw set sternly, Vesper made her way through the large front room of the cabin. She marched straight ahead, out the doorway, across the grassy path to the barn, where she paused only long enough to fill a wooden bucket with chicken feed before facing her nemesis.

Her spirit began to falter when she pried open the entrance to the coop. Several chicks with scrabby coarse feathers emerging from baby-soft down, fat brown nonlaying hens, and two wrathful roosters with imperious red coxcombs flew out of the coop, straight at Vesper. In fright, she dropped the feed pail, and the ground-up corn and grain spilled about her feet. The raucous birds, joyous to be freed from their nightly confinement, dashed for their morning meal. As if a spray of bullets were shot near her feet, Vesper hopped and leaped about, trying to avoid the sharp beaks of food-crazed fowl.

There was only one escape from the birds, and the girl, whose brave determination had melted to quavering fear, ran into the chicken coop. She was met by the suspicious glances of the laying hens, who seemed to spread themselves even more broadly over their nests at the presence of this intruder.

"Come, biddy, biddy, biddy," Vesper whispered in a cracked voice.

Clearing her throat, she accidentally emitted a loud barking sound, and the hens flapped their wings in disapproval.

"I'm sorry, chickens," Vesper begged, suddenly wondering about the sanity of a grown woman who would apologize to dumb birds.

She remembered Cord's indulgent teasing and firm support earlier that morning. She would stand firm and prove her worth to him.

"All right, you biddies," Vesper said, stalking her prey. "I want those eggs and I want them now."

She circled the coop, giving each hen a baleful stare. Without warning she lunged at one hen. The hen cocked her head and with perfect timing pecked at the delicate webbing between Vesper's outstretched fingers.

"Ouch," cried the girl. "You think you're so smart. Well, I'll get your eggs."

She waved her arms like a floppy scarecrow in the wind at the hen. The hen closed her eyes, blotting Vesper out of her existence. Frustrated, Vesper turned toward another reddish brown hen, who squawked in alarm at the approaching menace.

"Buck-buck. Buck-buck," Vesper intoned in her best chicken imitation.

The bird eyed her warily but sat passively as

Vesper slid her hand beneath the bird and into the nest. She'd succeeded! Vesper couldn't believe it. Her hand searched the nest timidly, then frantically. The hen lazily hopped from her roost to the floor of the coop. Vesper's eyes went wide with dismay. The nest was empty. No wonder the damn bird was so cooperative, Vesper thought.

Dull anger simmered within Vesper. She whirled about and caught sight of a hen who sat on her nest, preening her feathers.

"I'll get you," the girl muttered grimly.

Swiftly she stepped up to the chicken, still intent on grooming. With one hand Vesper grabbed the bird by its fat, compact neck and held it at arm's length while with the other hand she dived for the treasure trove of three eggs clustered in the middle of the nest. Eagerly she scooped up all three eggs and dumped the shocked bird back on her nest. The other hens were in an uproar at this outrageous action, but Vesper felt triumphant.

"Scrambled eggs for Cord, tra-la," she sang exultantly.

Vesper felt for the deep pocket of her skirt and carefully, lovingly, placed the eggs within. She turned to leave the coop when a look of disbelief froze on her face. She had forgotten the hole at the far end of her pocket. No, no, she cried in silent prayer. She had neglected her sewing all week, and now retribution was upon her.

As if in slow motion, Vesper felt each egg slip past the widening tear, fall against her leg, and drop down. The sharp sound of three successive cracks hit her as loudly as the thunder of cannons. There on her right boot lay Cord's scrambled eggs. She erupted in a flood of tears and ran from the coop, leaving the amazed chickens to digest and gossip about this latest brouhaha.

Vesper ran blindly for the stables, thinking only about the protection of Cord's comforting arms. But she stopped short as the white-fenced training ring came into sight. She couldn't tell Cord she'd been routed again. She wouldn't embarrass him by complaining in front of his Indian friends. Vesper sat down on an old stump and idly picked at some fallen leaves at her feet until a brilliant flash of inspiration came to her. She'd go berry picking and bake Cord fresh fruit muffins as a surprise.

Vesper jumped up with renewed purpose to find a pail. Her path ran along the edge of the big woods, where the open prairie began. Above her spread the wide canopy of blue sky with its patches of puffy white clouds. Rich green grasses, thick groves of trees, cheery-faced wildflowers growing from the iron-red earth, surrounded the girl and cheered her anxious heart.

Hours later she glanced up at the sun. She'd searched high and low for berries, not knowing that the season had not yet begun. It was getting late. She finished gathering the few chokecherries she had found and raced home. Vesper was out of breath by the time she reached the cabin. Cord was nowhere in sight, but something was there waiting for her.

On Cord's morning rounds of the far grazing lands, he must have had time to hunt, for by the front door lay a brace of rabbits. She picked them up gingerly, amazed by their heavy weight, and carried them inside. All right, she said determinedly to herself, Spring Willow showed me how to skin a muskrat. Rabbits can't be too different.

She armed herself with all the utensils she thought she might need. Laying the rabbits on a table, Vesper took up a sharp knife. She looked down at the soft, sweet brown eyes of the first bunny which stared sightlessly at her. Vesper shuddered. Quickly she turned the rabbit over on its back and watched the two little white front paws flop limply onto its chest. Vesper looked away as she forced her hand with the wavering knife closer to the motionless animal. Twenty minutes later, with her stomach churning, she gazed at the mess she had made.

Nausea won over determination and endurance. She fled from the cabin, wanting to scream and cry and forget all at once. She flung herself down along the gritty pebbled shore of a forest lake and took great sobbing breaths of the clean, clear air. Her hands formed tight fists as she swore over and over at herself. She was a fool. She had eaten meat all her life. The only difference now was that she was closer to the reality of it. She must get used to it. She'd force herself if she had to. Painfully Vesper raised herself and walked slowly back to the cabin.

It was dusk. The lovely sky, painted in an array of rosy pink and lavender swatches, was giving way to the velvety deep blue of approaching nightfall. Cord bade farewell to his Santee Sioux brothers. Coming home was different now. He used to eat with Running Wolf or, if he was too tired, throw together some greens and dried beef and settle down to his account books.

But now, since Vesper had become his bride, Cord hurried through the days, still loving his work, but anxious to be with his helpmate. She was more precious to him each day, and her efforts to please him, whether successful or not, had already shown him how right his choice was. He only hoped that she was content.

Cord pushed open the door to his happy home. In the half-light of dusk, Cord blinked, disbelieving the sight before his eyes. The large room, with its huge fireplace, sideboard, bookshelves, tables, and chairs, looked as though a hurricane had hit. The contents of the cabinets had been spilled onto every tabletop, and the clutter had then spilled onto the floor. Unrecognizable bits of food clung to burned pans, stained rags, and, yes, Cord noted in amazement, even the walls. The flue in the chimney had jammed and fetid smoke was filling the room. Coughing, he ran to the windows and opened them. Vesper, where was Vesper?

Catching his breath while he fanned the dark smoke out of the house, Cord glanced toward the alcove and back at the holocaust. Then, with eyebrows arched, he deliberately strode toward the bed. She lay there, curled up in a ball, nursing a bandaged finger.

"Well, Vesper?" Cord said sternly.

"Well, Cord?" she echoed.

He chose his words as carefully as his mood would permit.

"Perhaps you could explain yourself . . . the house . . . this mess."

"Yes, isn't it," she said lightly.

But the defeat behind her voice sabotaged her facade. In a moment, she was crawling into Cord's arms seeking her heart's haven.

"I tried so hard, Cord. I wanted to be the perfect wife. But the hens pecked me and the eggs fell on my shoes and the rabbits stared at me and I hacked them into a bloody mess and then the squirrels got into the nut sacks and my muffins wouldn't rise but I baked them anyway and burned them and my finger . . ."

She held up the greasy bandage as if it were the proof of her whole misbegotten day. Cord had never seen such a forlorn expression on anyone's face, and never had he heard such an outrageously strung together tale of woe. He clenched his jaw so as not to laugh. She clung to him, starting to cry with great howling sobs and gasps. Her whole body shook. Abruptly she pushed him away from her. Tears were streaming down her cheeks, but her face was contorted with wild laughter.

"Oh, Cord," she said, "after a while I couldn't believe it myself. It was like one of Running Wolf's spirit gods having a joke at my expense."

Cord burst out laughing too, relief pouring over him. The tension of trying so hard to be perfect was finally broken, and now, Cord knew, it would never be quite so hard for her again. The first, most difficult step had been taken, now that she had laughed at herself. They collapsed onto the bed in each other's arms and let the waves of shared worry ebb in the stronger passion of their love.

Wanting to possess her, to be possessed by her, Cord rolled on top of his willing wife. Even with their clothes on, they both felt the tempestuous swell of hunger for each other smolder through. Leaf-green eyes locked on amethyst eyes. Impatient, he hoisted himself up and tore at the buttons of her blouse. She shifted her weight, helping him to remove the long sleeves from her arms. She wriggled her hips forward as she slid her skirt off.

"Wait," she said suddenly.

He paused, wondering if she were embarrassed to make love before the sun went down. She sat up and leaned over him, draping her breasts on his bare arm. A smoldering shock went through him, but she was laughing, lying down again in his arms.

"Here, darling. The sole fruit of my day's labor."

Vesper handed him a muffin so tiny it fit in the center of his cupped palm. The miniature muffin was still warm and its fruity aroma filled the air. Cord tilted back his head and laughed uproariously.

"Vesper, don't ever change. You already are the

perfect wife," he said between gulps for air. His laughter subsiding, he grew more serious, adding, "You are everything I want. I love you for who you are now, my dearest. Give yourself time and you'll see I'm right."

He looked down at the muffin still in his palm. Carefully breaking it in two, he fed half to Vesper, the other half to himself. Then he kissed her, savoring the nutty taste mixed with Vesper's own sweetness. Now it was Vesper's turn to tear at Cord's clothes. Shirt, pants, boots, all were off in short order.

Soon they were lost in the spiraling glory of rediscovering each other. In the sun of Cord's passion, Vesper had put aside her innocent shyness. She blossomed in his embrace and matched him kiss for kiss, caress for caress. Their hearts were completely open to each other, and at the moment when their bodies came together, they gazed into each other's eyes, secure in their love, stronger in their commitment, and satiated in their need.

Through the last vestiges of spring and into the fertile summer season, Vesper grew in her role as Cord's partner. She stayed at his side, watching, learning, practicing with diligence and patience the skills of a frontier woman. From the first moment she had known she loved Cord, Vesper had thought the immensity of her emotion could never change. But each day that she lived with this sweetly fierce bear of a husband, she found new and unexpected reasons for her love to grow and grow.

Vesper was unceasingly amazed at the endless store of Cord's knowledge about the cycles of woodland life. Some of their sweetest moments together were on quiet walks through the Indian Woods. Her respect for Cord's deep commitment to the Santee continued to increase. He averted many a useless skirmish between the settlers and the hotheaded young braves. Cord's galvanizing spirit was no less apparent in the mystical rapport he seemed to have with his horses. Vesper felt as though she would burst with pride for her dearest, most stalwart husband.

As the year moved forward into autumn Vesper finally felt she had become a helpmate to Cord. She had mastered the daily routine. Those chores which had first reduced her to tears of frustration were now commonplace. She was up at dawn to feed the chickens, milk the cow before leading her to pasture, feed the big, lumbering plowhorses and ready them for the field. Then it was back to the house to prepare an enormous breakfast for Cord. There was just time to clean her kitchen before she made her daily check of the larder, prepared a bag of darning, and took her fishing pole to one of the nearby lakes.

Later, she was off to the fields to pick the ripest vegetables. Before sundown, she had the horses stabled, the cow milked again, the chickens back in their coop, and dinner cooking. Still, at the end of her long day, Vesper found a few moments to write a letter to Aunt Lucinda or read one of Cord's books on horse breeding.

Although Vesper felt bone-tired after their evening meal, when Cord's leaf-green eyes lingered on her curves or when his playful pats turned into suggestive caresses, all her weariness vanished. She marveled, as the months went by, how her body's need for him grew. Their nights were storms of fire and beauty as they tossed on a sea of passion, all of their own making.

With the arrival of winter and its heavy white blanket of snow covering the once-verdant land, Vesper and Cord truly withdrew into their own private Eden. The horses, safe with the Santee Sioux in their winter quarters many miles away, no longer occupied Cord, and he had plenty of time and attention to lavish on Vesper. She had emerged into full womanhood, independent, strong both physically and emotionally, capable of expressing the full range of her feelings in her husband's arms.

They shared everything during their first winter together, so closely that each became adept at guessing the other's needs, words, thoughts. Through the long winter nights, the cabin seethed with passion where every look, every touch, led to a locked, heated embrace. But nothing meant so much as their first Christmas Eve together.

After a luminous white day in their snowbound world, Cord and Vesper ate sumptuously on pheasant, wild rice, chokecherries, and muffins light as clouds. Replete, they bundled themselves into their heaviest clothes and stepped outside onto the long porch Cord had added to the front of the cabin. They stood, arms about each other, braving the bone-chilling twilight, to stare at the brilliant red and purple hues of the setting sun which seemed to set the snow afire. The sunset splendor gave way to the sparkling twinkle of a million faraway stars glittering against the backdrop of the jet-black night sky.

Cord and Vesper exchanged no words. They didn't need to. As they turned to each other, the miracle of the stars gleamed in one pair of green eyes and one pair of amethyst eyes. In their winter paradise, they kissed and, in all-embracing love, knew a deep and complete oneness.

# Chapter Ten

PALE LEMON SPRING SUNLIGHT FILTERED THROUGH THE cabin windows, bathing the big room in a soft verdant glow. Demoiselle, the Traverses' pet fawn, followed her mistress around the room, butting at her legs and bleating piteously.

"I know you're hungry, baby," Vesper said, nimbly sidestepping the animal as she carried a dishpan of soapy water to the front door and emptied it. "As soon as I finish here, we'll go for a walk and find something for you."

It was only a few hours after sunrise, but already Vesper's morning tasks were done. She eyed with satisfaction the line of clothing and bedding, newly washed, drying outside in the breeze. Half a dozen loaf pans, their rising dough covered with clean cloths, stood on the windowsills.

"Come, Demoiselle," Vesper called, opening the

door and standing aside as the half-grown deer leaped out.

She picked her way down the dirt path past the vegetable garden, the barns, and the horse paddocks. The rich red-brown ground was muddy from last night's rain. By the time Vesper reached the forest margin, her moccasins were heavy with wet earth.

"Demi, wait," Vesper called to the careening fawn, who leaped off the side of the path and piled into the wet bushes.

At the sound of her voice, the soft-eyed baby trotted back to her mistress. Vesper picked up a white, sharp-edged rock, balanced with one hand against a tree, and was scraping her moccasins clean when Demoiselle shook the rainwater from her hide, showering Vesper.

"How could such a small beast get me so wet?" Vesper scolded lovingly, kneeling down to hug her mischievous pet, who licked Vesper's dripping cheek with a wide velvet tongue.

"Come on," said Vesper, straightening. "Let's find some fiddleneck ferns."

The two scampered down the forest path together, lighthearted as children, for spring had finally broken through winter's long hold on the Indian Woods. Demoiselle had dashed far ahead, but now she raced back to her mistress, terror in her huge liquid brown eyes and a quill sticking out of her soft black nose.

"Silly girl," Vesper chided, removing the quill. "I told you you can't sniff everything."

She stroked the pricked nose until Demoiselle stopped trembling. Just ahead in the undergrowth, Vesper made out a stand of newly opened fiddleneck ferns. Picking a handful of the newest ones, she held them out to Demoiselle, who tickled her mistress's palm with soft pulling nibbles.

There was a sudden silence. The tapestry of birdsong had ceased and even the red squirrels had stopped their incessant rustling chase. When Vesper heard the slither of a moccasin and a small branch crack, she knew the visitors were Indians.

"Welcome," she called in Sioux as Spring Willow's eight-year-old twin grandsons emerged from around a bend in the trail.

"Good morning, Eyes-of-Violet," Striped Lizard responded shyly.

"Your fawn is looking well," said Small Fox politely.

Then Striped Lizard, who was the elder by only a few minutes, said, "There is a thing you should see, Eyes-of-Violet. White hunters killed a mother wolf and her cub. But another cub was not found. It is alone now and has no one to help it grow."

Vesper's heart contracted at the thought of yet another abandoned wild baby. For the past year, she had watched helplessly as the encroaching settlers crashed through the woods, blind to the natural order, intent only on plunder. They shot not only for food or protection, but apparently for the sheer wanton thrill of bringing death. Only last week Vesper had stumbled across the body of a gray squirrel, heavy with young, pinned to a tree by a bullet.

Running Wolf's words came back to her: "They will be judged by the Great Spirit and their deeds will walk before them."

"Children, take me to this cub," Vesper ordered, her soft mouth thinned to a grim line.

The twins each slipped a warm little hand into hers and led the way to a small clearing where a two-week-old pale gray wolf cub lolled listlessly at the mouth of a burrow. Vesper rushed over to the baby and knelt before it, cradling its weak little head in her hands. The shivering infant, its fuzzy, coarse fur matted with wet mud, slowly opened its slanted, cloudy blue eyes. Blazing amethyst eyes met soft sapphire ones, and the bond was forged.

The wolfling opened its tiny mouth and emitted a piteous whimper, licking Vesper's hand with a pink wisp of a tongue. Demoiselle trotted to Vesper's side at the baby's call and nuzzled the cub comfortingly. Vesper picked up the trembling baby, stood, and cradled it against her breast.

"I'm going to take it home," she told the two children, who smiled with satisfaction and bade her farewell, promising to visit the cub very soon.

She worried over the wolfling most of the morning, making it comfortable in a bed of soft rags and getting it to suckle from an old worn glove soaked in milk and honey. Leaving the cub in the contented glow of satisfied sleep, Vesper made for the fields and the plow. All afternoon she worked on the corn patch, making straight furrows, dropping the seed, managing the powerful plowhorses. At the end of the last furrow, she stretched her sore back and shoulders. The work was hard and exhausting. But the results were worth it. In a few months, tasseled ears of corn would be rustling in the summer breeze. Even more important to Vesper, she had proven again her capability. She could throw herself into her task now, trusting in her power to succeed.

And then one had to recover, Vesper thought ruefully, surveying her sweat-stained, dirt-spattered clothing. As soon as she had unhitched and watered down the horses, she hurried to her favorite bathing spot, a secluded deep pond.

The rock-edged pool, with its natural awning of leaning trees, had seldom looked so inviting. Where sunbeams shone through the emerald leaf cover, the water glittered white-gold against the rippling bronze of its shaded surface. Vesper peeled the grimy clothes from her tired body, rinsed the garments briefly, and spread them out to dry on a wide flat stone.

She plunged gratefully into the cool, beckoning water. The endless fingers of wet caressed her from her scalp to the soles of her feet, playing wordless streaming songs against her sensitive skin. It was sheer heaven. Vesper dived and surfaced, twisted and floated, sporting on the water's breast as lithe and sinuous as a river otter.

She was floating on her back, arms outstretched, with only her peaceful face, her lovely conical breasts, and the tips of her toes showing above the surface, when Cord came upon her. After a long morning with the horses, he too had felt the call of the pond. When he saw the naked body of his wife, he threw his clothing pell-mell onto the rocks and plunged into the water after her.

Vesper started at the sound of a heavy body striking the water, disturbing her peace. But before she had time to react, her husband's handsome chiseled face popped up beside hers, a playful gleam in his leaf-green eyes.

"Cord!" she yelped happily as he grasped her by the waist and lifted her high into the air.

She ran her hands over the still-warm, heavily muscled surface of his upper arms.

"Put me down, you idiot."

"Ask me nicely," he demanded.

"Pleeease," she squealed.

Obediently he dropped her into the deepest part of the pool where the water was icy. She fell so fast that water rushed into her mouth and she choked.

Bent on revenge, Vesper swam away underwater until she approached him from behind. She rammed herself with all her might against the back of both of his knees. She surfaced quickly to watch her massive husband flail for balance and finally tumble backward into the water. When he surfaced, she was laughing gaily.

"You little devil," he swore, a boyish grin splitting his face. "You've asked for it now."

Vesper hastened away from him, swimming for the far side of the pond as fast as she could. Twice she was able to elude his grasp. But finally he caught her and, holding both of her hands above her head, he tickled her ribs unmercifully until she had to beg him to stop.

"Had enough, sprite?" he asked.

"Yes," she gasped. "Enough."

As soon as he released her, however, she stretched out an arm just under the surface of the water and whirled, splashing his face with a huge wave. Vesper gurgled at the comical look of surprise on his face before she plunged deep into the pool and undulated away. Cord charged after her, his powerful strokes closing the gap between them. When his fingertips had almost grasped her toes, Vesper reversed direction abruptly so that she was swimming toward him, but underneath him.

The full length of his magnificent golden body stretched above her, its provocative contours dappled by the changing patterns of light on the water's surface. Drawn as a moth to the flame, Vesper swam up close to him and turned so that she was moving in the same direction as he but with the front surface of her body facing his. She rose until their flesh touched from ankle to chest and slowly slid her way forward, feeling shocks of desire as his skin stroked against hers. When she had passed him, Vesper could not resist rising up out of the water to look into his eyes.

What she read there startled even as it excited her. Gone was the playful boy, and in his place was a deeply aroused male, green eyes turbulent with desire. Vesper shivered in mingled fear and delight as she watched her husband take a deep, ragged breath. What would he do now?

Without a word, Cord took off after her, putting his full strength behind his strokes. Vesper shot away from him, her heart slamming in her breast. The power of her anticipation propelled her furiously through the water, but he caught her easily, grabbing an ankle and pulling her effortlessly back to him.

He held the entire length of her trembling flesh against his, running his hands up and down her body with a conqueror's touch. One of his massive palms turned her face up to meet his scorching lips that plundered her mouth with furious intensity. She twisted in his arms, half afraid of the hunger she had unleashed even while some primitive urging deep within her gloried in his power over her.

Cord sensed her resistance and let his arms go slack.

"Do you really want to escape?" he demanded, his eyes boring into hers.

Bereft of the heat of his body, Vesper felt astonishingly empty.

"No," she breathed, and hurled herself back into his embrace. "Take me," she begged as his hands began wandering over her waiting skin. "Make me yours."

His fevered lips traveled over her face, down the pale apricot skin of her neck, and up again to her delicate shell-like ear.

"How I love you, Vesper Travers," he whispered huskily. "Beautiful, beautiful creature."

All she could say was his name, over and over, as the stroking of his tongue, his fingers, the heat of his demanding body, and the unending cool lapping and caressing of the water built into an almost unbearably glorious symphony within her. Finally he positioned her above his throbbingly erect manhood and paused. Every fiber of her being cried out to be pierced by his love.

"Look at me," came his passion-roughened voice.

Her eyes flew open and were caught in the triumphant emerald blaze of his. Slowly Cord lowered her onto him, watching ecstasy transform her beloved face. He gave himself up to the timeless eternal rhythm between them. Rocking together in the spring-swollen river, they climbed higher and ever higher.

Her wild cries mingled with his groans as they felt some force greater than they had ever experienced lift them high and hurl them outward, beyond all boundaries. Cord poured himself into Vesper, filling her with his seed, and she cried out his name as she received him into her deepest recesses.

Afterward, they floated on the calming breast of the water, bathed in happiness. Cord lay on his back, one arm curled around his wife, the other making languid movements to keep them from sinking. She lay against his heart, its steady pounding the sweetest music she'd ever heard.

"Sometimes I feel so happy it almost scares me," Vesper said, watching the leafy shadows flicker over Cord's bronze skin.

He leaned down and pressed a long kiss to her temple. "I never thought I would ever find you. You were a dream I had locked at the bottom of my heart, the ideal woman every man wishes for but rarely finds."

Vesper nestled deeper into the pelt of golden hair on her husband's chest.

"My darling, if this is a dream, never let me wake up."

"Maybe it was all a dream until now. You feel uncommonly real to me."

His hand softly stroked down her water-spangled arm, along the side of her velvet hip.

"So very real," she murmured, arching back against his gentle caress like a satisfied cat.

They floated into the shallows, where Cord rose and carried Vesper out to the sun-toasted rocks. Tenderly he laid her down and, taking up his shirt, dried the water from her sculptured curves. Cord looked down at his gently smiling wife, lying so trustingly before him, and the words welled up in him.

"I think we've found Eden, my darling angel. Heaven could be no better."

"Eden," she breathed dreamily, taking in the perfection of the sky and sun and trees, and the glorious man who looked down at her with love-filled eyes.

"Eden indeed."

It was two months later, as the trees burgeoned with their lush summer dress, when Vesper knew she was pregnant. Taking an afternoon off, she had urged Cord to go berrying with her in the woods. Their pails filled with ripe sweet raspberries and their hands and mouths sticky with crimson juice, they went to their pond to rinse off.

The fiery pearled surface of the water reflected the sunset, and they sat on a rock, hand in hand, to watch the colors spiral and dance down the sky. To the piercingly sweet accompaniment of a caroling thrush, Vesper told Cord the wonderful news. His face lit up and he took her into his arms, holding her as if she were made of the most delicate porcelain.

"A child," he murmured into her black hair. "New life coming from our love."

Cord was filled with wonder. He pulled back to look down into her glowing face.

"I didn't think I could feel any happier, my love, but—"

He broke off, bending to plant a worshipful kiss on her waiting mouth.

Joy filled Vesper to bursting, bringing tears to her eyes. Tenderly Cord kissed each of her trembling eyelids, sliding his mouth down the tracks of her tears. His own eyes were moist as he looked at his wife, highlighted against a pale green sky spangled with early stars, and imagined her growing heavy with their child, saw her holding their babe to her breast.

They held each other there in the murmuring darkness, the future glowing before them brighter than any stars.

The weeks hurtled by, each more golden and perfect than the one before. The Santee Sioux would speak ever after of this Summer of Plenty. The luxuriant trees and bushes teemed with baby birds, the streams ran riotous silver with fish, and even the rows of vegetables seemed to ripen overnight to mouthwatering richness. Many of the mares dropped twin colts, swelling Cord's herds. Everywhere Vesper looked there was new life, burgeoning, potent, plenteous.

One soft summer night she was awakened by a bright outpour of moonlight, spilling in through the window onto their patchwork quilt. She looked at the precious face of her sleeping husband and felt, for the first time, the flutter of life within her.

Her hand flew to her belly as she whispered a delighted "Oh!"

Into her mind slipped the image of a little boy with a rounded version of Cord's strong face, his eloquent green eyes, his thatch of bronze hair. A strong child, unafraid, yet loving. Vesper couldn't sleep. She was too full of happiness. Quietly she rose from the bed and seated herself at the kitchen table, lighting a candle and pulling out writing paper. Into a letter to her Aunt Lucinda, Vesper poured her feelings.

Dearest Auntie,

I suppose I should be sleeping because tomorrow is the day I'm determined to clear out the storeroom, if Cord will let me. But I was just feeling so extraordinarily happy that I couldn't keep my eyes closed. Cord is so careful and gentle with me that sometimes it brings tears to my eyes. Our life together has exceeded my wildest hopes. How has this happened? It is something I have learned from my husband—that we are truly capable of creating the world of our dreams, if only we have enough imagination and persistence.

Now all our efforts have been crowned by the coming of the baby. I felt movement for the first time tonight, and the glory of it is still running through me. Together we will raise our son (for I am certain it is a boy) to be a citizen of this new world we are making. His challenge will be to conquer himself, his fears, his hesitations, all those things that can fall between a person and his dreams. How wonderful it will be to guide and watch that fruitful struggle. I can hardly wait to meet him!

All my love,
Vesper

* * *

Vesper stood at her husband's side in the doorway of their house, listening to the lonely beautiful cries of the wild geese flying overhead, headed south. There was a frosty bite to the air, a restless stir to the tawny and copper piles of fallen leaves that swirled along the hardened ground. On her other side stood Demoiselle, who had matured into a soulful, soft-eyed quiet yearling. Cord absently stroked the thick ruff of Romulus, the half-grown wolf, whose long, slanted yellow-green eyes sparkled with intelligence and trust.

"Here they are," Cord rumbled.

Running Wolf and Spring Willow rode up to the cabin on a pair of stately horses, their twin grandsons perched in the saddles before them. As soon as the boys saw Rom, they hesitated only long enough for their grandparents' indulgent nods before scrambling down from the horses. The wolf's long, bushy tail began wagging frantically as his playmates joined him in one last romp.

"We have come to bid you farewell until spring," said the chief. "The young braves have led the horses to their winter pasture. Soon comes the hour of the snows and my people must take shelter even as the fiercest bear retreats to his den."

Cord and Vesper both smiled at Running Wolf's play on the white man's Indian name.

"May the wolf and his mate find peace and pleasure in the long white nights," answered Cord. "We will see you again, come spring."

Spring Willow's deep black eyes were warm as they swept over Vesper's swelling body.

"You carry strongly, my child. Know that I will be back with you when the babe enters the world. All will be well."

Vesper felt a pang of melancholy. She would miss

this kind, stalwart woman who had become like a mother to her.

"Thank you for all you have taught me," she answered. "I hope the winter be an easy one for you and yours, Spring Willow."

"If there is any trouble with the whites," added Cord in his deep bass, "send for me."

"Our thanks to you, Fierce Bear," said the chief. "If there is need, you will know."

He took up the reins lying slackly along his pony's neck.

"May the Great Spirit keep watch over you."

The children, cheeks flushed from their games, gave Rom one last hug and clambered back onto their ponies.

"Good-bye," they cried as their grandparents turned the horses back down the forest track.

Cord and Vesper watched until they were gone.

It was less than a week later that the first blizzard arrived, out of a clouded midnight sky. In the morning, Vesper awakened to look out onto a world transformed. Gone were the familiar paths, the rich colors of the earth. A pale blue-gray sky softly met the white expanse of the land, broken only by a smoke-colored tracery of bare branches.

"What will I do every day without my field chores?" Vesper asked wistfully from the toasty warm bed.

"I'll find ways to keep you busy," came Cord's soft growl as his massive hand gently stroked her rounded abdomen.

Vesper slid back down under the comforting quilt, sighing with pleasure as her husband's sensitive caresses traveled over her lush swelling breasts, the softened fuller contours of her hips and thighs.

"Your skin feels just like velvet now," he whispered. "My beautiful Vesper."

He leaned over her to plant a row of kisses from the valley between her breasts to her navel. Vesper quivered under his practiced touch, wanting to fit her body to his but being stopped by her protruding belly.

"Oh, Cord," she wailed, "how can we make love when I keep growing? Soon you won't be able to get within a foot of me."

A deep laugh rumbled in his chest.

"We will simply have to be a little more inventive, my angel."

He grasped her and Vesper gave herself up to his unyielding embrace. She could tell he still found her arousing. He was trembling with need as he stroked her warm secret hollows. Every touch of his hands, every lave of his tongue, made her feel more beautiful, more treasured. Gladly she surrendered all that he asked, lost herself further and further in that mystic place where two souls strive to become one. When they reached the precipices of joy, gladly did she hurl herself over the last barrier, flying with Cord to that secret paradise which only they could find.

Safe within his arms, Vesper floated slowly back on a cushion of bliss. She looked at him hazily. His eyes were closed. On his lips was a small, delighted smile. How handsome he was as he lay there beside her, utterly satisfied.

"I hope the baby looks just like you," she whispered adoringly.

"Even if it's a girl?" he muttered, only half awake.

"Oh no, it's going to be a boy," she insisted. "And since he's your son, he'll probably ride before he walks."

"And if she's your daughter," came his warm, sleepy reply, "she'll never let anything defeat her."

With a sigh of deep contentment, Vesper sank within the nest of the bed, curving her rounded body against her husband's firmness. Outside, the snow began to fall again, blanketing the world in soft white velvet.

# Chapter Eleven

VESPER, WHO THOUGHT SHE HAD LEARNED EVERYTHING there was to know about snow last winter, was amazed at the vast totality of the blizzard's blinding force. During the day, there was an eerie beauty to the luminous white curtain, etched by vague rays from the white-gold winter sun. In the late-afternoon hours, the drifts of snow, piling high against the barn and stalls, house and trees, took on violet shadows. Night fell quickly, with pitch-black darkness blotting out the icy lakes and empty trees. Only the constant muffled sound of swirling, descending snow, frosting the windowpanes, knocking at the door, reminded Vesper that a world beyond the four safe walls of the two-story log and sod cabin existed.

Her world within the little house was complete and utterly satisfying. Every day, she experienced the thrust of life grow stronger and more intense inside her belly. She thought of her unborn babe constantly, her arms often cradling her protruding stomach as if she could already hold and rock the precious lad. Vesper was more and more convinced she would bear Cord a son. She insisted through the long winter evenings that he etch *Cordie* into the head of the cradle the proud father-to-be was busy carving from an aged spruce log.

One afternoon in the dead of the season, the Travers family was busy, as usual. Vesper was filling the shelves of her new pie cabinet, a gift from Cord before the first snowstorm. As tall as Vesper and pragmatically ornamented with a snowflake pattern of holes puncturing the tin doors for ventilation, the freestanding cabinet was brimming over with meat pies and fruit pies. The tantalizing blend of aromas brought Demoiselle and Romulus from the storage room to Vesper's side. Their bright eyes darted from Vesper to the cabinet and back again.

With a low chuckle, Vesper said, "There, there, my pets. Stop drooling for just one minute and I'll see what dainties I can spoil you with."

Hovering awkwardly on tiptoe, her belly prominently forward, Vesper clutched the edge of the tin door with one hand as she reached for a delicacy each animal might enjoy. She knew the delicate deer would patiently lick at a rhubarb pie, and as for the eager wolf, a hearty lamb pie would be to his liking. Setting down each dish by the fire, she called to her beasts. Docilely, somehow holding back their impatience, they padded toward Vesper, watching for her signal. She snapped her fingers and they each pounced on their treat without a whimper or growl between them. Vesper laughed, delighted and still amazed by this evidence of Cord's and her peaceful kingdom.

"Don't reward those fiends," Cord called out from the attached storage shed. "I'm about to tear them limb from limb."

"What are you talking about?" his wife asked in dismay, anxious at the lack of any humor in Cord's voice.

"This," he growled as he entered the warm, cozy kitchen, exhibiting a tattered tangle of paper packages before him. "It was meant to be a surprise for your birthday, my dearest girl," he added in an ironic tone. "But you will insist on believing those two scoundrels couldn't survive in their natural environment, even with woolen booties on."

"Oh, Cord," Vesper cried animatedly, "I raised them by hand. How could you expect them to return to the wild?"

As she spoke he rummaged through her basket of sewing and held up several pairs of oddly sized baby socks. There was a wicked gleam in his eyes that Vesper, even in her vehemence, could not ignore. Unwieldy in her weight, she threw herself at her teasing husband and snatched the remnants of her surprise from him.

"Enough, Cord," she begged through her tears of laughter. "I know I'm ridiculous about Demi and Rom, but I do feel motherly toward them . . ."

"And a fine mother you are and will be," affirmed Cord.

He smacked her playfully on her rounded rear and pulled her onto his lap in the big easy chair the fort commander's wife had given to Vesper. She snuggled in, glad her expanding curves still found a home against Cord's muscular body. But he frowned and turned Vesper toward him.

"You're not going to smother our son, are you?" he asked sternly. "I mean, he's got to go hunting and fishing with me and learn all the skills of expert horsemanship."

Just as sternly Vesper promised, "I'll permit it all, Cord Travers, as long as you wear your woolen booties too."

Putting the torn packages aside, she withdrew two large socks from the stack of unfinished darning, poked her fingers down to the toes, and wiggled them through the impressive holes she found.

"But no more of this, my good man," she scolded, shaking a finger at him.

At the fireside, the deer and the wolf lingered over the last infinitesimal lick of tasty pie, flicked their tails in gustatory comfort, and curled up together for a nap. Catching this little vignette out of the corner of her eye, Vesper felt a lump in her throat and motioned Cord to watch the two animals, natural enemies in the wild, settle down in perfect amity.

"We're so lucky, my darling," Vesper whispered in Cord's ear.

"We have found paradise," he echoed, gently stroking her raven tresses.

They sat there together in wedded bliss and silence until Vesper remembered the half-spilled contents of Cord's ruined surprise.

"Did my eyes deceive me . . ." she began, reaching for the chaotic tangle on the floor. And then it was, "Oh, Cord," in soft, hushed tones of awe as she sorted the rich variety of cloths, yarns, and baby-fine woolens. "Oh, how wonderful. I love you. The baby will love you. I've had so many projects in mind."

With effort, she heaved herself slowly out of Cord's lap.

"I'll start right now. But, Cord, have you noticed? It's getting dark so fast."

Vesper walked to one of the windows near the

front door. She pulled aside the lacy curtains and the thick muslin liner behind and peered through the glass.

"It's starting again. It looks like the wind is blowing as much snow up in the air as it is bringing down."

"It's all right, honey. We've got enough supplies for another ten blizzards. Mother Nature can't get to us, no matter how hard she tries."

Cord beckoned to her. "C'mon back by the fire. There's a spot behind your left ear I haven't kissed since this morning."

But Vesper stayed at the window, staring into the ominous bleakness of the unrelenting blizzard. She shivered, not because she was cold, she told herself, but something . . . not quite right . . . was out there . . . and coming closer. She swore she could see something moving amidst the wild swirling snow. She strained her eyes, blinked, and looked harder.

There. She was right. She had a momentary glimpse of feathers and a frosty cloud of breath.

"Cord?" she called in alarm, her heart beginning to flutter. "I'm not sure . . . Come quick, Cord."

Her tone changed to disbelieving joy.

"I think it's the Santee, come to visit!"

Cord shook his head. "I don't see how it's possible, sweetheart," he said gently.

But when Cord reached her side, placing his massive hand protectively on her shoulder, his eyebrows arched and he frowned. Vesper appeared to be right. A small group of braves was heading straight for the Traverses' cabin and, strangest of all, seemed to be rigged out in full warrior dress.

"It is the Santee, isn't it, Cord? I'll get the lantern so they can find us more easily."

As Vesper lumbered off toward the storage-shed

door, Cord racked his mind, trying to figure out why his Indian brothers would set out in the height of a blizzard, prepared for war. Peering into the storm, Cord could only conclude that white settlers or soldiers at Fort Snelling had raided the Santee Sioux's winter villages and Running Wolf needed Cord's help.

He felt a cold thrill of danger slice through him. He couldn't upset Vesper. Nor could he leave her alone and go with his adopted tribe. Until he knew more, he wouldn't tell Vesper anything.

Vesper returned with the big lantern and lit the tallow inside.

"Was I right, Cord? Are they from Running Wolf? Do you think they're in trouble, coming so far in the snow like this?"

Cord turned and smiled encouragingly at his perceptive wife. "Honey, your eye is as good as mine." Then he looked away from her. "Looks like a foraging party. That's all." He laughed, hoping he had fooled her. "They must have lost their way."

"They'll be cold and wet, Cord. Let's make them stay with us a few days. I'm dying to hear about Spring Willow and the twins."

There was earnest concern on Vesper's face and wariness on Cord's as they threw open the door and waved the lantern slowly back and forth, signaling to the party on horseback emerging through the gray storm. The Indians, for indeed both Cord and Vesper recognized the Santee war paint now, seemed to break into a dead run, bolting for the pale beacon which shone through the snow.

"Come in," the woman was calling. "Over here. You're safe with us."

In the last moment before the braves came out of the blizzard's blinding force, Cord caught a clear glimpse of their faces. And in that last moment he realized these men were no Santee Sioux from Running Wolf's tribe. The short hairs bristled on the back of his neck. They were not Indians at all.

The seven pale faces of the men stood out from the garishly painted war stripes and their expressions had a peculiar mercenary glee about them. In the extra split seconds it took Cord to register this incomprehensible fact, it was too late to turn back. In vain, he tried to push Vesper through the open doorway into the safety of their home. Cord yelled to Vesper to run and hide in the attached storage shed, but her clumsy body reacted too slowly. The disguised white men had already swooped from their horses, cocked their rifles, and made a beeline for the confused couple.

Cord hurled himself over Vesper, shielding her from the explosive gunfire. Somehow he managed to pick her up and get both of them through the open door. There wasn't even a second left to bolt the door. The seven marauders were too quick and pushed in behind a frantic Cord and Vesper. One man, whose face paint was already beginning to smudge, took one look about the parlor, smiled viciously, and took deadly aim at the quaking form of the petite deer. In the next awful instant, Demoiselle breathed a single startled sigh and keeled over, bleeding profusely from a hole in her chest.

"Demi, my Demi," Vesper screamed in disbelieving agony.

A primitive instinct took over, and she rushed at the gunman, flailing her fingernails at his face.

Then all hell broke loose as Cord went into action, making use of Vesper's hysterical attack as a diversionary tactic. He dived for his rifle which stood by the huge mantel and grabbed Vesper out of the way before the killer could shoot again. Before the man knew what hit him, Cord had pumped a bullet into his heart.

"Get behind me," he shouted to Vesper as he tried to back them toward the storage room.

The six remaining intruders rushed at Cord, momentarily nonplussed by his hair-trigger reflexes. But Cord let blast two more rounds and the two men leading the pack fell to the floor in a dead heap. The other four stopped in midstep. For a moment of uneasy truce, they eyed Cord warily.

"Who are they?" Vesper whispered, her voice barely audible. "What do they want with us?"

Then one of the men, obviously the ringleader, wiped his arm across his forehead and smiled crookedly. He signaled to the other three, who split up and slowly, cautiously, began to steal toward Cord and Vesper. From the depths of the room, seemingly out of nowhere, an unearthly howl filled the air. The armed men looked wildly about, and in that instant a huge gray wolf with glittering blue eyes leaped with all his strength at the ringleader. Rom spun the man around like a child's top, catching him at the throat and ripping the flesh open.

"Damn," one of the men swore softly.

"What in hell?" cried another, screaming as the furious beast turned and lunged for him.

The third man fired twice, stopping Rom in midair, halting the wolf's protective frenzy forever. The wolf fell, riddled by bullets, at the feet of his mistress.

Vesper sank to the floor in absolute terror and grief. Her two wonderful pets, precious gifts of nature, were gone, brutally slaughtered before her eyes. She clutched convulsively at her belly, more frightened than she had ever been in her life. Her

eyes wide and staring, she knew she was useless to
Cord. She prayed with all her might that her brave
husband would rescue them both from this horror.

"Vesper, quick. Get up. Run," she heard Cord
urging her.

He was tugging at her with one hand as he held his
rifle with the other, training it on the two men still
coming at them from opposite sides of the room.
The gunman who had just killed Rom pivoted and
saw his moment. He lunged beyond Cord, succeed-
ing in nabbing Vesper. He hauled her to her feet as
she shrieked at the top of her lungs.

"Vesper! Vesper!" Cord shouted.

He dropped his rifle and rushed for his wife, all
thoughts of his own survival gone from his mind. He
stepped from the precarious safety of his corner
position. The other two men jumped him from both
sides, one kicking Cord's rifle across the room. He
struggled in their grip, trying to shake off the
murderous scum.

Vesper's heart was in her mouth. Nothing could
happen to her invincible Cord. Please, God, she
prayed, let nothing happen to Cord. She pushed
against her attacker feebly, her strength sapped by
her terror. The man holding Vesper yelled something to his comrades.

They nodded and suddenly Cord was free. But
only for a moment . . . one agonizingly long, drawn-
out, time-frozen moment. As he reached for her,
their fingers almost touching, their eyes on each
other alone, one of the gunmen circled behind Cord
and pinned both his arms. The other man, a sneaky,
shifty grin spreading over his face, raised his rifle.
Sure and steady, his finger squeezed the trigger.

Vesper watched in utter horror, her entire body
jolted. A look of puzzled astonishment broke out on
Cord's face. The man holding him from behind

released Cord and stepped back hesitantly. Cord seemed to straighten, imposingly tall as ever.

"Vesper . . ." he breathed, half questioning, half demanding.

She found her strength and pulled from her assailant's solid grasp. But he recaptured her easily, and as she stretched one hand imploringly toward Cord, the other clutching at her breast, her beloved husband crumpled to the ground. A great pool of thick dark blood streamed from a wound in his head and settled about him.

No, no, it was too impossible to believe, Vesper told herself. This can't be happening. But there was no way to pull back the hands of Father Time and alter their fate. She wrestled with her assailant, trying to get closer, to touch and tend to Cord's body.

It took both gunmen to drag her out the front door of the cabin, and she kicked and screamed the whole way. Abruptly she was gagged and her hands were bound with coarse rope. She was shoved up onto the back of a horse with her legs caught together and tied at the stirrups. Snow pelted her like a shower of bullets as she sat imprisoned in the saddle.

Certain she was secured, the two surviving murderers removed crude torches from their saddlebags and disappeared back inside the house. Vesper strained desperately, pulling her muscles taut, an enveloping ache growing within her, as she tried to see what was happening.

When yellow-orange bursts of color shot up from inside the cabin, sickening dread paralyzed her thoughts. The two men ran out and threw the last of their flaming torches up onto the roof. Despite the blanket of snow, despite the wet cabin logs, despite the fervent, strong, loving hopes which had been built into Cord and Vesper's home, fire exploded throughout the house, destroying everything in its path. Vesper felt as if she were dying as dank black clouds of smoke and red-hot cinders rose in roiling fury above the inferno.

The gunmen watched in silent satisfaction and nodded to each other. Hurriedly they dashed toward Vesper and their waiting mounts. Catching up the reins of her horse, they wheeled about for one last parting sight.

"Gotta hand it to yer man, little lady. He shore put up one helluva fight fer you. But when the boss hears how many of the gang he killed . . . well, ah surely wouldn't want to be in yer shoes. Yer gonna pay, little lady. Yer gonna wish you was by yer husband's body, goin' up in all them purty-colored flames."

Laughing coarsely together, they kicked their horses into motion, leading Vesper's horse between them. If she could have spit at them and clawed their eyes out, she would have. But, shackled as she was, she could only twist about to stare at the charring remains of her life. *I would die with you, Cord, my love, if I had a choice.*

Her eyes sought in vain to keep the burning structure in sight. But the wind churned up huge curtains of snow and the sound of it howling was like ghosts crying in the night. She shut her eyes to cut the pain. She conjured a picture of Cord, his strong, chiseled features a blend of pride, wonder, and ecstatic happiness as she told him she was carrying his child. But the vivid image of Cord lying lifeless in his own blood was etched irrevocably in her mind and she could find no escape.

Freedom. Where was it now? she asked herself, longing for it. What good was it now? She choked on her gag, realizing she wasn't even free to feel the burden of her agony. She stared into the misty chaos of swirling snow, letting it blind her and blot everything from her mind. As the rhythm of the horse's hoofbeats lulled her into limbo, nothing else existed for Vesper. Cord's crumpled form, the fiery holocaust, the freezing cold about her, even the passage of time, grew distant and without meaning.

The two men rode on, intent on completing their mission and oblivious to Vesper's condition. They rode all the rest of the day, that night, and into the next day. They knew well that the weather could be an enemy as well as a friend. True, it eradicated the telltale evidence of their tracks. But it could also be a killer, numbing and freezing one to death. Their aim now was to get the woman to St. Louis—alive and well. Those had been the boss's orders.

It wasn't until the middle of the second day, when the blizzard ended, that they realized they might not be able to complete their end of the deal. The woman had been hunched over her saddle all morning, eyes closed, fingers limp. She hadn't even acted grateful when they removed the gag from her mouth.

"Hey, lady, you want some jerky?" offered one of Vesper's captors.

He shrugged and looked helplessly at his partner.

"Try givin' her some water," the other man suggested.

When the first man shoved his canteen at her and she still did not respond, he got angry.

"Yuh think yore too good fer us, is that it?"

He slowed the horses to a halt.

"C'mon, speak up. Cat got yer tongue?" he taunted.

He grabbed at her hair and jerked her head upright. Glassy lavender eyes, racked with pain, looked through him without seeing and a low animal moan escaped her lips.

"Hey, Brady, sumpin's wrong."

"Shut up. No names, remember?"

"Ferget it, Brady. She can't hear us. She's sick or sumpin'. Look."

Brady edged his horse close enough to Vesper's to touch her. In the icy chill of winter's wrath, Vesper was sweating profusely. Her face was flushed and her clothes soaked. Another moan, louder and more intense, broke from her chapped lips.

Frightened, the first man slapped her and yelled, "Shut up. Shut up. You want that gag again?"

"Stop it, Harner. She can't hear you. Somethin' is wrong, and we're in fer big trouble with the boss if we don't take care of her."

Harner scratched his head.

"You've got the brains, Brady. What do we do now?"

Before Brady could answer, Vesper lurched abruptly in her saddle. If she hadn't been tied down, she would have fallen out. Somewhere from the depths of her misery, Vesper was seeing again the terribly vivid moment of Cord falling . . . falling . . . falling into a broken heap . . . with blood, a torrent of rich red blood spurting from him, leaping high like flames . . . She heard a voice screaming in agony, drowning out the horrendous picture. The agonized woman never knew the voice was her own.

"Git her down quick, Harner. She's havin' a fit."

The bonds were removed just as Vesper was racked by a massive spasm of pain deep in her belly. Cramping, knotting, twisting, something tore within and she screamed again, piercing the still air. Her body clenched up into an angry fist. The two men, unable to control her convulsions, lost their hold and she fell heavily onto the snow-packed ground.

"Oh my God," croaked Harner, pointing down. "Look, Brady."

The two men stared at the pool of blood seeping

from between Vesper's legs, turning the snow a brilliant crimson.

"She's pantin' like a dog," Harner said, horrified.

"Hurry, man. Get the extra blankets."

Harner rushed to follow Brady's orders. He shivered, hoping Brady knew what he was doing.

The fresh, cold snow on her heated, sweaty body felt good to Vesper and, in the back of her mind, she could have sunk into blissful sleep and never woken up. But the fiery pain kept pounding at her, bringing her back to hated reality.

She felt rough hands turn her over, pull at her clothing, part her legs. No, not another indignity. Hadn't she suffered enough? Hadn't she lost everything already? And then the truth of her physical pain struck her. She was losing the baby. Little Cordie was being taken from her too. She wailed in protest, her hands flying to the mound of her belly.

"Too soon . . . too soon," she cried.

Gladly Vesper surrendered to the dark, deep pool of forgetfulness which engulfed her. She never knew when the helpless little body slipped from her onto the icy, loveless prairie. Brady was there, wrapping it quickly in a blanket. He handed the bundle to Harner.

"Bury it fast. And deep."

"What about her? Do yuh think she can ride?"

"Harner, yore a damn fool. Tie these blankets together and harness 'em to her horse. We'll have to travel slow and drag her to the next cabin we come across, abandoned or not."

Harner started away to do his dirty work, then paused and looked back at his partner.

"Brady, you think we'll make it to St. Louis?"

"The question is, Harner, will she make it there."

# Chapter Twelve

LIFTING HER EYELIDS WAS ONE OF THE MOST DIFFICULT tasks Vesper had ever been faced with. They were so heavy it seemed they were glued shut. When she finally managed it, a pale spotted blur swam into view. She struggled for focus until it resolved itself into a tall blue-and-white vase, filled with gold asters. Near it swayed a dark rocking chair. But before Vesper could make out the occupant's face, her eyelids trembled with the effort of remaining open and fell closed.

Swathes of time passed. When she awoke again, Vesper found herself bathed in a wash of pale sunlight streaming in from a muslin-curtained window. It was hard to see anything beyond the glare until she turned her head with great effort. She focused on the dark wooden bedpost, thickly carved with cupids and vines. The wallpaper beyond was brightly striped with crimson and olive flower baskets. As far as Vesper could make out, elaborately framed portraits covered the wall.

A bedroom, she thought hazily. A bedroom not her own. Where was she? The words formed on her mouth, but no sound emerged. What had happened? Her body did not seem to belong to her. She fought to regain control, to make a fist of the white, spent-looking hand lying limply on the gay coverlet, and succeeded only in waving her fingers slightly.

"Oh, you're finally awake," chirped a voice. "I'm so glad. I've been waiting ever so long, you know. . . ."

A face loomed over her. It was a plump young woman with the bloom of apples in her cheeks and dark brown braids twisted in a thick coronet around her head. The voice chattered on like a forest squirrel exclaiming over spring. But what was she saying? Vesper couldn't quite understand.

"I've never seen anything like it. . . . You've been drifting in and out for two months, you know. And you were bleeding something fierce when they brought you in. The doctor really didn't think you were going to live. But I said to myself, I said, Polly, where there's life, you know . . ."

Polly bustled about the bed as she spoke, tucking in the coverlet, plumping up pillows, throwing Vesper a quick smile.

"Your uncle's just been beside himself. I've never seen anyone so devoted. He comes to visit every single day. You must be very close to him. There, now. All neat and cozy."

Polly stepped back, hands on her broad hips, surveying her handiwork.

Uncle? Vesper thought, puzzled. Automatically her hand moved to caress her abdomen. She recoiled in shock to find it flat.

"My baby!" came her horrified murmur.

"Baby? What baby?" asked Polly, her round, earnest face showing confusion.

Vesper's memories came flooding back: the cabin in flames, Cord slumped lifeless in a pool of his own blood, her body racked with pain as a small bundle was buried beneath the snow. Vesper was torn by piteous sobs, her thin hands weakly covering her face. She wept as though her heart would break. Now she had nothing left of her precious Cord at all. Even their child, the dream of their future, had been wrenched from her. Everything was gone.

There was a knock at the door, then the sounds of a gruff male voice and loud masculine footsteps, crossing the floor.

"How is my little niece today?"

Though the words were meant to convey concern, there was a hard edge of impatience to them.

Polly rushed over to the visitor with the good news, her words tumbling over each other in her excitement.

"She's come to at last! So I'll leave you two alone, sir," she finished, breathless with her recital. "You must have so much to talk about!"

"Make sure that you close the door," came the visitor's voice. "That's a good girl."

Vesper was alone with the unknown man, who approached the bed with alacrity. Through the blur of her tears, she sensed that he was very big. A faint alarm bell rang in her mind as his hand tugged at his waistcoat.

Vesper looked up. Augustus Bledsoe leered down at her triumphantly, his tongue snaking into a corner of his mouth. She froze, fear rushing through her veins, even as a helpless woodland creature waits, quaking, when a ruthless predator comes to the end of its stalking and faces its hapless prey.

"So we meet again, Vesper Lawrence."

His anger-shrouded voice stressed her maiden name.

"You were foolish to think you could escape me. Now I have you," he snarled.

His hands clenched until the thick knuckles shone white.

"Your clumsy hulk of a husband has been killed by my men, and his heir very obligingly died on the way here. It's just you and I, as I planned." He smiled unpleasantly, adding, "There's only one difference."

Bledsoe's fleshy hands darted out and grabbed her wrists, forcing her hands away from her tear-strewn face.

"Had we married in Washington, I would have had to treat you with some respect, as a senator's daughter. But here in St. Louis, no one knows who you are or where you're from. As far as the innkeeper, his daughter, and your doctor—whom I very kindly paid for—know, you are my poor niece, rescued from a terrible Indian raid."

His pale little pig eyes bore down into hers.

"I can take my revenge any way I please and no one will be the wiser."

His hands forced hers down on either side of her head, pinning her against the mattress. His hateful face, with its heavy jowls and sweating forehead, drew closer to hers. She was enveloped in his stale winy breath.

"I will break you, Vesper Lawrence. By the time I'm through enjoying your body, you'll forget Travers ever touched you. I will erase anything you ever had with him. All that will be left of you will be a lust-crazed slave, too afraid to refuse anything. You will do anything any man asks of you, and love your bondage."

His eyes glittered hungrily with his imaginings.

"And when I'm finished, I'll give you to my men for their amusement."

He released her wrists contemptuously, standing over her again.

"Heal quickly, my dear," he sneered. "I can hardly wait to begin your reeducation."

His heavy tread receded, and the door slammed shut.

Blind, unreasoning panic shot through Vesper, blotting out all but a terrified need to escape. She attempted to lunge out of bed but gasped when her most strenuous effort hardly moved her body at all. Hoping she was only tucked in too tightly, she plucked at the blankets, but her arms moved slowly and listlessly. She couldn't even rustle the bedclothes. Her ragged breathing quickened to pants as tears of frustration sprang to her eyes. Soon she was covered in sweat. She was shaking from head to toe with her ineffectual efforts.

This was the ultimate nightmare. Even her helpless screams came out as weak, breathy bleats. She felt completely at the mercy of the revenge-crazed madman who had already killed her husband and child and who was gleefully planning to crush the integrity of her being. And impossible, ghastly as it seemed, she was incapable of escaping her bed, let alone his clutches. In her mind rose an image of herself as Bledsoe's creature, cringing, broken . . .

A piercing elemental refusal sprang from the wellsprings of her soul. He would not have her. He would not win. Whatever the cost, Cord Travers' murderer would not have his wife. The fires of revolt spread through Vesper, igniting a primitive need to avenge her loved ones. She would find a way to right the scale, she swore to herself. She would heal, and Bledsoe would pay.

By sheer force of will, Vesper pushed herself free

of the blankets and swung her shaking legs over the side of the bed. Ignoring the protesting pain of long-unused muscles, she clenched one hand into a triumphant fist and shook it at the closed door.

"No matter how long it takes," she whispered.

Two weeks had passed, and Vesper's healthy young body, fueled by her fierce determination, had healed. She fought to keep at bay the deep depression that welled up whenever a vivid memory of her green and golden seasons with Cord surfaced. Polly was amazed at her patient's recuperative powers but was stung to silence more than once by Vesper's grim refusal to discuss anything about her past. The innkeeper's daughter could not know what it cost Vesper to maintain her seemingly distant demeanor while the past tore and clamored at her. But Vesper knew that if she yielded to her sorrow, she would weaken herself. She had to muster every ounce of her strength to fight off Bledsoe's plans for her.

One afternoon, Vesper stood at the open window of her locked bedroom, overwhelmed by a powerful inner picture of the blaze of joy on Cord's face when she had told him she was carrying their child. Sorrow knifed through her. He was gone. All their love, all their dreams, their babe nestled in her womb . . . Vesper forced back the sobs, throwing her head back defiantly.

She renewed her vow to make Bledsoe pay. He would suffer as she suffered now, agonize with pain. He would learn, to his everlasting dismay, just how strong Cord had made her. She was so intent on her inner battle that she didn't hear a key turning in the lock on her door.

Augustus Bledsoe insinuated himself into the room, and stopped in astonishment at the picture Vesper made at the muslin-edged window. Gone was the timid, insecure girl he remembered from Washington, and in her place stood a proud, fierce woman, beautiful, strong, and independent. Travers' mark was all over her. It infuriated Bledsoe to see how far from him she had grown. What intense pleasure it will be to beat her back into a sniveling wretch, he told himself.

Vesper sensed that her enemy was watching her. Though her heart leaped into her throat, she made herself turn slowly and remark in an aloof voice, "You come early today."

Bledsoe's jealousy impelled him toward her. He grabbed her jaw in both hands and held her face up to his with bruising force. There was a momentary glint of fear in her eyes that disappeared swiftly, whetting his appetite to see her broken.

"You look surprisingly well today, Vesper."

His oily voice sent tremors through her. She tried to ease away from him, but his fleshy fingers only tightened.

"Yes, I believe you are strong enough to receive my attentions. We will begin your lessons tonight."

She couldn't quite conceal her start, but she forced herself to regain her stillness.

"I doubt you will look so haughty later this evening, my dear, after I've ridden you several times."

He spoke slowly, relishing his words.

"I'll begin by stripping you and tying you down. Then I will handle every part of you that Travers ever touched. It will all be mine, his no longer."

As he spoke he watched her face go white, her amethyst eyes blaze out at him. He leered triumphantly.

"You'll do everything I tell you to do. There are many things I'm sure your simple husband never even heard of, things only a real man can make a woman do."

Vesper could no longer contain her overwhelming fury and fear. She tore herself from his grasp, shrieking, "Don't touch me, you filthy, perverse monster! Go away! No! No . . ."

Her hair whipping around her head in a wild angry cloud, Vesper threw herself past her tormentor, lunging toward the door. Bledsoe reached out and grabbed her flying hair, pulling her in, playing her like a drowning fish on a cruel hook. He drank in her humiliating loss of control with a connoisseur's delight. Vesper pounded hysterically on his heavy arms with her fists, overcome by anguished disgust at his touch.

"Let me be. Let me go." Her words tumbled out in shuddering gasps.

Grinning, he pinioned her arms down, imprisoning her against his corpulent flesh. Only her head was free to toss helplessly from side to side in an agony of terror.

"Tonight we begin our association, my pretty. Prepare yourself for me."

He released her contemptuously, and she stood with bowed shoulders and bent head before him.

At the door, her satisfied, gloating captor threw out, "Enjoy your last private afternoon."

After a last relishing leer, he closed the door and turned the imprisoning key.

Maddened, Vesper rushed to the door. Her flailing fists thudded against the heavy wood to no avail, and finally she sank, beaten, to the floor. She lay in a huddled pile, her tears pouring forth in a hot stream, punctuated by moans.

"No . . . no . . ."

She had nothing left to summon that could stem

the tide of utter horror sweeping her away. The pictures her captor's words had planted in her mind throbbed with unrelenting intensity. Inwardly she quailed, a victim of the brutalizing hours to come.

Then, faintly, from far away, Vesper seemed to hear a voice calling to her. Her weeping quieted to occasional shudders, and finally calmed. The voice seemed to strengthen as she listened. It was a beloved voice, the one she wanted most to hear in all the world. From the depths of her memory, Cord spoke to her.

"Each of us is capable of much more than we realize. Inside you, my darling, is an endless pool of inner strength. You can draw on it whenever you need it. Trust me, Vesper. You can do anything you must do. Anything at all."

How many times had she heard her husband, his eyes blazing green fire, say those words? How many times had his strength lifted her from despair? Augustus Bledsoe may have taken his life, but Vesper would never lose communion with Cord's spirit, that unique power that was his alone. She felt courage tingling back in her veins, lifting her from the floor, bringing new life to her cramped limbs.

Her tears dried as she examined the locked door in front of her. It was easy enough to pull a splinter from a loose floorboard and poke inside the wide keyhole. When the catch clicked upward, Vesper felt a pulse of fear.

Was there a guard outside the door? She would have to avoid all of Bledsoe's men. Taking a deep breath, Vesper reminded herself that any risk was better than waiting passively for her captor to return.

She was in luck. The corridor was deserted. Flitting from shadow to shadow, Vesper made her way to the inn's ground floor, searching for Polly. I must have her help, Vesper thought. But what can I say to convince this scatterbrained, romantic little soul?

She found the red-cheeked, busy young woman washing cutlery in the scullery. Vesper paused in the shadows, conceiving a plan, then stepped forward and called to the girl. Startled, Polly relaxed as she recognized Vesper.

"Land sakes, what're you doing down here?" her cheery voice boomed.

Vesper put a finger to her lips and whispered dramatically, "Please. I must speak with you. You're the only one who can help me."

She paused for a moment, widening her eyes deliberately.

"Things are not what they seem."

Polly, captivated, dropped her handful of forks and tiptoed toward Vesper.

"What do you mean?" she whispered back.

"That man who calls himself my uncle?" Vesper hissed. "He's no relative of mine."

Polly's eyes grew rounder and rounder as Vesper unfolded her story.

"He's an evil man who stole me away from my husband."

She paused to clasp Polly's wet hands in her own.

"Please, oh, please, help me. I must find my dearest husband again and return to our happy little home. Take pity on a helpless woman who did nothing to deserve her fate."

"Oh, I just knew there was something funny about that man," Polly fumed. "I told myself, I said, Polly, he's up to no good. I could feel it in my bones. But what was I to do? You poor, poor lady. How you must miss your husband." Polly patted Vesper's cheek consolingly.

Vesper didn't have to pretend. "More than you'll

ever know," she said in a husky undertone. Two tears trickled down her cheek, and she wiped them away brusquely.

The sight of Vesper's tears propelled Polly into action.

"You stay here," she whispered. "I'll get you a boat. My brother's got an old rowboat he bought with his summer's catch. You can use my cloak and no one will recognize you. We can wait until it gets dark. Don't you worry. I'll take care of everything. I wonder if those oars are still . . ."

Polly bustled out of the scullery, leaving Vesper to wait the long hours until sundown. From the tiny scullery window, Vesper watched the swollen wintry Mississippi River swallow the last rim of the sun. Her mouth was dry with worry. Would Bledsoe discover her absence before Polly returned? She tensed as footsteps approached the pantry door.

"The boat's all ready," came a reassuring hiss.

Vesper stole out to join her sympathetic coconspirator. Polly's eyes danced with excitement as she handed her romantic heroine a dark, coarse cloak.

"Put this around you," she whispered. "Here. I'll help. Everything is going to work out fine."

Vesper cast a furtive look around the deserted storeroom through which Polly led her and followed the trail of the girl's excited whispers. When the creaky back door released the two women into a cobbled street near the docks, a deep, ragged sigh flew from Vesper. First step accomplished. She was free of the inn itself.

As Vesper and Polly hurried to the river, Augustus Bledsoe, seated before the scattered remains of the inn's finest available meal, took one last sip of his port and pulled the linen napkin from under his chin. A small cat smile appeared on his heavy face as his eyes pierced the gloom of the hallway at the top of the stairs.

Taking up a coil of rough hemp rope, he rose and made his ponderous way toward Vesper's bedroom, stroking his lips with one frayed end of the rope. But his lecherous inner vision of Vesper's nude, rope-bound body was shattered by the sight of her door swinging open. Rage flooded Augustus Bledsoe. His prey was gone. He took the stairs two at a time, bellowing for his band of henchmen.

Vesper eyed the crudely made boat and its warped oars with some trepidation but, at Polly's urging, stepped into the rowboat and fixed the oars into their locks.

"Remember what I've told you. She pulls a little to the right," came Polly's cheery whisper through the gloom. "Now, make for the next town down-river. After the second sandbar, take the thin fork to the right. Oh, I just know you'll be with your husband again. Take care. Take care."

Polly's voice faded as Vesper mastered the crooked boat and sent it shooting downstream.

"Thank you for everything," she called back.

But her voice choked as she saw Bledsoe's three hired gunmen climbing into a boat less than one hundred feet from where Polly stood.

"No," Vesper whispered to herself, and bent all her energy to propel the boat faster.

In her panicked haste, she forgot to compensate for the old boat's pull and started rowing in circles, each one tipping the boat rim closer to the water. Horrified, Vesper leaned and then stood to correct the imbalance, but she stumbled as the boat lurched.

Still onshore, the gunmen watched Vesper topple into the black, freezing Mississippi River and sink out of sight. They knew that the icy water could kill within minutes. At first they watched hopefully for a hand to grab hold of the side of the boat. But long moments passed. She didn't appear again. The river had claimed another victim.

Shaking their heads, the men hurried back to the inn, dreading their boss's reaction to the news of Vesper's death. His reaction was even worse than they feared.

"Dead!" he roared. "Dead?"

His hands clenched and unclenched in front of him like vulture talons as a long, jagged scar flared livid on his face. One heavy hand swung around and knocked a gunman to the dining-room floor. The man moaned, his jaw broken.

"Get him out of my sight," Bledsoe muttered to the other men.

Alone, his coarse invective filled the air. Vesper Lawrence Travers had escaped him again, and this time there was no way to bring her back. Augustus Bledsoe demanded a bottle of whiskey from the terrified innkeeper and sloppily drank his way into crass oblivion.

# Chapter Thirteen

SHOCKING ICY FINGERS OF THE RIVER PULLED GREEDILY at Vesper, but she managed to surface on the far side of the overturned rowboat. One hand gripped an oarlock while the other tore at the sodden cloak threatening to sink her again. Freed of its dangerous folds, Vesper knew she would soon die if she didn't get out of the water. Already the winter current was stealing precious heat from her weakening body. A log swirled by and Vesper ducked too slowly. It knocked her from the boat and she sank again, unable to fight her way back to the surface.

I can't die like this, she cried inwardly. Not before Augustus Bledsoe suffers as I have suffered. Though dizzy from lack of air, she forced her legs to scissor her upward and managed to reach the surface again. Gasping for air, she caught hold of a floating bale of

167

cotton. Every second was precious. Her body would not take much more chilling.

Vesper's desperate eyes fastened on a huge white steamboat looming out of the frosty dusk. With her last strength, she kicked off in its direction. But she was too late. The last ounce of power ebbed from her numb limbs as her fingers loosened on the rope of the bale. Even the icy pain of her body faded. Soon she would feel nothing.

"Hey!" came a shout. "Dere's somebody in de river!"

A rope splashed down near her. A blind instinct for survival took hold of Vesper, and she grabbed the rope and was dragged to the side of a ship. Eager hands pulled her aboard, up over the scrolled railing and onto the cargo-packed deck.

Her legs were unable to hold her up. Vesper sprawled on the white-painted decking, shaking uncontrollably in the early-evening breeze. Someone threw a coarse woolen blanket over her, and rough hands rubbed the icy water from her quaking body.

"Doan take de skin off'n de lady," admonished a soft musical voice. "Heah—drink this."

A battered tin cup was thrust into her hands and Vesper gulped the amber liquid. The strong brandy made her cough violently, but it warmed her insides wonderfully. In a short time, she was able to scramble to her feet and smile gratefully at the ring of seven cocoa-colored faces. The men were roustabouts, Negro porters and cargo loaders who lived on the big white steamship and performed most of the menial labor on board.

"Gentlemen," began Vesper, "you saved my life. Please accept my heartfelt thanks."

Their eyes grew wide as they took in her cultured tones, the gracious, upright stance she automatically assumed.

"Lawdy, dis lady cain't stay down heah," said Elijah, the perplexed man with the big moon face who had offered her the brandy. He cast a dismissing eye over the cluttered, dirt-caked main deck of the large steamboat, where the lowest-class passengers slept among the gear, lines, and freight.

"Well, den where she goin' to go?"

"We'll take her to Massah San Mahteen," was the reply, which seemed to meet with all the deckhands' approval.

Her guides led Vesper, still clutching the ragged blanket around her for warmth, up a white-banistered staircase at the front of the ship to the boiler deck, where most of the wealthier passengers had their staterooms. She was ushered into a long candlelit room with crimson-flocked wallpaper and dominated by a huge bar at the far end. Vesper's escorts led her directly toward two men playing cards at a small green baize-covered table. But the small company halted when they sensed the intense air of concentration surrounding the two poker players.

The man dealing the cards was dark and lean, with a thin black mustache and a full, vital head of blue-black hair. His coal-black eyes never left his opponent, yet there was no expression to be read on his tobacco-colored aristocratic face. He was dressed in the height of fashion, his long, sinewy body shown to fine advantage by the perfectly tailored black suit and snow-white river of ruffles that cascaded down his chest.

He exuded fastidiousness from every pore, from the high polish of his precisely trimmed fingernails to the bland perfection of the pearl-and-onyx stud on his shirtfront and the understated elegance of his embroidered waistcoat. Yet Vesper instinctively sensed that this man was no dandy. There was a danger to him, a hooded, watchful power that suggested he would be a tough man to challenge.

His opponent was a soft, round middle-aged gentleman, expensively overdressed in a pale gray planter's suit that at this moment was badly stained with nervous perspiration. His big watery blue-gray eyes protruded fishlike from his pasty face as he stared at his five cards, one facedown and four, including two jacks, up on the table. His little mouth kept pursing as he moved his fingers towards and away from his remaining pile of greenbacks.

"Well," drawled the planter, pushing all his money to the center of the table, "ah'll pay to see what y'all have."

The dark man casually flipped an equal amount of money onto the pile and turned over his own hole card. It was a queen, which gave him a higher pair and the win unless the planter had a good hole card. Vesper was fascinated. There was almost two thousand dollars riding on that one card, and yet the dealer acted utterly nonchalant, as if it mattered not at all whether he won or lost. Not so his opponent, whose pudgy fingers trembled as he turned over his six of hearts, which meant he had lost.

"Well, suh, y'all cleaned me out," he told the dealer in obvious dismay.

There was a long, desperate silence while the planter's shaking hand moved to his breast pocket and then withdrew again. The defeated man swallowed several times before he said, "Ah'll tell you what."

He fished in his breast pocket for his wallet, drew out and unfolded a large crisp piece of paper.

"Now, here's the deed to my plantation. Ah'll stake it on the next round."

The dealer held up one long, dark hand.

"I never take a man's home," he stated in a voice

low and cultured. "I suggest you return to your plantation and raise some more cotton."

His clear-eyed, cynical gaze held a gleam of humor.

"I'll be happy to relieve you of your money again next year."

He leaned back in his plushly upholstered chair and took up a cigarillo as the defeated plantation owner retreated from the salon. For the first time, the dealer became aware of the deckhands waiting in a polite semicircle at his side.

"What can I do for you, boys?"

Elijah answered, "Boss, we done pulled dis lady out of de rivah an' we doan know what to do wid her."

Raoul St. Martin's inscrutable black eyes met Vesper's with probing force. One eyebrow arched upward as his examination continued, traveling slowly down and then back up her wet body. When his eyes met hers again, she felt naked not only physically but emotionally. With one raking glance, he seemed to have penetrated to her innermost thoughts. Vesper's hand tightened on the rough blanket as she strove to reassemble her defenses, to present this dangerously perceptive man with as cool a facade as his own.

Raoul watched her struggle for impassivity. He saw the pale, elegant hand instinctively move to shield her breasts as her enormous violet eyes looked back unflinchingly into his own. Though she was clearly on the verge of exhausted collapse, the woman held herself proudly erect. Her spirit shone from her lovely face and touched him, in spite of his long-held cynicism about women. He was astonished to find himself wanting to protect her.

"You did the right thing, boys, bringing the lady to me. I'll take over now."

Elijah and his fellow workers doffed their ragged caps, bowed to Vesper, and returned to the lower deck.

"If you'd like to change out of those wet things, mademoiselle," Raoul suggested, shooting an urbane smile at Vesper, "may I suggest the privacy of my cabin?"

He offered his arm to her, and Vesper, beginning to shiver again, took it, not knowing what else to do.

His cabin consisted of a tastefully furnished suite of two rooms, the first an elegant sitting room and the second a bedchamber. Leading her to the inner one, Raoul told her, "I don't normally travel with women's clothing, but I happen to have bought a gift for an old friend."

He favored her with another raking glance as he took a large beribboned box from the closet shelf. A twinge of alarm shot through Vesper at the familiarity of his look. She was alone with a masterful stranger in his bedroom. Wouldn't he expect his kindness to be repaid? She had no money. What else would he accept?

"I doubt you usually dress in this style, but at least it will be dry."

He sent her another one of his easy, charming smiles. Before Vesper could remonstrate, he let himself out of the room and closed the door.

As she shivered Vesper fought a short battle with her sense of propriety. Either she accepted the dark stranger's help or she would be sick from exposure before the night was out. Hurriedly Vesper removed her soaked clothing, rubbing her chilled flesh and her dripping hair with a thick, warm towel. Besides, she thought, there was something about the man that led her to trust him, even if his eyes held hunger when he looked at her.

As soon as she opened the box, she realized what

his last words had meant. The dress was a rich orange moiré silk, lavished with enough ribbons, lace, and jewels for half a dozen gowns. She stepped into the wide skirt with its five separate flounces edged with wide gold lace and a narrow black velvet binding. When she had pulled and tugged enough at the tight bodice to mold it to her, Vesper stopped in shock.

Instead of covering the slope of her shoulders, the neckline was cut so low it exposed the top half of her breasts in front and fell to a very low vee in back. Three lush orange velvet and chiffon roses liberally sprinkled with paste diamonds emphasized the daring of the gown's cut. One was sewn between her breasts and the other two were attached where each cascading gold lace sleeve met the skintight bodice. The gown was very low-waisted, coming to a jewel-outlined point at her navel. It was a dress so suggestive it was vulgar, and Vesper swallowed hard as she pinned up her hair and turned to examine herself in the full-length mirror.

A stranger stared back at her, a bold, hard, glittering figure capable of anything. If only I could really be like her, Vesper thought, no one would ever make me a victim again. She narrowed her eyes, spellbound by the formidable expression that stole over the face of her mirror image. How sultry, how fascinating, that image was. Was this creature really herself?

Suddenly Vesper remembered how awestruck the young men at her engagement ball had been. She recalled the soldiers outside the jail succumbing to her immediately. Cord had told her many times how beautiful she was, but Vesper had assumed he thought her beautiful because he loved her. Yet only a few minutes ago, this dangerously handsome Creole had stared at her, wet and filthy as she had been, with heated eyes. As if for the first time, Vesper looked at herself.

"I am a beautiful woman," she murmured, haltingly at first, and then with increased confidence.

Though Augustus Bledsoe had ripped from her everything she held dear, she still had this power over men. It was all she had left to exact her revenge, so it would have to be enough. She looked at her reflection one last time, feeling strangely comforted by the completeness of her transformation.

The mirror lady looked cold and sure, capable of revenge as Cord's Vesper could never have been. A calculating little half-smile appeared on her face as she turned decisively and opened the door to join the man awaiting her.

He had just lit a cigarillo when he saw her, and the match paused in midair for a long moment before he shook it out. This gesture was not lost on Vesper. Even more than her mirror, his reaction told her of her newly discovered power.

Raoul was astonished. Was this the pretty bedraggled mermaid he'd hoped to beguile into spending a few nights with him? She looked like the ultimate courtesan, with her ice-goddess face and hauntingly ripe body. He sensed strongly kept secrets locked behind those magnificent amethyst eyes and felt the determination that drove her. She was no respectable matron fallen on hard times but an outlaw with her own code, even as he himself was. Instinctively he knew her to be his equal, and all thoughts of an easy dalliance fled, though she intrigued him far more than before. He bowed to her.

"Mademoiselle, I have been remiss. Allow me to introduce myself. I am Raoul St. Martin, the owner of this steamboat."

Vesper was surprised to hear herself say in a low

voice, without hesitation, "You may call me Morgana."

Raoul raised an eyebrow. "A theatrical choice, my dear." He stepped back to survey her as he mused, "The dark lady of Arthurian legend."

"It suits my purposes," Vesper said, meeting his amused glance with a cool one of her own.

He smiled at her with real pleasure.

"Where are you traveling to, may I ask?"

"Wherever this boat is going," she answered.

"Then why not go in style?"

He settled himself on the pale green watered silk cushion of his French-style sofa and flicked the end of his cigarillo into a delicate porcelain tray.

"You're welcome to stay here as my guest."

He slanted a look up at her.

"A woman traveling alone, particularly one as evocative as yourself, requires protection. I offer you mine."

Vesper thought fast. He did not strike her as an unselfish man. What would he want in exchange for his protection?

"And where would you sleep?" she confronted him.

He patted the corner of his sofa.

"Here, of course."

He was clearly enjoying her directness. His black Creole eyes were dancing.

She considered him measuringly. Normally a woman would be a fool to trust those words coming from a man who boldly admired her. Yet Raoul St. Martin seemed different. She sensed an unflinching code of honor in the man. Under that distant, amused surface, she felt a passionately held belief in what he knew to be right. If he promised not to take advantage of her, he would take nothing she didn't offer. She felt strangely safe with him.

"Your hospitality is too timely to refuse," she said finally, a rueful smile crossing her face as she considered the sum of her worldly possessions lying in a sodden heap on his bedroom floor. "I hope I will be able to repay you very shortly."

"Your company is payment enough," returned Raoul gallantly, gesturing gracefully at her voluptuously revealed form. "Shall we have dinner, my dear Morgana?"

Taking his arm, Vesper allowed him to lead her to his boat's surprisingly elegant dining quarters, where she made short work of the huge meal Raoul ordered for her. He ate sparingly, clearly enjoying the gusto with which she attacked her food. She spooned up the last bit of her second jelly cream from the bottom of its tall glass and sat back with a satisfied sigh. It had been a long time since she had had any appetite.

Raoul finished his wine and placed the glass precisely back onto its doily. He uncoiled himself from his seat and held a hand out to Vesper.

"Come, my dear. It's time for me to go to work. Perhaps you will bring me luck."

There was a self-deprecating grin on his face.

"Luck? For your ship's logs?" Vesper was confused.

He laughed.

"I'm the owner, not the captain. No, I am what you might call a gentleman gambler. I earned this boat at the poker table."

His sardonic gaze met her startled one, daring her to condemn him. Vesper smiled coolly.

"I'd be pleased to watch you play."

An eager group of wealthy planters and New Orleans businessmen awaited Raoul at his customary table.

He seated himself, opening a fresh deck of cards,

and said, "Gentlemen, may I present a friend of mine, Miss Morgana?"

To a man, they stared agog at the vision perched with unconscious imperiousness on an arm of Raoul's chair. She was a woman of ice and fire, half naked in a dress of flame. Her moist pearled skin, the color of rich cream, begged to be touched, but the disquieting violet jewels of her eyes warned she was not to be tamed. She had the lush, pulsing curves of a woman and the slender grace of a young girl. Thick midnight coils of hair framed her perfect fine-boned face, giving her a haughty, regal air.

Vesper's knowing little half-smile turned dazzling as she acknowledged the men's hungry worship. Her newly discovered power was so satisfying after weeks of being under Bledsoe's cruel control.

"Please don't let me disturb you, gentlemen," she said in a low, thrilling voice. "I'll just watch while you play, if you don't mind."

A chorus of assurances met her words, and she bowed her head in acknowledgment of their invitations to remain. When she looked up, she caught Raoul's smile, a complex blend of pride in her and amusement at the other players' blind adoration. He began to deal.

Vesper knew enough about the rudiments of the game to realize that Raoul's first hand was quite poor. The conservatively dressed businessman to his right had him beat even without his hole card. Yet in the final round of betting, the bony redheaded merchant made the mistake of watching Vesper stand and smooth the folds of her gown more closely over her hips. Swallowing several times, he stared at his cards as if he'd never seen them before and announced he was backing out of the hand. The stakes were too high.

Raoul sent him a puzzled frown as he took the first

pot. The merchant's fair, freckled face was deeply flushed as he fought a losing battle to tear his eyes from Vesper's sensuous curves. Raoul's glance followed the man's to the tantalizing female seated on the chair arm. Inwardly Raoul laughed, though only a faint gleam of humor showed in his ebony eyes.

As the evening progressed Raoul's greatest difficulty was restraining his amusement. With only average cards, he cleaned out every man at the table. Vesper's reaction was different. It took her several hands to realize that she was the cause of the other players' poor judgment, broken concentration, and outright befuddlement.

When the extent of her body's power over these supposedly hardheaded businessmen finally dawned on her, her amazement was quickly followed by exhilaration. Power was a heady business, Vesper realized as she deliberately touched an index finger to the neckline of her gown and watched a city magnate's mouth fall open as his cards dropped from suddenly nerveless fingers.

The last round was hard fought, with Raoul and his single opponent's cards matching after every draw. The pot built to almost five hundred dollars before the final card was dealt. Raoul lifted his hole card and glanced calmly at it, and then at his opponent. With an inscrutable expression on his dark Creole face, he put another hundred dollars on the table. The round, balding doctor who sat across the table from him narrowed his eyes as he considered his options.

But then Raoul's luscious female companion bent forward to examine Raoul's hole card herself. When she replaced it facedown, she looked up at the medical man and gave him a sweet, commiserating smile. Undone by the combination of sympathy and her swelling breasts, he threw his cards down, muttered a curse, and stalked out of the salon.

Raoul's laughter finally escaped as he gathered up the small fortune from the table and bade the rest of the players a good night. He was still chuckling as he offered Vesper his arm to escort her back to the cabin.

"I must thank you, my lovely Morgana, for all your help tonight," Raoul said in a voice brimming over with amusement. "They acted as if you'd cast a spell of enchantment over them."

They walked toward his rooms, down the long white corridor polished to silver by the moon. Vesper shared his enjoyment.

"They were staring so hard at me you could have emptied their wallets directly and saved yourself the trouble of dealing out the cards."

They had reached his door. Raoul paused, one hand on the polished bronze knob.

"You are well worth staring at," he told her.

His eyes were warm as he looked down at her moonlit beauty.

"It's mostly the dress," returned Vesper quickly, not wanting to encourage his tentative advance. "Not exactly an everyday gown, is it?"

There was an awkward pause as they entered his suite, which Raoul covered by offering her a glass of brandy. They sipped the fine liquor, chatting companionably about the different players and their various fumbling mistakes.

How witty he was, Vesper thought pleasurably. How intelligent and perceptive. She enjoyed their sparkling repartee.

"And now I'll wish you pleasant dreams," said Raoul, collecting both their glasses.

The revelations of the evening still coursed

through Vesper's veins, leaving her far from sleepy, but she rose obediently and gave her rescuer a last smile before retiring behind the closed door of his bedroom.

As she peeled off the provocative gown, blew out the light, and slid naked under the luxuriously thick feather comforter, Vesper felt as if she had stripped off her assumed Morgana identity as well. And, surprisingly, the feeling brought not relief but apprehension. Never again could she appear as Vesper Travers. Her only safety lay in Augustus Bledsoe's belief that she was dead. And as he paraded about the streets of Washington, playing the gallant gentleman, she would find a way to destroy him.

Vesper tossed restlessly. She was without funds, possessions, or any help. Yet tonight had shown her that she possessed a power far more potent than any of these—she could bend men to her will through the challenge of her body. Vesper shrank from the obvious implications of this fact. She would not become a rich man's mistress. She would not sell herself.

A mocking little voice inside her asked, "Even if that were the price of Augustus Bledsoe's ruination?"

Vesper wrestled with herself as the hours passed, but her conclusion was firm. She would not, could not, give the body that Cord had made his to any other man. There would have to be another way. Vesper's clenched fists beat on the lush pillows. How? she demanded of herself as the hours ticked away. How?

A few feet away, her benefactor also lay sleepless on his elegant couch. What an extraordinary woman Morgana was, he mused. She pulled men to her as inexorably as the welling tide. Yet she had seemed greatly surprised by her own power tonight. It had been easy to read the astonishment on her face, followed by her almost childlike delight in the new game. Her innocence touched him profoundly, even as her utter womanliness stirred his own manhood. He would not let her walk out of his life.

But how could he keep her at his side? Raoul stared wide-eyed in the darkness as he felt his fine-honed gambler's instincts rouse. There was money to be made, chances to be taken, though how he couldn't fathom. Images of the evening's gambling flickered through his mind. A wisp of an idea was born in the shadowed night, and he pursued it intently through the hours.

Finally Raoul caught it. With growing satisfaction, he examined the plan from all angles. A smile of pure delight appeared on his face. It was perfect. In the morning he would set his scheme in motion. Now he could sleep.

# Chapter Fourteen

A DISCREET TAP AT THE DOOR AWAKENED VESPER FROM the fitful sleep she had fallen into sometime after dawn. She wrapped herself in a sheet and peeked outside. The sitting room was deserted. On the floor near her feet was a wide silver-chased tray with breakfast, an envelope, and a single scarlet rose in a crystal vase. A pile of boxes tied with ribbons was stacked neatly at the side of the tray.

He certainly treats his guests in princely fashion, Vesper thought uneasily as she carried the offerings into the bedroom. I couldn't have better service if I'd paid for my passage.

The croissant was delicious, its buttery flavor set off perfectly by the dark, bitter taste of the thick coffee. And in the boxes Vesper found an attractive yet inconspicuous morning dress of lavender linen with white lace at the high collar and wrists. She also found undergarments, petticoats, shoes, and a silk shawl. Somehow Vesper was not surprised that the clothes fit her exquisitely.

Vesper wavered. Certainly she needed them. She could not very well wander about in last night's gaudy evening gown. But every gift she accepted put her further into Raoul St. Martin's debt. Her eyes lit on the note, still propped up on her breakfast tray. She read the short, intriguing message.

My dear Morgana,

Enjoy your breakfast, your new dress, and your leisure. Send for me when you have dealt satisfactorily with all three. I have a proposal for you which you might find interesting.

Raoul

She would accept these clothes, Vesper decided, suiting words to actions as she began her toilette. But they must be the last gift. She might already have strained his sense of honor too far. Vesper sighed as she fastened the long line of pearl buttons up the front of the gown and coiled her lustrous black locks into a matronly chignon.

A wave of longing overtook her for the rough, practical calicoes of her frontier past. If only she could have been back in the pasture, watching Cord . . . Don't look back, Vesper warned herself as she felt the tears begin to gather. She must have all her wits about her when Raoul St. Martin made his proposal.

A few words to a passing cabin boy brought Raoul to the door of the suite. Vesper was struck anew by his arresting combination of elegant aloofness and danger. He was dressed all in white this morning, which emphasized his seal-brown skin and luxuriant inky hair. She watched small flames light in his onyx eyes at the sight of her and braced herself for his proposition.

Raoul felt his heart begin to pound as he drank in the breathtaking woman before him. In the demure new clothing, her vulnerability was far more apparent. The lavender shadows under her wide, soft amethyst eyes only added to her air of feminine fragility. To him, she was the picture of the gentle woman who waits for every man, standing at the door to his private castle, to welcome him back into her arms after all his dragons are slain.

Raoul shook his head to rid himself of his surprisingly romantic imaginings. He reminded himself that, for all her seeming vulnerability, Morgana seemed to have great courage and pride. If he wanted to bend her to his will, he must orchestrate his presentation masterfully.

Taking her elbow and steering her to the couch, Raoul said lightly, "Good morning, my dear. The dress looks quite lovely, though I am sorry you slept so poorly."

Vesper colored. "How could you know that?" she demanded indignantly. "Did you spy on me?"

"No," he assured her smoothly. He leaned forward and touched the shadowed skin beneath her eye with one elegant finger.

Startled, Vesper jerked back. "Please, Monsieur St. Martin," she remonstrated.

He raised one eyebrow. "I can't help but see what is right before my eyes."

It was decidedly uncomfortable, Vesper thought, to be read so effortlessly by this man. How much had he already guessed about her? And she was indebted to him as well. She struggled to regain her composure, to extract herself from the intimate web he seemed to weave around her.

Summoning up a distant, faintly amused glance, Vesper said, "You did say you had a proposition, I believe."

To her relief, he leaned back against the sofa and became all business.

"Last night, due to your provocative presence, I made the easiest money of my life. Though several of those men were good poker players, you caused them to forget everything they knew. What I propose is to hire you as a gambler in my salon. Your opponents will be so taken with you that they won't mind losing."

Vesper's mind was awhirl with objections to his bizarre proposal.

"But I don't know the first thing about cards."

"If you can endure my perfectionism, I would be happy to teach you," responded Raoul with a slight bow.

"Monsieur St. Martin," Vesper said in an astonished voice, "the only women I know of who deal cards are . . . well . . ."

"Tarts?" supplied Raoul in a calculatedly casual tone. He knew this was the greatest hurdle to be overcome. "I suspect you would make a poor slut, but certainly your morals are up to you alone."

Vesper gnawed her lip, stymied for the moment. "Men would assume that I was available to them. I'd be constantly fighting off their advances."

Now he must reassure her completely, Raoul warned himself. His onyx eyes glittering in seeming anger, he demanded, "Do you seriously believe that any man in his right senses would molest a woman who was under my protection, on my boat?"

Raoul's air of danger had never served him better.

Vesper eyed his elegant form, felt the reckless power that lay coiled just beneath his polished surface. Yes, she admitted to herself, he would keep her safe. But the whole idea still repelled her.

"But I would have to dress . . . provocatively, would I not?"

"You seemed to enjoy that, last night," he returned with a probing look.

Now, Raoul realized, was the moment to play his trump card. His finely honed gambler's instinct told him she was a desperate woman. He watched her closely as he dangled the bait.

"However, if the costume disturbs you, think of the enormous amount of money you'd earn."

Vesper's eyes grew wide. She struggled to hide her surge of interest. "Enormous?"

"Last night," Raoul added helpfully, "I walked away from the poker table with fifteen hundred dollars in my pocket. A rather sizable wage for a few hours' work, wouldn't you agree?"

Vesper swallowed. "Quite sizable."

The preposterous proposition was sounding considerably more reasonable to her as Raoul batted down her objections with seeming nonchalant ease. She looked straight into his eyes.

"You have been solicitude itself, Monsieur St. Martin, feeding and clothing me, even giving me your bed. And you've asked for nothing in return. But you must expect something if I go to work for you. Am I not correct?"

"Of course." He grinned engagingly at her. "We would be partners. In vulgar parlance, we'd split the take. You're going to make me a very wealthy man, my dear."

She sensed he was hoping for something more. Her eyes became very hard.

"Were I to live on your steamboat, under your protection, dress as you describe, and be your gambling partner, everyone would assume that I am also your mistress."

"Very probably."

He tapped the ash from the end of his cigarillo with deliberate nonchalance.

"But I wouldn't be." She faced him squarely. "That would have to be part of our bargain."

He frowned slightly.

"Let me put my cards, if you will, on the table as frankly as you have. You must be aware that I desire you. But I will do nothing to force you into my bed. One day, I know, you will come to me. If that is satisfactory, then our partnership can proceed."

Vesper stared at him, openmouthed. She had never imagined a man could talk of his own passion so remotely. But he was waiting for an answer.

"This is quite a proposal you've presented me with," said Vesper, striving for a tone as cool as his own. "I'll need some time . . ."

"As much as you wish, my dear," said Raoul, settling back against the cushions and lighting another cigarillo.

Vesper rose and paced the room. It was amazing how Raoul's plans dovetailed so perfectly with her own. To avenge her beloved Cord, to tear out the filthy heart of his murderer, she would need a small fortune. And she would need a new identity. Raoul was offering both. But Vesper would have to give up her reputation.

She shot the impassive Creole an appraising look. He was waiting patiently enough, watching her. From the first moment she had met him, Vesper had trusted Raoul St. Martin.

What do I care what people think, Vesper asked

herself fiercely, as long as I know the truth? And as long as I can pay Augustus Bledsoe for shattering everything I loved.

Raoul watched the war in her face. For all her supposed hard-as-nails facade, he concluded, she had come from a gentler world. What had she endured? he wondered. What had she lost? One day he would hear her story, when the trust between them was consummated. For now, he pitied her even as he eagerly awaited her answer.

"I'll do it," she told him, her eyes glittering, icy as gemstones.

Joy leaped within him, quite apart from his pleasure as a businessman. He offered her his long, thin hand, and she took it up determinedly with her delicate ivory one. It was as equals that they shook hands, two proud loners. They were scarred, each filled with dreams unshared by the other, but bound together in mutual strength and mutual need.

The rest of the winter was spent in hard work for both Raoul and Vesper, though Raoul thoroughly enjoyed teaching his beautiful protégée everything he knew about the gambling arts. Vesper learned to play the popular games of faro and poker expertly, to read her opponents' faces while keeping her own expression blank, and to recognize and expose cheaters.

She proved to be an excellent pupil, working grimly at her lessons, honing her judgment of both odds and people. Then, when spring turned the river turbulent, Raoul gave Vesper her final test. She would have to beat him at a game of poker.

They sat in his sitting room, facing each other across a highly polished table. Hand after hand went by, and she found her pile of greenbacks dwindling

at an alarming rate. Vesper grew desperate. She had
to win, to show him she was worthy of being his
partner. But she simply could not read Raoul's face.
He was as inscrutable as fate itself. Even the more
subtle cues he had taught her—the clenched fingers
on a winning hand, the shifting set of the shoulders
—did not change, whether Raoul had good or bad
cards.

With only enough money for one more round,
Vesper resorted to a ploy of her own devising—one
Raoul had never taught her. She ran a single finger
gently along the back of Raoul's brown hand as he
held the deck of cards.

"You will deal me something exciting this time,
won't you?" she asked in a low, husky voice.

Startled, Raoul looked up into her huge, glowing
amethyst eyes, at her beautiful mouth with its sensuous lower lip swelling in a pout.

"That's all in the hands of Lady Luck, as you well
know, my dear," he said, one eyebrow raised, but
his voice was shaking slightly.

She leaned toward him, picking up his hand and
removing the deck of cards from it.

"I like this hand better," she murmured, stroking
his palm lightly.

She could feel his skin heat up, the pulse at his
wrist, buried in white lace, begin to beat frantically
as she rubbed over the spot softly again and again.
In an awkward gesture, quite unlike his usual suavi-
ty, Raoul pulled his hand back from Vesper.

"We must finish the game," he insisted.

Vesper threw him an amused look.

"By all means, Professor. Deal the cards."

Raoul played the next round like a rank amateur.
In the next rounds he fared no better as Vesper
continued her seductive wiles. Soon she had won

back all her greenbacks and had made considerable inroads in his. Suddenly Raoul threw down his cards, loomed over Vesper, and plucked her out of her chair.

"Temptress. You have asked for this," he grated as he held her against him and covered her mouth with his hot, searching lips.

For a moment Vesper was too stunned to respond. Then she struggled in the unfamiliar though expert embrace, pulling away as far as she could.

When his mouth released hers to wander hungrily over her face, Vesper cried, "No, Raoul, you don't understand. Let me go, you fool."

"Fool?"

He released her and stepped back, his eyes dangerous with anger.

"We are neither one of us children, Morgana," he told her in clipped tones. "If you did not want my kisses, why did you invite them?"

"It was the only way to beat you at poker," she explained hurriedly, wanting badly to erase the coldness in his eyes. "Remember that first night when none of the men could concentrate and you won so easily?" she asked sheepishly. "Well, you're a man too. I had to pass my final test, so I figured it was worth a gamble."

Vesper watched the anger fade from his face, to be replaced with rueful comprehension and, finally, amusement. Raoul St. Martin burst out laughing.

"There has never been a woman like you, Morgana," he told her as his laughter faded. He took up her hand in his and planted a deeply admiring kiss on her long fingers. "Together we will be absolutely unbeatable."

Vesper raised her eyes to his, brilliant with her triumph.

"Now we are truly partners," she exclaimed, and

the smile she gave him was radiant with pride and anticipation of their victories to come.

Raoul and Vesper proved to be an unconquerable and fascinating duo. As their reputation on the river grew, so did their bankroll. In her honor, Raoul refurbished and renamed his huge white steamboat *The River Siren*. Over the months that followed, he made clear that he would welcome a personal relationship as intimate as their professional one, but Vesper was too locked in her bitter memories and revenge plans to respond to his gentle overtures.

She had hired a mercenary investigator, Joaquín Delgado, to ferret out incriminating evidence against Bledsoe. But, much to her dismay, Delgado had uncovered nothing of substance though he had prowled Washington, D.C., for nine months. As Raoul had predicted, Vesper had finally told him about the death of her beloved husband and stillborn babe, which made the gambler all the more gentle with her. But she never revealed her true identity or the plot she had concocted to make her nemesis pay for his crimes.

What Raoul did know was that the restless, unsatisfied, deep-seated sadness in her eyes had not abated. His incomparable protégée had not been healed of her wounds, but seemed instead locked up in her tragic past, unable to live in the present where he waited for her.

His own feelings toward her had changed considerably. He hadn't realized to what extent until one night when he heard Morgana scream out from her cabin, which now adjoined his. Raoul went to her bed to comfort her and found her in the grip of a nightmare.

"My love. My love," she cried out and held out her arms to him.

In that strange place between sleeping and waking, she yielded voluptuously, gratefully, to his warm embrace. Shaking with pent-up hunger, Raoul lay down next to her and rained kisses on her heated body. His hands slipped inside her translucent chemise, exploring adoringly what he had only imagined for so many months. She clung to him, moaning with pleasure, and whispered another man's name—Cord.

Though Raoul knew he could have taken her, and every fiber of his body ached to do exactly that, he forced himself to stop. She truly came awake then, finding her clothes awry and Raoul fully aroused.

In a voice straining to retain some control, Raoul said, "I can't take you like this. While it would be easy to do so, you would certainly regret it in the morning. And if you did, then so must I."

"Raoul, I . . ." Vesper began in confusion.

"Hush, my lovely. Pretend it was all a bad dream."

Her eyes were warm with gratitude, but he could see sadness in her face. Was it for him? he wondered. He held his own disappointment in check, cradling her until she fell asleep again.

Unable to go back to his empty bed, he walked outside in the cool night air. At the ghost-colored railing, staring at the dark river, he realized that Morgana's happiness had become more important than his own. He had fallen in love with her.

# Chapter Fifteen

OVER THE NEXT MONTH, THE LINES OF DISTINCTION between Raoul and Morgana's business partnership and their personal relationship blurred even more. Raoul had again redecorated her stateroom aboard the luxurious *River Siren*. Now it was fit for a queen, he told her. Or at least a king's mistress, Vesper mused ruefully one evening as she stood before an ornate mirror, its frame carved in leaping dolphins, and surveyed her domain. Raoul had insisted on redecorating in the latest French Renaissance revival.

Though her own personal taste would have dictated a far simpler, perhaps less elegant style, in a strange way Vesper found herself preferring the gaudy, overstated, and massive pieces the Creole had chosen for Miss Morgana, the notorious riverboat lady gambler. There was an unquestionable, overpowering solidity to the gilt, dark-wooded, heavy curved furniture. It gave Vesper an immediate sense of security. Raoul was convinced the style had authority, even a sort of regalness to it.

*The River Siren* had become a regal, pristine white, floating palace of pleasure on which the handsomest, most-talked-about couple on the Mississippi River relieved weary yet eager travelers of their money in the most entertaining ways possible. And regal Vesper would be tonight.

Typical of their partnership, Raoul had presented his latest scheme after a champagne toast to their very considerable and continued success. In the salon during the hours before dawn, they had counted the take from their last jaunt up the river. It was Raoul and Vesper's most intimate moment together, and it was the closest Raoul had ever gotten to courtship.

Raoul had made Vesper laugh at his grandiose plans for a sumptuous masquerade ball, describing it in his driest, drollest wit. Of course he was to appear as Louis XIV, and Morgana would be none other than the Sun King's favorite mistress, Madame de Montespan. Their eyes had glistened at the thought of the financial benefits to be reaped from such an extravaganza.

Now Vesper stared at her image in the large looking glass that dominated one wall of the dressing chamber. Once again, as it had done many times before during the past years, her reflection revealed something new and different about herself and the way life had changed her.

This time, she swayed to the left, then to the right, taking sharp critical measure of the woman in the reflection. The costume fit her as though she were born to it. Raoul had seen to that. He had taken Vesper to the finest seamstress in New Orleans to fashion the perfect gown.

The woman had created the epitome of baroque ornamentation. The bodice of brocaded coral velvet had a square, low-cut décolletage, and the swirling pattern of the brocade was emphasized by tiny seed pearls. Seed pearls also dotted the elbow-length layered ivory lace sleeves. A matching overskirt lined in forest-green satin pulled back from the waist and draped over her hips, displaying an elaborate petticoat festooned with white velvet braid and fringe, fleur-de-lis appliqués, and more lace.

The dress was ridiculous yet at the same time quite effective, Vesper thought. In the spirit of the intriguing ball to come, Vesper selected two beauty patches of gummed black taffeta. She placed one along her left cheek and the second more daringly next to the peak of her cleavage. She eased her feet into dainty high-heeled slippers. Tonight she was the king's mistress. So be it.

Vesper frowned. Where had her headpiece gone?

"Daisy?" she called out. "Are you still fiddling with that flowery marshmallow?"

A tallish, severely thin ebony-skinned woman with a pronounced limp and a worried expression emerged from the bedroom with an enormous concoction of powdered wig hair, lace, and ribbon, eighteen inches in height.

"Lawdy, Miz Mo'gana, you gonna be able to dance wid dat thing on yo' head?"

Vesper smiled at Daisy's display of genuine concern. It wasn't often that the slave girl spoke at all, despite Vesper's kind coaxing. Daisy smiled a little too, and Vesper warmed to the shy girl.

Several months previously, Raoul had brought a

disheveled ragamuffin to the steamboat and given
her to Morgana as a gift.

"You're a woman of substance and importance
now," he had said to her. "In my world that means
you should own some property. I have *The River
Siren;* now you have a slave."

Vesper had thanked him uneasily. While the buying and selling of human souls had always repulsed
her, here in the lenient world of the Mississippi it
was easy to allow her conscience to become calloused about one more issue. In a strange way, she
knew she had sold herself to Raoul in order to
finance her plans for revenge. She had convinced
herself that whatever means served the end she had
in mind for Augustus Bledsoe were justified. And if
it made Raoul happy to give her a slave, then it was
just one more part of his world she had to accept.

But she resolved to treat Daisy Cotter as an equal,
a friend. It had taken Vesper months to win the
reticent slave's confidence. Only in the last few
weeks had Vesper's patient, friendly manner begun
to win over Daisy's wary reserve.

Vesper answered the little maid's question with
vivacious cunning.

"Maybe I ought to try it out first, Daisy. What do
you say to a spin or two about the room?"

She plunked the extravagant coiffure on her head
and whirled Daisy around, humming a catchy polka.
The headpiece tilted precariously but, to both wom-
en's surprise, held firm in Vesper's thick tresses.

"Oh, Miz Mo'gana," the slave girl puffed, "you
done took mah breath away."

A look of pure distress covered the young woman's wide features.

"What'll Mistuh Raoul do to me if'n you ain't
finished off when he come fo' you?"

"I'll be good, Daisy. I wouldn't want either one of

us to have to answer to Mister Raoul's black moods," she added, winking conspiratorially.

Vesper went obediently to her vanity table. She sat down before a smaller mirror to touch up her makeup, letting Daisy secure the lopsided headdress firmly in place.

"But you know?" Vesper added, laying a golden glove on top of Daisy's battered hand. "In all the time I've been with Monsieur St. Martin, I've never seen him hurt a fly."

She leaned forward toward the mirror, her eye intent on Daisy.

"He'd never hurt you, honey. I promise you that. No one will hurt you as long as you're with me."

Vesper lifted the girl's hand again and stared at it, slowly shaking her head. Ugly welts and needle-thin scars marked the knuckles. Daisy abruptly withdrew the mangled hand and slipped it into an apron pocket.

"Please, Miz Mo'gana, I doan lak to think 'bout it no mo'."

Vesper twisted around in her intricate seat of interlaced carved bands.

"All right, Daisy. I only want you to be happy."

There was a sharp knock at the door, and Daisy went to answer it. In dazzling resplendence, Louis XIV had arrived to escort Madame de Montespan to the ballroom.

"You may go, Daisy," he said, dismissing the girl from the stateroom, never taking his burning gaze from his costumed partner.

Bowing low to his lady, Raoul took Vesper's hand and brushed his lips across her fingertips. Caught up by Raoul's infectious verve, Vesper joined in the mirth.

"My lord, my king, my sovereign," she humbly enjoined, sinking into a deep curtsy.

"Arise, chatelaine, and see what pretty bauble I have brought you as a reward for your undying loyalty and virtue."

Vesper shot Raoul a sharp glance, for there was none of the accustomed irony in his voice tonight. Before she had a chance to retort, he withdrew from his bejeweled and braided coat an extraordinary necklace of coral and emeralds. The stones were a perfect match for the velvets of her ensemble and his as well. She gasped and turned automatically for him to fasten it around her neck.

The two of them faced the large, dominating mirror. He stood behind her, observing the face of the woman he had come to love. Perhaps tonight his haunting dreams would be made real and she would come to him. But as he brought the circlet around her slender neck and lightly stroked her swansdown skin, Raoul despaired of ever possessing his mysterious Morgana.

Her expression had changed and her eyes were focused not on him, here in close physical proximity, but instead on the dim, unreachable past. What was she thinking? he wondered. Was it still the old matter of the dead husband and babe? It was at moments like these that Raoul wished he were not so expert in reading faces. The truth hurt far more than ignorance.

At the touch of his fingers, Vesper snapped out of her reverie. She would not think of Cord or Bledsoe tonight, she vowed to herself. She owed it to Raoul to be his completely in mind and spirit, at least for one night. The clasp locked into place, Vesper turned and looked tenderly at this man who had done so much for her.

As if seeing him clearly for the first time, Vesper was stunned by the raw vulnerability apparent in his coal-black eyes. Gone was the mask of cynicism.

What remained undimmed were the Creole's innate nobility and his sense of honor. And shining bright as a beacon was his desperate hunger for her.

She stroked his cheek.

"Come now, my dear. This is a night of triumph, a night for celebration. Haven't you told me often enough to put aside sadness and seek the joy of the moment?"

His expression belied the war of emotions so unusually displayed on his face.

"Raoul," she said sincerely, "I know I owe you everything."

"I don't want your gratitude, Morgana," he rasped with unaccustomed difficulty. "I want your love."

Vesper was silent. She was well aware of how Raoul had taken care of her, now cared for her, yet demanded nothing in return. She leaned toward the darkly handsome Creole in king's clothes and kissed him with a tenderness she thought had died in her. He pressed her to him in delighted wonder, deliberately restraining the passion with which he would have liked to embrace her. They stepped apart, eyes locked together. There was no need for words. An acknowledgment of a newer, deeper intimacy passed between them.

They were two of a kind, partners in everything but bed, Vesper thought. Why had she kept such distance from Raoul? What was she saving herself for? Perhaps after all this time, her husband dead, lost to her forever, perhaps it was time to let herself feel for a man again. With new eyes, she looked at Raoul. Perhaps I love him already, she ventured to herself.

Bowing deeply, he offered, "My queen."

"My consort," she returned with unmistakable meaning.

He presented his arm to her, she accepted, and together they swept off to the grand salon where the party was in full sway. As the king and his madame entered the ornate gilt and silver-chased room, a drumroll sounded from the gay band Raoul had hired for the occasion. All eyes turned toward the couple, and an audible gasp arose from the crowd. Had Raoul and Vesper been dressed in rags, their natural majesty would still have shone out.

As it was, with *The River Siren*'s notorious couple sumptuously decked out as French royalty, the effect on the ship's guests was spontaneous and magnetic. They swarmed toward Raoul and Vesper. Even the most jaded, who had been everywhere and seen it all, were drawn irresistibly by the leonine pride the pair exuded. Men fawned over the incomparable Miss Morgana, offering her compliments, each more extravagant than the next.

Always on the ready to defend her against would-be Lotharios, Raoul never moved from Vesper's side, propelling her expertly through the throng of her admirers. Tonight she was at her best. She maneuvered her way with her own unique brand of deferential sensuousness. She was gracious but untouchable, and she seemed to have eyes only for him. Keeping her arm firmly in place on his, she was driving him mad with her appetizing nearness.

The same undeniable hot emotions were plaguing Vesper. Raoul had never seemed more desirable to her than on this night. The wiry strength of his body was shown to best advantage by his costume. The tailored velvet coat, fitted at the waist, then flaring deeply, emphasized his long, sinewy torso. His muscular thighs were clearly outlined by knee-length breeches and tight hose. Even his peruke of cascading curls, which on other men might have seemed foolish and effeminate, gave Raoul a lush dignity.

Above all, it was his eyes that aroused Vesper, prowling across her like those of a glistening coal-black panther.

She noticed with an unusual sting of jealousy how the female guests could not seem to tear themselves from the fascinating Monsieur St. Martin. They sought his attention by playfully tapping at the jeweled buttons of his coat, stroking his grand peruke, and giggling girlishly at each suave comment he made. That women were attracted to Raoul did not surprise Vesper. She was used to that. But that she should mind . . . This new feeling shook her, and she trembled with anticipation at the only possible conclusion of their evening together, for his eyes were on her and on her alone.

The band began playing again and struck up a lively galop. Raoul shook his head and signaled to them. They stopped midnote, whispered among themselves, and Vesper heard instead the gentle strains of a sentimental waltz. As king and queen of the ball, they danced alone through the first refrain, oblivious to their audience. Soon they were joined by dozens of other swirling couples, but their eyes were only on each other.

Raoul held Vesper artfully, matching her body to his as the hypnotic rhythm swept them up into the waltz's intimate lilting motion. Vesper was heady from her partner's enveloping musky scent. Intoxicated, she moved closer to him. Through her gloved hand, she could feel the muscles of his back working, and a thrill of animal anticipation coursed in her veins. She felt more alive here in Raoul's arms than she could last remember. His lips brushed her forehead, her temples. His hot breath tickled and teased her ears.

As they whirled and weaved about the lavish salon, Raoul gripped his partner more tightly to him, so that her breasts were crushed against his chest, her nipples hard and erect. Their steps grew smaller, closer together. When the music stopped, they were locked in each other's arms. While the other couples enthusiastically applauded the band, Raoul and Vesper exchanged a wordless, meaningful glance. He swept her from the room, taking her to the privacy of his suite.

In his bedroom, Raoul passionately embraced Vesper, communicating the force of his hunger for her. He rained kisses on her upturned face, and Vesper received them willingly, awash in reawakened sensations. Achingly he drew her from him, his eyes burning and nostrils flared.

"I've waited too long for this moment, my lovely Morgana, and now I will make it last forever."

With excruciating slowness, he undressed both of them, releasing their heated longings with each piece of apparel. His touch ignited her sensitive skin and she throbbed with pent-up desire. Their clothes peeled from their bodies, Raoul carried her to his huge four-poster bed and gently laid her down. His hands roamed over her full breasts, her taut belly and silken thighs. Urgently her fingers traveled up and down Raoul. She felt him eager, trembling, pliant in her grasp.

"Torturer," he groaned, his eyes closing in ecstasy.

He lay down beside her, increasing the tempo of his caresses. Vesper turned toward him in welcome, wanting what he wanted, ready to pull him to her. But a pervasive numbing sensation took root and spread inexorably over her. She closed her eyes, willing herself to accept Raoul, the man who loved her, desired her, was with her now.

She moaned, not from frenzied need but from misery. It was Cord she wanted in her arms. It was

Cord she would always, only, want. Abruptly she tore herself from Raoul's fervent embrace and sat up, burying her face in her hands.

"I can't, Raoul. I can't give myself to you. I'm sorry, so sorry."

Her sobs came, convulsive and unnatural, as if yielding to this emotion were as difficult as surrendering herself to another man.

Raoul stiffened. It was the ghost of Morgana's dead husband come between them again. The Creole was forced to realize, once and for all, that Morgana, with all her capacity for passion and life, would never belong to anyone but her husband.

"I've been patient, my love," Raoul finally said in a deathly quiet voice. "I hoped that between time and my own enduring charms"—his voice held the old ironic tone for just an instant—"your wounds would heal. But it appears I was wrong."

Vesper turned toward him, her eyes purple pools of defeat. She reached out to touch his arm, but he drew back as if she had stung him.

"I hate myself for doing this to you, Raoul. I never meant to deceive you. I honestly thought I could . . ."

She had to look away as he strived to control the accusing pain which twisted his face.

"I can't keep looking at you and not have you. So you'll understand if I keep my distance. . . ."

He reached for a silken dressing gown thrown recklessly over a chair near the bed. Slipping it over his head, he left Vesper's side.

"We'll continue as business partners, Morgana," he said, his back to her. "The benefits are too lucrative to give up."

His voice broke slightly.

"In that way, I suppose I show my weakness for you."

With great effort, as though his emotions still fought his wiser reserve, Raoul turned and withdrew to another room in his suite. Vesper started to call out to him, but she had nothing to say that he would want to hear. Wearily she gathered her finery, separating the two discarded costumes into discreet piles. She slipped from Raoul's bedroom through a specially built door which joined her stateroom to his. Once on her side, she stared at the closed door and slowly drew the bolt into its locked position.

It will never be the same again, she thought with a wistful sadness. For all their trips up and down the river to come, Raoul and she would only meet in the gambling salon to conduct their mutual business. They would smile. They would be polite. But the lines of separation were drawn, and their eyes would never meet in shared warmth again.

She was losing more than a friend and a partner. Raoul had been her protector, her teacher, her constant companion. Without him, how could she maintain the hard, sparkling facade essential to her plan? Life would seem so bleak without his wit and his intelligent, discerning eye.

Vesper's head began to ache terribly, and she pressed her hands to her temples. Again, tears welled up in her eyes. She shut them tight, forbidding the feelings of hurt and guilt to spring forth. She walked slowly through the stateroom, wrapped in a veil of self-pity. But an intrusive sound interrupted her misery.

Someone was bitterly sobbing from the depths of the bedchamber. Vesper stopped in her dressing room just long enough to pull on a silk wrapper and light a candle. In the dark bedroom, she made out a hunched-up form, huddling on the carpet between the elegant canopied bed and the oversized armoire.

"Daisy?" Vesper whispered. "Is that you?"

There was the sound of hurried snuffling and the form straightening itself.

"It is you, Daisy," Vesper cried in alarm. "What is it? Has someone hurt you? Come here, now, and let me see."

Daisy shuffled forward, her head cast down.

"Ah didn't mean nuffin' by it, Miz Mo'gana. It's jes' an ol' mis'ry."

Vesper put a motherly arm around the thin girl.

"No, no, honey. You're obviously upset about something, and I want to know what it is. Come on, now. Sit here and take this."

She handed Daisy a glass of water and beckoned to an old oak gossip chair. Vesper lit the sconces about the walls, then returned and sat by the girl.

In the light, Daisy warily surveyed her mistress's face. She saw the familiar concerned expression on the lady's face, but Daisy was startled to see a sadness there she had not noticed before. Miz Mo'gana looked like a person who could be trusted, who really cared. Daisy suspected, no, she knew, she could say anything to Miz Mo'gana, even tell her the awful truth. Daisy opened her heart to the kind soul before her and poured out her sadness.

"It were a year ago when I fells in love wid a house hand at de next plantation up ribber from my massah's house. Noah, he were a good-lookin' man and good to me, Miz Mo'gana."

Daisy stared earnestly at her owner, then lowered her liquid brown eyes to the floor.

"Noah's mistress and my mistress be friends. My mistress would take me wid her in de buggy to visit, cuz I be good wid needle and thread."

She flashed her eyes in an old instinctive pride.

"Dat's how I met up wid Noah. Soon, he ax me to marry him and he tell me 'bout his grand plans to git back to Africa. It sound wonderful to me, Miz

Mo'gana. He fairly turned mah head round wid his big talk. He tol' me it'd be easy to excape . . . said he'd done it three o' fo' times already and jes' come back cuz he missed me."

Daisy could sit still no longer and paced back and forth. Her limp seemed to worsen with each hectic step.

"Ah was scared. The night I lit out, my heart was poundin' like a jungle drum. But ah loved dat man and I promised to go to de ends of de earth wid him. Ah got as far as de ribber near an ol' holler cottonwood tree when I seed a little fire. Ah thought ah could see Noah in de tree, wavin' to me. I ran fast then, right into de arms of de Butcher."

She paused in her tracks.

"You hear tell o' de Butcher, Miz Mo'gana? He de evilest man ever. He and his devil gang, they had Noah up dat tree, all right, hangin' by his neck wid his eyes poppin' out. Ah screamed an' fell to my knees. You know what dat Butcher done? He laugh, Miz Mo'gana, he howl, lak nothin' ah ever hear on dis earth. And dis jaggedy scar on his cheek fairly jump off'n his face."

Daisy's shoulders went slack and her voice was reduced to a croaking whisper.

"He took me right dere in front of mah true love's dead body, and den he passed me to his gang. Ah'll never fo'get deir faces. When they be finished wid me, he chain me to de same tree dat Noah be swingin' from and he whup me and stick me till ah cain't see nothin'. De next mornin', Butcher and his gang took me back to my massah. But jes' befo' dey reach de plantation, de Butcher took dis long, mean knife and cut into my leg real deep."

Daisy lifted the hem of her skirt and showed Vesper an ugly gash below her calf. The Butcher had made sure that Daisy would never run again.

"I never walked right since. I been sold three times since then. Ah never feels safe again til Mistuh Raoul buy me fo' you here on de ribber."

There was a long moment of silence. Daisy stole an uneasy glance at her mistress, whose elegant hand was tightly cupped over her mouth and whose big violet eyes brimmed with anguish. In the next moment, Vesper rushed to the beleaguered young woman and pulled her into a tight, soothing embrace.

". . . to suffer so much . . ." Vesper mumbled in Daisy's ear, made wet by her mistress's tears.

Vesper's emotions were in tumult and her unwilling mind dredged up vivid pictures of her own pain, in many ways akin to Daisy's. Images hurtled past her eyes of lost loves, of fire's grim light destroying the future, of devilish men in disguise, and the faint recollection of a livid scar. . . .

"Oh, Daisy, I know what it is to have the life cut out of you," Vesper grieved in empathy.

She told Daisy a little of her own unbearable sadness, mentioning her murdered husband, the lost babe, and now the fresh wound of hurting Raoul, her only friend in the world.

"Miz Mo'gana," Daisy murmured shyly, "ah be yo' friend."

Gently she reached out with her scarred hand and petted the velvet black masses of Vesper's hair.

"Dere, dere," she continued in a low, soothing voice. "Doan cry no mo'."

The two women sat together, hugging and rocking each other, each feeling better for having eased the other's heavy burden.

# Chapter Sixteen

ICY JANUARY GUSTS RUFFLED THE DARK WATER OF ST. Louis's harbor and lifted snow off *The River Siren*'s railings, whirling it toward Vesper. Standing in the doorway of her stateroom, she shivered in her thin satin dressing gown as she waited for the delivery boy to extract a letter from his ragged pouch. Joaquín Delgado's monthly report had arrived with its usual regularity.

After sending the inadequately dressed lad away with a whole dollar tip, Vesper locked her door, pulled up an olive-green velvet-covered stool to her escritoire, and broke open the black seal on the detective's letter. An irritated sigh escaped her. It seemed as though she had been through these same actions hundreds of times already, and for no reward. Would this letter be any different?

Dear Miss Morgana,

　　The suspect is extremely wary. More information is required before I can proceed further.

Yes, thought Vesper peevishly, that's why I hired you, dolt. Her heart sank. He wouldn't open a letter with that statement if he'd had any luck.

Have staked out his house, as per instructions. Subject has received several rough visitors late at night but I am unable to ascertain identities of said men. Bribed new groom who reported suspect rides out very late at times. Was able to trail suspect once. He met with group of men in uncleared swamplands of city. Unable to hear conversation but saw money exchanging hands. May be source of unexplained sums in bank.

"Damn," Vesper swore, looking up. "Why didn't he follow one of those men?"

The wan winter light stealing through the window fell on her pinched, discontented face. Gritting her teeth, she returned to the letter.

Could not track suspect in night woods, but am certain he is engaged in secretive activities, probably illegal. Will continue surveillance though it will be difficult to pin him down. Must wait for his mistake.

Enclosed is a list of monthly expenses.

J. Delgado

"I know he's engaged in illegal activities," Vesper shouted as she crushed the letter into a ball and threw it across the room. "He murdered my husband!" came her anguished cry.

What was the use of anything? she thought in despair as she buried her face in her hands. She'd become a hussy, flaunting her body at countless men, in order to revenge Cord, and not only was her revenge plan at a standstill, but she'd hurt another good man in the process.

Raoul's sad eyes haunted her. Instead of finding life amusing, as he had done when she'd met him, now he often turned wearily away from the antics of their passengers. Vesper knew she was to blame for his change of heart. It made her ache inside every time she looked at him. Vesper was engulfed by self-disgust.

Is there nothing I can do right anymore? she wailed inwardly as Daisy entered with a huge pile of freshly laundered petticoats.

"Mornin', ma'am," came the voice, soft as ashes.

Vesper gave her a kind smile.

The shy, self-effacing slave crossed the room to the elaborate wardrobe so quietly she scarcely made a sound. As usual, her drooping shoulders and her starved-cherub's face with its constantly mournful expression touched Vesper's warm heart. The girl was still so unhappy. Whether Vesper was kind or cruel to Daisy, she was still a slave.

Daisy belonged to whomever had the right price in his pocket. The wrongness of slavery struck Vesper once again. It was an institution Cord had never countenanced, and Vesper agreed with his fierce rejection. A man who valued freedom as he had, who had taught her to be free, could have little sympathy for any system that chained one human being to another.

Then why am I a slaveowner? Vesper asked herself, watching Daisy silently cleaning up the dressing-table clutter left by her discontented mistress the night before. Vesper realized that she had ignored her conscience about many things in the last year.

"Daisy, leave that mess."

Vesper patted the plush wingback chair next to her and smiled encouragingly. Daisy gave her a questioning little smile as she seated herself.

"I have come to a decision about you," Vesper told her. "I've decided to free you, honey."

For a moment, Daisy didn't move. When she raised her face, her eyes looked round as saucers.

"You gonna give me mah freedom?" she said in a voice choked with emotion.

The elation flooding through Vesper told her she was doing the right thing at last.

"Yes," she assured Daisy. "This very day."

Tears of joy cascaded down Daisy's taupe face.

"Oh. Ah am so . . . Thank you, Miz Mo'gana. Bless you fo' this."

Daisy's bowed back straightened, and for the first time Vesper saw her brilliant smile. Why, Daisy was a pretty girl, thought Vesper, amazed and pleased.

"Come on," she told Daisy. "Pick out my plainest dress. If we hurry, you'll be a free woman before lunch."

Daisy attended to her mistress's dressing, but she was so excited she couldn't concentrate. Vesper had Daisy sit down and kept up a stream of reassuring chatter, fastening the jet buttons on her gray calico gown and placing on her neatly coiffed head a black bonnet trimmed with gray and gold velvet ribbons. She pulled on a heavy black cloak and wrapped another one about Daisy.

It was a strange feeling to set foot in St. Louis again. Vesper had always remained on board *The River Siren* whenever the boat had docked in the city that reminded her so vividly of Augustus Bledsoe and his vicious plans. While Daisy floated at her side in a fog of joy, Vesper recognized the dock where his men had set out after her. She remembered the calculated cruelty of her captor's words, the utter panic she'd felt when he'd locked her in that last day. Though Vesper had escaped, she still felt strangely chained to Augustus Bledsoe. Her life was not her own to lead as long as he went unpunished.

But a look at Daisy's beatific face calmed her painful thoughts. At least I can free one victim, Vesper thought with satisfaction as they followed the directions of a helpful innkeeper to the municipal courthouse.

Vesper was not surprised that the officials were reluctant to free a slave. They presented her with form after form, delay after delay. One slight, cadaverous gentleman in black serge went so far as to challenge her identity. It was a tense moment, for Vesper had no papers that would prove she was Morgana. Another official finally confirmed that this beautiful woman was indeed the celebrated river siren. He had lost a bundle to her last summer aboard the big white boat.

It was considerably after the noon hour when Daisy, happy tears in her eyes, stood before a frowning magistrate with the writ of manumission open before her on his wide desk. Vesper had already signed, and now it was Daisy's turn. But the pen trembled so much in her hand that she could not even make an X.

Vesper stepped forward and took the pen out of the girl's sweating fingers, holding the shaking hand between her two gentle ones.

"Everything will be just fine, honey. All we need now is your signature," Vesper said in a soothing voice. "You can do that. You're a free woman now."

Daisy's hand stopped shaking, and with a flourish she signed the document. She seemed to stand straighter, Vesper noticed, as the disgruntled official folded and sealed the writ before handing it to Daisy. Vesper put her copy in her black knitted purse, watching her former slave's spirit begin to glow again in her eyes.

No matter what Raoul says, I'm glad, Vesper thought. She knew that he would object for both personal and theoretical reasons to her freeing Daisy, who had been his gift.

But as the two women made their way back to the steamboat, Vesper's steps grew heavy. She had freed Daisy, but who was there to free Vesper herself from the tangle of tawdry falsehoods and schemes she had locked herself into? She felt the whip of despair lick at her again as she watched Daisy walking proudly, pointing out interesting sights in the street. From time to time she patted the writ she'd tucked in her sash.

Vesper sighed miserably, and Daisy turned to look at her former mistress. Seeing the icy misery that bound the glamorous woman, Daisy sought to comfort the person who had been unfailingly good to her.

"No mattuh how bad it is, Miz Mo'gana, jes' think what happened wif me. Yo' luck can turn in a minute. Listen to me tellin' y'all that. You de gambler."

Suddenly Daisy grew silent. Vesper turned to her in surprise and saw that her companion's entire body was rigid with shock.

"What is it, Daisy?"

Without a word, Daisy pulled Vesper behind a wagon loaded with tall boxes that was parked on the side of the street.

"You see dat man? In de doorway of de saloon?" Daisy whispered fearfully. "He be one of de men what hurt me so bad, lak I tol' you."

She crouched fearfully in the wagon's shadow.

Vesper peered cautiously at the man, one arm comfortingly around the shaking Daisy.

"One of the men who tortured you after the Butcher . . . oh my God," she gasped.

Daisy crouched even lower and squeezed her eyes tightly shut.

"Is he comin'? Ah'd rather die . . ."

"No, no," Vesper said in a harsh whisper. "He . . . uh . . . just reminded me of someone."

But inside, Vesper was reeling. Daisy's assailant was one of Bledsoe's hired men, the one who had shot Cord! She watched him disappear inside the saloon as the pieces of her year-long puzzle fell into place. Augustus Bledsoe and Daisy's Butcher were one and the same.

It was so clear now. The scar. The immense cruelty. The unexplained sums of money. The meetings late at night. Bledsoe made his fortune capturing runaway slaves. He could be as sadistic as he liked with them, for who would object? In fact, some slaveowners would welcome a man with his reputation. It probably deterred many would-be escapees.

But in Washington, were it to become known that the influential Mr. Bledsoe tortured slaves for a living . . .

"Is he gone?" came Daisy's whisper.

"Yes. It's safe."

Vesper reassured her automatically, her mind still struggling to accept this wonderful stroke of luck. She had him now. Now she could break him.

Daisy looked up and stared at the unholy glee that contorted Vesper's face.

"You all right?"

Daisy took her by the shoulders, alarmed.

"Miz Mo'gana. What's wrong?"

"I'm fine, better than I've been for a long, long

time. But we must get back to the boat immediately."

She stood, pulling Daisy up with her.

"Hurry."

Vesper began to run, with a puzzled Daisy following in her wake. The most important letter of
Vesper's life needed writing, Vesper thought with
fierce elation. Once on board, Vesper excused herself to Daisy, pleading need for a rest after so much
excitement. She immediately locked the door to her
stateroom, then unballed Delgado's letter and
smoothed it out on her desk as she sat down and
took out pen and paper. With satisfying delibera-
tion, she created her plan to destroy Augustus
Bledsoe.

Mr. Delgado,

In your last letter, you wrote that we would
have to wait for the wary fellow to make a
mistake. I am pleased to report to you that your
subject has made two. He let me live and he
allowed a beaten runaway slave to see his face.
Believe me, he will regret the day he made those
costly errors.

I have irrefutable proof that the genteel, highly
touted Augustus Bledsoe has a different identity
here in the South. The horrors he perpetrates on
runaway slaves whom he recaptures have earned
our fine friend the nickname of the Butcher.

Before his alter ego is revealed to everyone in
Washington, I want him to sweat, to suffer as he
has made so many innocents suffer. You will
reveal his identity slowly. Begin by planting rumors in the lower-class watering spots. He will
find these easy to deny, but he will worry about
how the story started. I want him to have plenty
of time to worry. Wait until he's managed to

completely squelch the stories. Then send an anonymous letter to the editor of the Washington . . .

Vesper paused as the picture rose in her mind of the brutally powerful Bledsoe reading the newspaper at his garishly expensive breakfast table and being overtaken by fear. There was a yellowy wolfish gleam in her eyes as she imagined her nemesis struggling in the net which would draw tighter and tighter around him. In the end, when he was stripped of all dignity, she and Daisy would appear at his trial to tell their stories. Cord and the babe would be avenged.

As Vesper continued to detail her plan to Joaquín Delgado, she had no idea how predatory she looked. The feral, gloating expression on her face would have shocked her upstanding Aunt Lucinda, disgusted Cord, and astonished even worldly Raoul.

He'll hang, Vesper promised herself. He will die. And then . . . Vesper's pen paused in midsentence. What would happen afterward? A little voice inside her warned that even Augustus Bledsoe's death would not bring Cord back. The willful call to vengeance that had given life to Vesper's spirit since her husband's death would be silenced.

Through sheer force of will, Vesper pushed away this vision of coming emptiness. She could not think about that now. Her generous mouth held rigid in a thin white line, she continued etching out the details of Augustus Bledsoe's destruction.

On another part of the docks, an enormous man, whose bulging muscles showed clearly through his old black wool frock coat, was loading the last of a group of prize horses onto a barge. He had an obvious air of authority, but his green eyes were murky with pain, his face rigidly grim. Though he was doing a competent job of calming the skittish sleek horses, it was clear that he was simply going through the motions. There was a lifelessness to him, so that he seemed an empty hulk of a man rather than the powerful individual he was meant to be.

Beyond the shell of silence surrounding him, the two traders who'd bought his horses cheerfully exchanged gibes and tried to include the taciturn giant in their conversation. After all, he'd been their best customer for many years.

"Awfully good horseflesh," offered the shorter one, who had a headful of thick brown curls and guileless blue eyes.

His partner, wiry, with a flashing smile that featured two gold teeth, shot an amber stream of tobacco juice into the river. "Almost good enough to eat," he said, and guffawed at his own joke.

"Most expensive steak you'll ever chew," shot back the first buyer. "At the price we paid, be maybe ten dollars a pound, hey?"

He nudged the silent brawny seller. The big man winced at the joke about eating his horses, and ignored the horse trader's sally. Gently he urged the last horse, a roan filly with four white stockings, up the plank. Vesper had helped birth that one, he remembered painfully, and gave it a final lingering pat. He watched stony-eyed as the plank was taken up and the barge set off across the somber water.

"Well, that's that," came the cheerful voice of one of the buyers.

Yes, Cord Travers thought disconsolately, that is that. The last link with his past was severed. Though he would try to find a new life, he wondered whether it was worth the effort. Picking up a two-pound flint as if it were a pebble, he shifted it in his hand as if he were going to fling it out into the wintry river. Then he dropped the rock. His shoulders slumped.

The two lively dealers exchanged a glance.

"Hey, Travers," began the wiry one. "You're rich now, but keep those greenbacks in your pocket or Morgana will eat them up."

"Morgana?" asked Cord in a low growl.

"Yep. You're taking *The River Siren,* right?"

The first dealer added eagerly, "You never heard tell of Miss Morgana? She's the talk of the Mississippi. Gambling lady, son. So sharp she'll separate you from your money before it lands on the table, and so purty you don't rightly care."

"You got a real treat in store for you," said his partner. "Tell her Dugan says hello."

Cord shot the two grinning men a puzzled glance, as if they were talking a language he'd long forgotten. Then his face lapsed back into its granite lines. Without so much as a good-bye, he walked off in the direction of the huge white steamboat, his feet dragging at every step.

# Chapter Seventeen

THAT SAME EVENING, BOGGS FLETCHER SAT IN THE center seat at Miss Morgana's table in the grand salon. He gave his cards a last disgusted look before folding.

"Dang," he said in his gravelly voice, "these here five cards don't amount to a hill o' beans."

He cast a pleading look at Vesper, who had paused in her card dealing to give him a fond glance.

"Can't yuh see yore way clear to givin' ol' Fletcher here a decent hand? What do yuh say, Miss Morgana, honey?"

The old fur trapper raised a freckled, heavily calloused hand to scratch his hoary head as he made a comical grimace.

"It's Lady Luck you have to court, not me," Vesper told him with a warm smile.

Boggs had been one of the first passengers to

become one of her regulars when Vesper started as a professional gambler aboard *The River Siren*. Whenever he made a profit on his furs, Vesper could be sure it would end up in her pocket. Boggs was a terrible poker player. But, Vesper thought, he was an endearing old cuss. She exchanged amused glances with Raoul, who was standing nearby, lounging against the bar, in his usual proprietary position.

"Deal the cards, hussy," came the angry voice of a foppishly garbed young man sporting an aristocratic beak of a nose. "Make your assignations for tonight on your own time."

Raoul was on him in a flash, lifting the offender out of his chair by his expensive lapels.

"Apologize to the lady, sir, or swim to New Orleans," Raoul snarled. He set the shaken youth on his feet, adding, "If this weren't your first time aboard *The River Siren*, I'd let the alligators have you."

The chastened young man saw the iron in St. Martin's eyes and yielded. Hastily he bowed to Vesper, saying, "Please forgive my intemperate words, Miss, ah . . . Morgana. Were it possible to unsay them, you may be sure I would do so with alacrity."

"We all make mistakes, Mr. Thorpe," said Vesper, beginning her much-used gracious little speech. "I'm sure you won't make this one again. Won't you sit down and join us?"

Reassured by her words and beguiled by her glimmering smile, the young man returned to his place. Vesper continued to deal the cards. Her beautiful, provocatively clad body and her sparkling though impersonal flirtation kept the four men at her table bedazzled and losing steadily. Inwardly, however, she was visualizing her letter to Delgado making its way east into the detective's hands. Finally Bledsoe's destruction would begin.

Vesper caught her breath, staring down unseeing at her cards. She might soon play her last hand of poker. Once her enemy was vanquished, she would no longer need either the hidden identity or the money. From the relief flooding through her, Vesper realized that she had come to hate her manipulative, artificial job and would welcome its end. And perhaps Raoul would regain some of his joie de vivre, once there was real distance between them.

The mellow candlelight shining on her cards from the chandelier was blocked for a moment by what must have been an enormous man, filling the one empty seat at her table.

"Yore new round here, ain't yuh?" came Fletcher's rasping voice. "Must cost a fortune to keep yuh in shoe leather, friend."

With a sigh, Vesper began her well-practiced welcome to a newcomer. Slowly she raised her eyes, letting a slow, beckoning smile grow on her face. Her contrived smile froze halfborn as she recognized her long-lost husband, and her cards fell from suddenly numb fingers.

"Cord!" she cried out in unbelieving joyous tones.

Cord's bleakness disappeared in an instant as he discovered his beloved wife.

"Vesper!" he shouted, his murky eyes blazing green as spring.

She drank in his wonderful alive face as a parched wanderer gulps at a mountain stream. How had he survived the holocaust their cabin had become? She had seen him fall with a bullet to the head. How had he escaped death? Did it matter? she asked her-

self as she scanned his beloved features again and
again.

But his expression changed and hardened. Instead
of rushing to her, pulling her into his arms, Cord
stared at her in shock and growing disgust. Vesper
looked down at herself, at the low décolletage of her
purple satin gown, the formfitting bodice dripping
with strings of pearls and trimmed gaudily with gold
lace. Her face was artfully painted, her jewels
strategically placed to draw men's eyes toward her
long, elegant neck and ripe, pear-shaped breasts.
With dismay, Vesper realized how she must appear
to him.

He stared at her as if something precious deep
within him were shattering into a thousand bits. She
put out one imploring hand, but he was already
standing, towering over her and bristling with undis-
guised fury.

"Please, Cord . . . I . . ."

"How could you?" he said slowly.

Then his voice rose to a shout.

"You're nothing but a whore!"

He strode from the room, leaving Vesper surrounded by a sea of shocked, scandalized faces.
Crimson with chagrin, tears blinding her, she rushed
after him. In the corridor, she was stopped by
Raoul, who had hurried to intercept her.

"Wait," he ordered, grabbing her upper arms,
stopping her headlong flight.

He peered down into her face, reading the undeniable truth blazing from her amethyst eyes.

"That man is your husband, isn't he?"

"Yes. Yes!"

She struggled to free herself, but Raoul held her
tightly. He tried to affect a light tone to hide his
sinking heart.

"Don't you think you'd better calm down before you go storming after him?" He raised one eyebrow. "A man in his state is not easily persuaded to listen, my dear."

"Don't protect me anymore. Let me go!" she cried.

She twisted out of his hands and dashed down the corridor in the direction Cord had taken. Raoul was left standing alone.

She found her husband in a pool of moonlight at a deserted corner of the railing. His head thrown back, he was taking a long swallow from a battered tin flask. She watched him shudder as the fiery liquor went down, as if he were unaccustomed to its bite.

"Cord, let me explain," she began, hurrying to take his hands in hers.

He wrenched them away.

"There's nothing to explain," he snarled, a slight slur to his words. "I can see as well as the next man."

His obvious disgust made her words stumble.

"But I'm not . . . I never . . . It's only a disguise . . ."

"You disguised yourself for a while as my wife, it appears," Cord said slowly, the venom thick in his voice. "Now it's clear what you are."

He took another draft from his flask and fixed her with a harsh look.

"At least your stepsister Roxanne was planning to sell herself for a wedding ring. What do your customers pay you with? A fancy dinner?"

Vesper was sobbing now. Each cruel word cut at her, flaying her inmost feelings. Cord was struck by a sudden thought. His voice became very hard.

"Our child . . . You did have our baby, didn't you? Is he here, or did you abandon him long ago?"

"He's dead," she choked out, covering her face with her hands.

Cord reeled as if from a body blow.

"Due to your loving neglect, no doubt," he gritted.

Vesper was stung to silence by his frightful words. Her face turned white. Her hands clenched in agony. Cord tore himself away from his wife with a cry of anguish he could no longer stifle and stumbled toward the opposite side of the ship.

The joy of rediscovering the woman he had given his heart to had been obliterated by a painted whore who would sell herself for a drink or a pair of sparkling earrings. Had he ever known the real Vesper Lawrence, or was her love for him only an illusion, a pretense to escape from a less than satisfying lover?

Cord found himself standing at the door to his cabin. His hand paused, irresolute, on the handle. Vesper, whose violet eyes had haunted his every dream, was only a moment away. He could return to her, hold her . . .

"No," he roared.

He strangled his terrible urge to take her back at any cost and wrenched open his cabin door. Stumbling inside, he fervently wished he had taken any boat except *The River Siren,* played at any table except hers. His love and his hatred tore at him like ravening dogs, giving him no peace until he fell into a liquor-fogged sleep.

Vesper did not sleep that night. She paced her stateroom, from tousled bed to silver moonlit window and back again. How ironic it all was, she thought bitterly. Cord had come back to her, like the miracle she had long given up wishing for. And instead of bringing her joy, he had tossed her into scalding misery. He had taken her shining memories of their years together in the Indian Woods and smashed them beyond repair.

Had he ever loved her? Vesper asked herself in anguish. Had it all been her illusion? No man who truly loved a woman could believe her capable of abandoning their child. On through the slowly moving night hours Vesper paced, tortured by the pain of her husband's return.

When Raoul came to her room the next morning to see how she was feeling, he was secretly shocked at Vesper's haggard air. In the pale lined oval of her face, her eyes were bruise-dark and her mouth was drawn with suffering. Sliding an arm around her waist, he led her to the couch and sat her down at his side.

"Tell me the whole story, my dear," he said, "and this time, why don't you tell me the truth?"

Vesper's judgment had been blurred by her sleepless night. She saw only Raoul's coolheaded calm and forgot the intense man who lurked beneath that surface. She blurted out her entire history, including the revenge plot she had always kept from him. There was a long silence when she finished her recital.

Then Raoul said, in a voice iced with disdain, "All these months you've been carrying out this dirty little scheme, and never once mentioned it to me."

He looked down at her, his mouth thinned by contempt.

"Has no one ever told you, Vesper Lawrence Travers, revenge is never sweet? To stoop to this Bledsoe's level and to play by his rules, you must inevitably become as vicious as he."

He paused, his eyes very hard as they searched her face.

"I'm very much afraid I was laboring under the illusion that you were made of finer stuff. Fool that I am, I believed that I could trust you."

He chuckled mirthlessly, shaking his head. His scorn cut Vesper to the quick.

Hotly she demanded, "Since you're apparently so superior to the rest of us mere mortals, suppose you tell me what you would have done if the woman you loved had been torn from you. Wouldn't you have done everything, anything, to keep that love alive?"

For a moment, Raoul's face was nakedly vulnerable. Vesper saw the man of passion that he might have been.

"When I was young, it so happens there was such a woman. She wanted another man's money instead of my love. He offered to pay up all her family's ruinous debts if she married him. I decided not to enter into the auction for her hand. Perhaps I was too fastidious, but buying a bride offended me. She married him, and paid the price. She died in childbirth a year later. I have never forgotten Yvonne. You have something of her spirit, I fancy."

He gave her an ironic smile. Raoul's distanced approach to life had never irritated Vesper more.

"You mean, you tucked your tail between your legs and ran like a wounded puppy because you weren't courageous enough to fight for love. Well, let me tell you, Raoul St. Martin, that I believe love is worth fighting for."

Vesper's words touched a raw nerve in Raoul. Turning on her, he sneered, "You call reducing a man by inches to a quivering mass of fear 'fighting for love'? Don't fool yourself. You've run from your grief by turning it into hatred. You've nourished that hatred for Augustus Bledsoe until it has strangled your honor."

The truth of his observations seared Vesper to the bone and roused her to blind fury. She found her hands shaking, wanting to force the words back down his throat. Instinctively she reached out toward a vase to fling at Raoul.

He rose from the couch and stepped back, his dispassionate facade intact once again. One eyebrow raised, he said coolly, "You really don't want to break that lovely Sèvres vase, my dear. Here," he said, picking up an ashtray, "throw this instead."

Vesper was astounded by her own descent into violence. Slowly she placed both the vase and the ashtray on the table, and took a long, deep breath. She sensed that Raoul was watching her calm down like a theatergoer attending a particularly interesting play.

"Do you never feel anything, Raoul St. Martin?" Vesper hotly demanded. "Must you always be a bystander, watching from a safe distance?"

His smile mocked them both.

"I've had considerable difficulty finding a safe distance from you," he murmured.

Even as he said the vulnerable words, Vesper saw Raoul gather his aloofness around him like a protective cloak.

"It would never have worked between us, Raoul," she said. "You fell in love with Morgana, not

Vesper. But Morgana was miserable, only half a woman."

In a low voice, Raoul answered, "She was woman enough for me."

Vesper forced herself to face the raw pain in his eyes. What a terrible waste of a man, she thought as a wave of pity overtook her. Vesper stood, went to him, and stretched out her hand. He took it and met her sad gaze with a distant look.

"I take it that this is good-bye, then," said Raoul, and his voice had never seemed calmer.

"You could always read me like a book, Raoul," said Vesper.

She remembered that first night when she had been fished out of the Mississippi River. He had worn the same speculative and self-contained expression. But now, despite himself, Raoul's hand trembled slightly in hers. Vesper looked up into his black eyes.

"Will you be all right? They'll all think your mistress has deserted you for another man."

Raoul drew his hand out of hers and turned away, staring out the window at the gray, turbulent water. His voice was very calm, yet it held a tinge of sadness.

"The river has always been my mistress, Morgana. It does not matter what anyone else thinks."

"No," she said softly. "I suppose it doesn't."

But I will always think of you with gratitude, Raoul, she thought as he left the room. Gratitude and melancholy for the vital man you could have been.

# Chapter Eighteen

"MIZ MO'GANA, YOU GOTTA LET ME IN," CALLED Daisy. "It be almost time fo' you to go to de table."

The former slave, standing worriedly in the chill night air, frowned down at the breakfast tray and the lunch tray, lying untouched where she'd left them earlier. She knocked again on the stateroom door, which had been locked all day. There was no response.

Daisy thought, It's got sumpin' to do wid dat man, de one what called her a whore. The entire ship had been buzzing with speculation ever since that giant of a man had so grossly insulted their gambling lady.

"Miz Mo'gana, you cain't stay in dere forever," pleaded Daisy.

Poor lady, she thought. It was goin' to be hard fo' her to face all those eyes tonight. Daisy knocked again.

"Come on, now, honey," Daisy cajoled. "Let me help you git dressed."

"I'm already dressed," said a voice.

The door was flung open, revealing Vesper in an outrageous scarlet gown. Daisy's eyes opened wide.

"Oh no, Miz Mo'gana," she protested. "You said you'd nevah wear dat one. It makes yo' bosoms almost fall out."

Vesper's eyes were red-rimmed. In her set blanched face, two hectic red spots shone high on her cheeks.

"It's the perfect dress for tonight," she snapped.

She tore off the rim of black lace from the upper edge of the bodice, making the dress even more revealing. Hurriedly Daisy entered the room, shoving the door shut with her foot.

"Lawdy, Miz Mo'gana. You cain't do this," she protested in shock.

Ignoring her, Vesper turned back to her dressing table and sat down before the mirror.

"Pile my hair up high," she directed. "I want all of these stuck in it."

Vesper lifted up two handfuls of assorted pearls, feathers, jeweled combs, and ribbons and threw them on the table. Daisy's dismayed eyes met those of her employer's in the mirror.

"I cain't put all those in yo' hair. It's too much."

Vesper's eyes were hard.

"You'd better," she said.

Daisy swallowed. Her eyes fell to the floor.

"Yes, Miz Mo'gana," she whispered.

As Daisy reluctantly created a gaudy tower of curls and ornaments, Vesper worked feverishly on her face. Her hands clawed open rouge tins, boxes of heavy powder, and pots of kohl as she applied the makeup with a heavy hand. When both women were done, Vesper stood, waved Daisy aside, and looked at herself in her full-length mirror.

A lewd, tasteless image peered back at her. The reflected woman looked as if she could be bought for a cup of coffee. The scarlet dress clung to every curve of her torso like a coating of melted cherry candy. With every breath, her breasts, pushed up high and round, threatened to burst from the deep wide vee of the bodice. The skirt's flounces and the long, slender sleeves were black satin, which focused the eye back to the bodice. The garish hairdo and masklike makeup only accentuated the tawdry, inhuman air of a woman who felt she was worth nothing.

"He called me a whore," she burst out, strangling a bitter sob. "I'll show him what a whore really looks like."

Daisy gasped as Vesper, with a defiant sweep of her gown and her head held high, flounced out of the stateroom.

"Be careful, Miz Mo'gana," Daisy called after her.

The former slave wrung her hands, fearing that no one but she would see the agony that underlay the painted lady's cheap and blatant seductiveness.

As Vesper had expected, Cord was waiting for her. He was the only man seated at her table, his massive, rigid body dwarfing the black leather armchair. Her regular customers hovered near the round green baize-covered table, hesitant to seat themselves because of the almost tangible cloud of fury floating about the giant glowering man who had insulted Miss Morgana the previous evening.

"Why, gentlemen," Vesper called, turning on her most dazzling smile as she glided to her table. "I do hope I'm not late."

Every head in the room turned toward her. One of her regular customers, a thin, courtly banker with rich waves of white hair and a dashing mustache, reassured her.

"Ah no, Miss Morgana. We've simply been waiting for you."

She patted her overly ornamented hair, one finger drawing down a small curl to dance against her cheek.

"I wanted to look especially good for you boys tonight."

The banker's dark eyes were bewildered as he took in her changed appearance. The other three players feasted their eyes hungrily on her exposed breasts as they complimented her on her gown. But no one sat down at the table.

They all looked at the silent bronze-haired man whose eyes narrowed dangerously as he took in Miss Morgana's scandalous costume. Defiantly Vesper ignored Cord. Let him stare. In a husky, intimate voice, she addressed her skittish regulars.

"I would miss you all dreadfully if you deserted me tonight. Won't you play with your Morgana?"

She let her eloquent amethyst eyes pull at each of the four players. Her plea, with its seductive overtones, was irresistible. With a lot of chair scraping and nervous throat clearing, the men positioned themselves gingerly around the table, giving the tense, brawny stranger a wide berth.

Behind her, Vesper sensed that people were drifting back to their drinks and games. Inwardly she breathed a sigh of relief as she unwrapped a fresh deck of cards and let her professionally inviting smile dance impersonally around the table.

"Five-card stud, gentlemen?"

The condemning glare of her husband's eyes never left her as she worked, dealing and bidding with polished moves. How could she spend the evening half naked with a group of men? his hot eyes seemed to demand. How could she sell to strangers the body she had vowed would be his alone? Where was her pride? Where was her self-respect? His silent accusations fueled her sense of betrayal, and she flaunted herself more and more boldly.

When the player to her right, a sallow-faced, narrow-shouldered young man with the petulant face of a spoiled younger son, threw his cards down with a pout, Vesper leaned toward him until their arms pressed against each other, giving him a clear view of her wonderful bosom. She whispered into his ear loudly enough for everyone to hear, "Now, you know Mama will always give you more, right?"

Startled by her warm flowery breath on his neck, the young man jerked away in surprise. He sent her a surprised look that quickly changed to a leer. Licking his lips, he whispered back, "How much more will you give me, honey?"

He half expected Miss Morgana to put him smartly in his place. She had never welcomed anyone's favors before.

"Just maybe we'll talk about it later," she said, to the amazement of all her regular players.

Vesper accurately read their astonishment, but her defiant look was for her husband. His eyes betrayed nothing of his feelings, but a muscle in his jaw leaped as he watched her brazen behavior. A shaft of feeling that was both pain and triumph shot through Vesper. Score one for me, she thought savagely, beating back tears.

She continued outplaying her customers and charming them out of their greenbacks. Cord's pile of dollars, however, did not dwindle. He played a strong game, Vesper thought uneasily as he watched her implacably from behind his cards. Her wretched-

ness at his betrayal goaded her on to make him hurt
as badly as she did.

"Hey, Boggs," she chaffed one player who, shaking his grizzled head, was getting up to leave.
"Surely you're not going to yield the field to a raw
backwoodsman like our friend here, are you?"

Her nod indicated Cord, and her mocking smile
was bright.

"Forgive me, ma'am, but he's got a pile of greenbacks higher than a grizzly bear, and I'm wiped out.
Yep, he's a smart one, I reckon."

"Oh, pooh," she protested. "Mr. Travers here
just has a run of lucky cards. I'm sure, with all his
skinning and tracking and swindling Indians, he
hasn't had time to learn much past the names of the
suits. Isn't that right, Mr. Travers?"

She turned a patently phony smile on her husband, whose hands grasped the edge of the table
with bone-splintering strength. His knuckles went
white, as if he were struggling not to strangle the
smirking woman who sat across from him. For an
instant, Vesper felt real fear. Where will this all end?
she wondered. How could I have said that to him?

The smile he gave her was as cold as the grave.

"My prowess at cards should be easy enough to
determine. I challenge you to a single hand, right
here and now."

His eyes bore into hers, and the words crackled as
if they were on fire.

"Just you and I, alone."

The other players backed away in alarm from the
poorly contained fury they read in his face. Games
around the room stopped, conversations died down.
Everyone, sensing the drama of the situation,
watched the wrathful giant and the provocative
gambleress who shook with anger. Her wounded
pride pushed her to meet his challenge. He had

actually accused her of selling herself, of abandoning their child . . .

Indignation gave her the strength to say coolly, "Apparently you will get your wish, since your ill-mannered behavior has repelled all the other players."

"Deal the cards," he ordered.

Their eyes never stopped dueling as Vesper's practiced fingers dealt one card down and one card up for each of them. Her hand was high. She had an ace showing, though her hole card was only a three. Cord had an eight up. It was a routine enough beginning.

"Twenty dollars," Vesper opened.

Without a word, Cord laid three fifty-dollar bills over her twenty. There was a surprised murmur from the crowd of people that had gathered around their table. Why would the backwoodsman raise the stakes so high so early when there were more rounds to go?

Vesper frowned. Did he have a pair of eights? There was only one way to find out, though she was uncomfortable with the stakes being raised so quickly. She matched him and dealt each of them another card face up.

Vesper had to school her face to keep from smiling. She now had a pair of aces, and Cord, a useless eight and ten. He had forced her into a big raise. Now it was her turn. She put a hundred-dollar bill on the table and looked up at him with satisfied eyes. His face was calm as a distant mountain as he covered her money with ten hundred-dollar bills.

Vesper managed to turn her gasp of alarm into a cough as the buzz around the table swelled. She could read nothing in his face. But she knew that her husband was no fool. Why had he made such a foolish move? She told herself that his anger was blinding him to common sense, that she would beat him badly. But his implacable face looked all too controlled. Uneasily she matched the thousand dollars, feeling the tension coil between her shoulder blades.

Vesper tried to keep her wrists relaxed as she dealt herself a queen and Cord a nine. He still had nothing, she told herself, looking at the eight, ten, and nine before him. But when he didn't fold, she realized that he was working on a straight. His hole card must be a seven or a jack.

What utter idiocy, she thought. Any card out of sequence could destroy his whole hand. How could he risk so much money on such a small chance? Again, she opened the bid at one hundred dollars, not knowing what to expect.

He reached into a pocket and took out two thick packets of folded greenbacks, which he threw negligently onto the table. The money hit with a loud, solid thump. Vesper eyed the pile with alarm. There was a hundred- dollar bill on the outside. She made a rough calculation and shuddered. Her furious husband had just possibly raised the stakes by forty thousand dollars.

She managed to achieve a bored expression on her face as she asked, "What exactly is your bid, sir?"

He gave her a piercing glance and said slowly, "There were precisely four hundred bills the last time I counted. You haven't forgotten your arithmetic, have you?"

The crowd clamored with amazement. The backwoods giant might not know the first thing about cards, but watching him was better than going to the theater. And the crowd knew he had Miss Morgana trapped. How could she match that much money? The hulking man might win the hand even though Miss Morgana had better cards.

Vesper writhed inwardly under his challenging stare, maintaining her outward composure with a power she never knew she had. He would not beat her so ignobly, she vowed. Recklessly, knowing he had deliberately trapped her, she ordered the steward to write a voucher for the amount. Now all her savings were riding on this one hand, on the next card.

Licking her dry lips, Vesper slowly dealt Cord his last card. The onlookers were tensely silent as she turned up a seven. He could have the straight, she told herself despairingly, which would beat anything she could get unless she turned up another ace. But it was just as likely he had had nothing from the start, and had simply tried to raise the stakes beyond her means without realizing how wealthy she was.

Taking a deep breath, she turned over her last card. The crowd watched avidly. A queen. She had a good hand, an excellent hand, Vesper thought, unless he had a jack or a six in the hole. She looked up at him, seeing the power in his narrowed green eyes and flared nostrils. There would be no mercy from him. He had been pushed too far.

She slid her last hundred-dollar bill onto the pile. It was possible that he had cleaned himself out with that last bid. Please let that be true, Vesper prayed. She forced herself to meet his gaze.

Never taking his cold glaring eyes from her, Cord reached into another pocket and pulled out another thick wad of bills. Vesper stared at the pile of greenbacks and knew it spelled her doom. She looked at him, her shoulders slumped in defeat.

"Do you have the straight?" she whispered.

"It's easy enough to find out," he told her, a cold smile on his face. "Just match my bid."

"You know I can't do that," she flared. "That

hundred dollars was the last money I had in the world."

"The solution is simple enough for a woman like you," he said in a hard, triumphant voice. "Offer me a night of your time."

He ran his eyes insultingly up and down her body.

"You're probably pretty enough, beneath all that paint, but you'll have to use your whole bag of tricks tonight to pay back what you owe me."

Vesper turned her head from him as if he had slapped her across the face. Deep humiliation burned through her. How could he do this to her? How could he? She forced back the hot tears that were choking in her throat as seemingly hundreds of eyes drank in her degradation. Some rag of pride made her turn back to him, to disguise the ravages of his towering insult with another reckless smile.

"Why not?" she asked airily, as if selling her body were her nightly practice.

He turned over both his hole card and her own. His was a jack. He had won.

Vesper's hands were shaking as she watched him calmly gather up his winnings and shove back his chair.

"No . . . you can't expect me . . ." she began, the crowd hanging on his answer.

But before she could finish, he was upon her. With a single yank, he had her out of her chair, and slung over his massive shoulder. Her shriek of protest faded as he pushed open the salon doors and carried her away to his cabin to take his revenge.

Once inside, Cord kicked the door to his cabin shut and dumped his protesting burden unceremoniously on the floor. He seated himself on his bed as Vesper scrambled to her feet, smoothed her skirts, and tried to tug her bodice higher. When she stole a look at Cord, he was eyeing her expressionlessly, his arms folded on his chest. She took a deep, ragged breath and let it out, watching him warily.

"All right," he said calmly. "Take off your clothes so I can see what I bought for my sixty thousand dollars."

Vesper's eyes widened indignantly.

"You know what I look like. We were husband and wife for two years and there's not an inch of me—"

"Take off your clothes," he roared.

Vesper swallowed. He looked like an infuriated bear. He might do almost anything if she didn't obey him. She knew his strength, and there was no resisting it. Her eyes lowered to the ground, Vesper began the humiliating task of stripping before his icy eyes.

Cord watched her reluctantly unlace the black strings of her bodice, and his heart pounded as she freed her beautiful pear-shaped breasts from their confinement. He remembered so vividly the taste of her rosy nipples, the scent of her midnight hair.

"Stop," he ordered as she began peeling off the skirt.

She froze, still looking at the floor.

"Take all the trash out of your hair."

She obeyed. Her lifted arms pulled her breasts high and revealed the classic lines of her lovely alabaster torso. Her hair fell about her in rich clouds, making the skin peeking through look whiter still. Vesper pulled her hair around her in an instinctive gesture of modesty and sent her husband a pleading look from tear-drenched blue-violet eyes.

Pain coursed through him at what he was doing to his wife, but she had hurt him too badly.

"Go on," he snarled.

Realizing she could not move him, Vesper took off the rest of her clothes as quickly as she could, hoping to end her mortification quickly.

"Have I changed much?" she challenged out of her pain, her lips trembling. "Can you see the marks of my dissolute life?"

He winced as if she had struck him. In truth, she was as perfect as his memory of her. Her naked body shone in the lamplight like a Greek statue carved out of melted pearl. He was shaking at her nearness.

"Wash your face," he rasped.

Again Vesper obeyed. Her lithe, graceful walk to his washbasin, the subtle rhythm that was hers alone, tormented him with memories: Vesper running to fling herself into his arms at the end of a long day; Vesper bending over the helpless wolf cub, her gestures all tenderness; Vesper astride a bucking horse, controlling it easily, a happy, confident grin on her tanned face; Vesper naked, plunging into their lake, leaf shadows dappling over her flesh.

Slowly she put down the towel and stood trembling, defenseless to him. Only her eyes spoke, and they were eloquent with misery and betrayal.

What right has she to look betrayed, Cord asked himself furiously, when she had allowed so many men to see and touch what had been his alone to worship? With a muttered curse, he was beside her, laying hungering hands upon her flesh, forcing her back to the bed.

He tore open his clothes with one hand while the other pinned her struggling form to the mattress. His hands marauded over her nakedness, fueled by both primitive need and vengeful fury. Vesper cried out as he entered her, wounded deeply by his loveless possession. But as he moved, careless though he was of her needs, she found a warmth welling to life within her. She began to encourage him with throaty little cries, losing herself in the wonder of feeling his body on hers once again. She had been dead, and now she was alive again. Her body trembled with awakened intoxicating sensuousness. They reached the apex together, and Vesper plunged back down to earth bathed in an endless pool of passionate love for her husband.

She cuddled against his massive panting form, nestling her head against his heart, listening delightedly to his breathing gradually slow, as she had so many times before. Her love was with her, she exulted, and they would never lose each other again. She gave him an adoring smile, anticipating his words of forgiveness. But the eyes that met her melting ones were cold as shards of green ice.

"You've learned your tricks quite well," he sneered, forcing back his own wonder at the passion of her response to him.

No matter how real it feels, he warned himself, she gives the same to all the others. The thought was burning agony, pushing him to hurt her back.

"You were always a quick learner, weren't you," he snarled.

Vesper's body went rigid as stone. The pain of his rejection thudded through her, freezing her reawakening passion for him. As he took her again and again in the night, she was numb to his despairing needs, limp under his angry punishing of both himself and her. He finally slept, exhausted as much by the battering conflict of his feelings as by his physical exertions.

Vesper lay still, imprisoned at his side by one of his powerful arms. Her throat ached with unshed tears, but she couldn't cry. The tragedy she had endured was too deep to be relieved by tears. Tonight's brutality was all the worse, haunted as she was the whole time by her memories of Cord's wonderfully tender, extraordinarily passionate love-making.

As Vesper lay tearless and aching she felt Cord's palm stroke her cheek in an old gesture of tenderness. But when she looked at him, she saw that he was deep in dreams. Only in his sleep can he love me, she thought despairingly. A single tear traced its slow path down her face.

When Vesper awoke, she was alone in Cord's stateroom, her clothing in a heap on the floor. Rising, she was surprised to find not a single bruise on her body. For all his rage, she realized, Cord had contained himself in order to protect her. It was a ray of light in her dark memories of the terrible night before.

How could he have used me like that? she asked herself in leaden misery. The Cord of the Indian Woods would never have taken her cruelly. But am I the Vesper of those far-off days anymore? she asked herself. She eyed the gaudy heap of satin and velvet that lay where she had so reluctantly dropped it the night before. She would have to accept that those long-ago days of innocent love between them were gone forever.

Vesper slumped back onto the bed, remembering all too vividly how Cord had forced her unwilling body open. No matter what she had become, she did not deserve such heartless treatment. If their relationship were to be saved, they would have to learn to trust each other all over again, she told herself as she sprang up from the bed again and started sorting through the pile of clothing.

She pulled on the dress and fastened it, feeling as if she'd donned someone else's clothes. The gown seemed fashioned for a girl in a woman's body, someone who craved endless amounts of attention from men.

She only wanted one man, Vesper knew. And in order to regain his love, she would have to break down the walls of anger and mistrust that had sprung up between them. Somehow, she determined as she tiptoed back to her own stateroom, she would reach the inner Cord, and find again the Vesper she once was.

Daisy sprang up from the sofa when Vesper walked in.

"Oh, Miz Mo'gana, ah'm so glad yore all right. I was so worrit."

Vesper gave the girl a warm smile. Encouraged, Daisy asked the question everyone on the boat was wondering about.

"Who was dat big, handsome man what carried you off last night?"

Vesper swept past her, stopping at the wardrobe. Daisy watched with a puzzled frown as Miz Morgana pulled out dress after fancy dress, throwing them one by one onto the bed.

"Come help me find a decent gown," Vesper called to her.

"You got plenty ob good dresses," Daisy protested as she caught a flying emerald velvet skirt.

Vesper shook her head, having emptied her wardrobe. "I don't have a single dress that a hardworking frontier wife would wear."

"Miz Mo'gana . . ." Daisy began in total bewilderment.

"He's my husband, Daisy. Right now he hates me, but I'm going to win him back. And the name is Vesper, not Morgana."

Daisy stared at her, astounded.

Suddenly Vesper realized what she had to do.

"And you're going to help me, Daisy."

She began explaining her idea to the stunned girl, who eagerly fell in with the plan.

# Chapter Nineteen

FOR THE THREE SUCCESSIVE NIGHTS AFTER CORD HAD
so brutally claimed Vesper, he had the same dream.
She was with him, beneath him, and the achingly
familiar rhythm of their lovemaking was just reaching its peak. Cord looked into the face of his beloved
Vesper to see the strains of ecstasy sweep over her.
Her eyes were gauzy from his thrusting urgency, her
parted lips swollen from his kisses, her sweet breath
coming fast. He could hold back no longer, and,
knowing they had both been pleasured, released
them from their bondage to a spiraling freedom of
sensuous rapture. Their first ravenous yearnings
satisfied, still they clung to one another, unwilling to
part, even after their bodies grew quiet.

In the dream, Cord looked upon his dearest wife
once more and shrank back, first in disbelief, then in
loathing. Where had Vesper gone to? Who was this

cheap, hardened slattern who mocked him with glittering violet eyes lined in black and reddened teasing lips?

He found himself hunched over her, grabbing her by the shoulders and shaking her. He kept at it until tears spilled from her eyes. He watched, again in disbelief, then frightful joy, as the crystal-clear tears washed away the tawdriness and revealed his dearest Vesper once again.

"It's you! Don't ever leave me again. I've found you . . . I've found you . . ." Cord repeated endlessly, saying the words even as his eyes flew open and he was suddenly awake.

He stared at a gaudily framed Madonna and Child hanging on his cabin wall, lit by the first shafts of morning light. The dream was still vivid. His hand stole over to the spot Vesper had occupied only a few nights previously, closed into a tight fist, and pounded the bed with frustrated fury.

"Damn," he gritted.

Damn her for leading him on, and damn himself for wanting her anyway. He kicked the bedcovers aside and flung himself out of bed. With angry jerky motions, he washed, shaved, and dressed, dissipating only a little of the tense energy surging through him. He wouldn't spend another day locked in his cabin. One had been enough, and he had been ashamed of himself, admitting that Vesper . . . no, not Vesper but that witch Morgana . . . had any power over him.

The second day he had conquered his feelings, or so he thought, and sauntered about the steamboat as if he owned it. He was lucky he hadn't made a complete fool of himself, he thought ruefully. It was uncomfortable enough being stared at by the numerous passengers who had witnessed the tempestuous finale to Morgana and his poker game.

He had spent the third day down on the lowest deck among the slaves and journeymen. But there was no place for him. He had made a nuisance of himself, emptying, refilling, and emptying again his flask.

No more, Cord vowed. This was the start of a new day and he wasn't going to let the memories of Vesper or the haunting presence of Morgana gnaw at him anymore. With renewed purpose, he stepped out into the corridor and headed for the promenade deck. A good dose of river air would clear his head, he thought.

But his feet had a mind of their own and Cord found himself pacing at what had to be Morgana's stateroom door. He shook himself and forced himself to move on. Then he found himself at the gambling salon, where he eagerly sorted through the patrons for a glimpse of Morgana. He swore under his breath. She was no good for him and he'd only be asking for more pain. He steeled himself and turned away back to the outer decking.

Once again his impulses were too strong to ignore. Cord's eyes roamed to each fancily dressed woman he saw. But Morgana was nowhere in sight. He had almost given up hope of finding her, having circled the decks twice, when he paused and leaned his back against the painted white iron railing.

Across from him, under the protection of the extended ceiling, was a scattering of deck chairs. On one sat a young woman dressed in simple country style with a clean, shining, quiet radiance about her. Her face was lowered, intent on studying the intricate crochet with which her fingers were occupied. Cord felt a wrenching tug in his heart at this tiny vignette of domestic tranquility.

How often had he come across Vesper in the early evenings, sitting by the fire, in just such a pose. Her head slightly atilt just as this woman's was . . . her fifth finger held upward in a funny little crook just as this woman's was . . . one hand flying up to sweep back an intrusive curl just as . . . Cord's heart skipped a beat and he grabbed at the railing.

It couldn't be. He blinked, straining his eyes. Slowly, as if in a trance, he approached this irresistible vision of Vesper as she had been. For a moment, he hesitated and stood over the woman, breathing in a strangely familiar scent.

"Excuse me . . ." he ventured.

She raised her head, looked directly at him as if she had known it was him all along, and smiled. My God! he thought, staggered. It was Vesper. He stared into those luminous violet eyes, losing himself in their glow. He was home again, free to laugh, free to love.

Cord let himself bathe in the honest, tender aura of her spirit. How vividly he recalled her mastery of the frontier, matching his strength and respect for the land they had adopted as their own. He looked deeper and saw reflected with artless truth the love she bore him . . . then and now.

Her telling gaze filled Cord with the wellspring of life. For the first time in two years, his heart felt light and his breath came easily. The burden of despondency was replaced by an animated will to survive.

Vesper sensed the transformation in her husband. His murky eyes, his solemn expression, the tense anger in his body, all disappeared. His eyes seemed to lighten green as spring once again, and she thought somehow she could glimpse the verdant Indian Woods in them. With a single graceful motion, she patted the nearest chair and her eyes asked him to join her. He stepped forward, half eager, half hesitant.

"I've missed you, Vesper, missed you badly," he confessed in low tones.

She put down her needlework as he drew a chair close to her and fitted his long frame onto it.

"Cord," she murmured, trying to keep her voice steady. "I've only been half alive these months, thinking you were dead. How did you escape? I saw you with my own eyes, shot and bleeding to death. Then the flames devoured everything . . . Demi, Rom, our home, you . . ."

Vesper couldn't go on. Speaking the words made her relive the old agony afresh. Cord stared out in the distance.

"The Santee Sioux really did come," Cord began, nodding in response to Vesper's startled frown. "They had tracked our assailants through the snow but lost them just as the blizzard worsened. They reached the cabin and dragged me to safety with only seconds to spare before it became an inferno. Between the head wound and the burns to my body and lungs, I was sick for a long time. It took me almost a year to recover my strength."

Vesper longed to reach out to Cord, to comfort and nurse him now, making up for all the time she couldn't.

"It wasn't until I could walk and eat without help that Spring Willow told me the braves hadn't recovered your body. They had risked their lives, going back into the raging fire, but the heat and smoke were too intense."

He paused and a rueful expression swept over his face.

"I went on a wild rampage then, tearing everything from my path. Running Wolf let me rage until I was spent." With the old defiant honor displayed proudly in his eyes, Cord added, "I'm not ashamed to admit that I leaned on his shoulder and cried like a baby."

He sat forward, leaning his elbows on his knees, his fists on his chin.

"I tried to go back to the old life, living among the Santee, raising horses on their lands. But it was no good."

His voice broke.

"Without you and the baby, I couldn't bear it."

Vesper sat quiet as a statue, her mind racing. She saw what her loss had meant to him and how his grief had bent him. She pictured the gaunt, haggard man who had sat at her card table and recalled his empty, sad eyes, the light of life gone from them.

Cord continued. "One day, not too long ago, Running Wolf told me the time had come for the tribe to move westward. He pointed to the charred remains of our chimney. 'This place is forever haunted in your heart,' he said. 'You will never again be fierce as the bear until you return to your father's house. Go home,' he counseled me, 'and heal.'"

Cord looked up, traces of unhappiness still etched in his weathered face.

"I sold the horses and now I'm bound for Louisiana to see if there's a place for me alongside old Zachary Travers."

Vesper yearned to tell Cord how much she wanted him back alongside her. But she knew such a bald confession would spoil this delicate moment.

Instead she murmured, "If I could have saved you all this pain . . . if I had only known how much . . . how close . . . if I had been there . . ."

Cord heard the earnest plea in her voice. Looking into her tearstained eyes, he began to think the barriers between them might not be so great. With an impulse born from the love they once shared, Vesper drooped her head against Cord's shoulder, nestling into the hollow of his neck. They stayed that way, neither willing to break the fragile peace they had found.

But a stronger urge on Cord's part to measure and test their new footing caused him to shift in his chair and turn directly to Vesper. His hands reached toward her face. Slowly, tenderly, as if treasuring a priceless art object, he closed his fingers about her dear face. He inclined his head nearer and nearer until their lips touched. They stayed lost under the spell of the single searing deep kiss, reunited, the life force swelling in their hearts once again. When the sublime moment came to an end, Cord searched Vesper's violet eyes.

"Vesper, maybe we could—"

"Hey, when are you gonna be done with him? You promised me a night, too. But ah'm not gonna pay as much as this fool did."

Cord and Vesper looked up into the petulant face of the young whippersnapper who had played at Morgana's table the fateful night Cord had defeated her. She could feel Cord's body tighten rigid as stone. Vesper froze too, knowing their one moment for reconciliation was ruined. Tall and proud, Cord stood to his full height, staring hard at this foppish excuse of a man.

"You'll get her when I've had my money's worth," he sneered.

"That may take forever," pouted the spoiled youth. He slunk off muttering, "You'd think he owned her or sumpthin'."

Cord remained standing with his back to Vesper. She was the best, he acknowledged to himself, the best at her trade. His eyes narrowed to slits. She could pretend to be whatever a man wanted. She had made him forget the harlot Morgana and had taken on the form of his ideal woman. But there was no Vesper Travers. That woman existed only in his long-gone dreams.

Vesper hung her head. It was obvious from Cord's steely stance what he was thinking.

"Cord, please, forget that man, forget everything but us," she begged him.

He turned, fixing her with an ice-green glare.

"You almost did it again, but thanks to your . . . friend . . . I think I'm cured of Vesper, Morgana, and whoever else you say you are. You trapped me twice: first in Washington making me want you, taking you away from your family; then in the Indian Woods teaching you everything I knew, giving you my whole world. But never again."

Each word fell on her like a sharp slap. She had come so close to paradise again, only to have it destroyed by Cord's blindness.

"Cord, you don't understand," she said in a hollow voice.

"But I do, river siren. You were trying to get your precious money back. Let me tell you, you didn't have to go to these lengths," he said in cold bitterness. "I don't want your filthy money."

From the vest pocket below his heart he extracted the voucher Vesper had signed. Holding it close to her face, he ripped it into shreds. Taking a last look at her, he strode over to the railing, scattered the little pieces into the Mississippi River, and walked away.

Vesper remained in her deck chair, stunned, her breath stuck in her throat. She felt as though she had been flayed within an inch of her life. She watched Cord leave, knowing that nothing she said or did would alter his convictions. Raw pain seared her heart. Losing him again was as bad as the first time, and she had come so close to having him back. No words, not even tears, could soothe her this time.

As she sat tightly clutching the arms of her chair, only one burning thought kept her going. Bledsoe, damn his soul. He had succeeded in killing her love twice. With tensed jaw and ragged deep breaths, Vesper swore she would have her revenge.

Accompanied by Daisy, Vesper left *The River Siren* when it docked in New Orleans and took an apartment at the St. Charles Hotel in the Faubourg Ste-Marie district. She was eager to leave behind her Morgana guise. But she had to register as Miss Morgana so that Delgado's reports could reach her. And she could not expose her true identity for fear that Bledsoe would find her before she was ready to reveal herself.

Vesper had no worries about the three people who knew the truth. Daisy was the essence of loyalty, grateful to be a free woman and delighted to be earning a wage. Raoul's code of honor would never permit him to damage her reputation. As he had so often pointed out, that was for a lady to do to herself. And as for Cord, he considered Vesper dead to him. He wouldn't care where she was or what she did.

With the money she had earned on this final trip down river, as well as the money she had banked from her previous winnings, Vesper was a wealthy lady. Not quite a lady, Vesper quickly came to realize. Even when she wore her least ornamented gowns, men turned and stared. A few even dared approach the notorious Miss Morgana.

As a result Vesper and Daisy went to Royal Street one day to sell all of Morgana's expensive gaudy gowns and to purchase material for new plainer ones. While in Madame Adèle's emporium, Daisy said nothing. She merely followed Vesper about, her limp exaggerated by the heavy bolts of cloth she carried back to the dressmaker for measuring. But once in the safety of a horse-drawn buggy, Daisy scratched her head in puzzlement.

"Ah doan understand, Vesper. Why on earth did y'all buy thirty yards of black cloth?"

"I'm in mourning, Daisy," came the unexpected reply, reducing the free woman of color to silence.

Despite her new simply designed dresses, Vesper unconsciously created an even more arresting aura of tragic mystery. It was the same in the hotel as in the streets of the city. Men stared and elbowed each other when she passed through the lobby. Women whipped out fans to hide their whispers about her in the ladies' dining room.

By the end of Vesper's second month in New Orleans, she had retreated to the privacy of her own rooms, rarely venturing out, taking fresh air from her fourth-floor balcony window. Her life had become condensed into a dull routine.

She woke with a start each dawn. She would dress herself and perform her own toilette. Daisy would bring her a cup of chocolate and a steaming hot brioche, straight from the hotel ovens. Daisy would draw open the drapes, letting the sun filter in, and Vesper would sit by the balcony window watching the street below come to life.

First would come the young chocolate-skinned marchandes, swaying with their trays of freshly made cream cheese. Then came the fruit vendors selling fresh figs, flower sellers, and plump girls offering brown sugar and sweet pralines. All the color and activity of the passing parade was so lively, yet Vesper only felt inert and distant.

Later she would turn to her desk, preparing yet another letter of inquiry, complete with extensive suggestions, to Delgado. After her few chores were completed, Daisy would bustle about Vesper's sitting room and try to entice her friend to go out with her on some errand. Rarely did Vesper accept Daisy's invitation.

"I think I'd rather be here when the mail comes," Vesper would say and then turn back to the window facing the river to watch the big white steamboats go in and out of port.

Vesper invariably napped in the afternoon, the hours slipping by in painless somnolence. When Daisy would wake her to dress for dinner, Vesper's face would light with animated anticipation.

"Is there a letter from Delgado?" she would eagerly ask.

Daisy always mumbled the same reply, looking away from those anxious, imploring eyes.

"No, Vesper, not today."

She would glance quickly at her companion, just in time to see the life force drain from her face.

"Maybe there'll be one mo' deliv'ry today, honey."

The young woman, whose beauty seemed more fragile than ever, would wearily nod and hoist herself from the bed, trudging with heavy steps toward her post by the window. She be lak an old woman, Daisy thought in alarm. Sumpin's gotta change, and change soon.

Vesper would stare out past the city streets, out to the river, watching the beacons light along the riverbank as darkness enveloped the muddy waters. Far into the night she would sit, listening to the haunting steamboat whistles crying out to one another, reminding her of the piercing moans of exiled lovers.

# Chapter Twenty

IT HAD TAKEN CORD TRAVERS A FEW DAYS TO SETTLE his affairs in New Orleans. He'd almost taken a room at the St. Charles Hotel, but the sight of the grandiose granite structure reminded him too keenly of the gaudy palatial boat he'd just left. The smaller, less pretentious Hotel Verandah suited him better. Except for mandatory visits to the Travers family banker and lawyer, Cord secluded himself behind the closed draperies of his second-story lodgings, steering clear of the city's exotic nightlife. He'd had more than he ever bargained for aboard *The River Siren*.

His business completed, Cord had no reason to put off the last leg of his journey home. He could have borrowed or bought a horse to ride to the plantation. He could even have rented a carriage. But something within the man, perhaps his pride, his spirit, or maybe his undaunted principles, made him return home the way he had left it.

On a misty morning, Cord trudged down the long road from New Orleans to Fairlawn, carrying only a leather satchel in one hand and a cloth bag in the other. The dew quickly evaporated as the sun rose higher, bringing unseasonable heat with it. When he could stand it no longer, he took off his coat and collar and cut through the tangle of cattails at the roadside. He slipped down the sandy banks of the ever-present streaming waters. Kneeling, he cupped his hands into the shallows and brought them up to his sweating face. He kept on in that way, stopping every few hours to wash the grime away till midafternoon when the Gulf breezes began to blow. It wasn't far now, he told himself.

Then, suddenly, in a nearby field, Cord saw a dozen dark heads bobbing up and down, kerchiefed in blue madras. He shielded his eyes from the glaring sun and stared. So his father still insisted on the old ways. Field hands had to wear blue. Undoubtedly, the house hands were capped in red. Had it been fifteen years since Cord had left? In some ways, it felt like fifteen minutes.

More and more familiar sights greeted him as he neared the main house. Along the live oak–lined lane, a double-seated buggy driven by an ebony-skinned man with an incongruous top hat over his red kerchief careened by. Cord was reminded of his father's stern voice demanding the precarious pace of the horses pick up. It had been like that every Sunday. Cord had never been sure whether his father was racing like the very devil to run away from the boring minister or to run to the plantation to deliver his own more fiery sermon to the slaves.

In the distance Cord caught a glimpse of the rounded peaked roof of Fairlawn's summerhouse and, just beyond it, an old palmetto. As a lad he had climbed it on a dare only to overhear his parents arguing about the neighbors. Young Cord hadn't understood anything they'd said, but his face grew hot and his chest tightened when he saw his father slap his mother and she burst into heartrending sobs. Long after his parents stormed out, he'd stayed in that tree, not knowing what to do but hating the whole world.

Now Cord came to his mother's grave. He paused, remembering the awful day he had been made to watch her casket descend into the damp clay soil. He had planted a willow sapling next to the fresh mound, thinking, as children do, that she would thank him someday for the cool shade he'd provided her. But it was his father's face that day that Cord recalled most vividly. Grim and tightly drawn, displaying no emotion, the man had refused to post even a marker.

Mother's grave had changed, Cord realized, shaking himself back to the present. The little willow had grown into a majestic tree with a crown of heavily ridged dark branches. And all about the boundaries of the grave was a profusion of wild pink roses. At the base of the willow stood a stone marker with an angel on top.

Cord arched an eyebrow. Perhaps his father had mellowed over the years, he speculated. So much had happened to Cord in fifteen years' time. He knew he was a changed man. How could it be any different with his father?

Cord walked on, his pace a little quicker. There . . . there was Fairlawn, magnificent and stately as ever, with its tall slender white columns and its wide sweeping verandahs. And there, sitting alone on the front verandah with a glass in one hand which he raised to his lips and an unmistakable thick cane grasped in the other hand, was his father, Colonel Zachary Travers.

The man had been in his prime when Cord left home. But now, even at a distance, the signs of age were obvious. His once-shaggy head of hair had whitened and thinned, his tanned complexion was florid, and there was a discernible tremor in the fingers resting on the knob of the cane. Cord stepped closer, drawn by the distinct change in the old man's eyes. The implacable glare was gone, and in its place Cord saw an unfamiliar softness.

The old gentleman suddenly put down his glass, blinked, rubbed his eyes hard, and blinked again. He struggled to his feet, leaning heavily on his cane. After a few hesitant steps, Colonel Travers threw the cane down and took the stairs from the verandah to the expansive lawn two at a time. He waved his arms toward the tall, powerfully built man who possessed his son's unforgettable features.

Cord came straight to him and was wrapped in a bear hug. The unexpected tide of his father's emotion overwhelmed Cord. Yet he was stunned by the old man's feeble physique. He was less robust, less hearty, than Cord had ever imagined possible. But Colonel Travers was lost in the joyous discovery of his son, first pushing him back, then clasping him again, pounding him on the shoulder.

"Mah boy, mah boy, is it really you? After all these years . . . ah'd given up hope. Let me look at you."

The colonel held Cord out at arm's length and studied his son. What he saw pierced him to the core. Here was a man of real experience, with hands scarred from the proud marks of his labors. Cord's muscular body was proof of the hard conditioning of a life spent out-of-doors.

But there was an odd slump to Cord's shoulders

that didn't make sense until the old man peered into the murky depths of his son's eyes. Misery, pain, and a vast emptiness welled forth, and he had to look away. Yes, the colonel thought, this man has made his own way and suffered for it. He placed a paternal arm about Cord's back.

"Welcome home, son," Travers said quietly and led him into the big house, their two heads bent close together.

For the next two weeks, the colonel left Cord to his own devices, having learned the hard way that only time and one's own survival urge heal all wounds. But there was a curious aimlessness to his son that old Zachary could not quite figure out. At table, Cord was polite enough, but his comments were perfunctory and unrevealing.

During the day he was nowhere to be found, although Colonel Travers had received several reports from his overseer and heard gossip from the well-informed house slaves that young Mistah Travers had been seen restlessly roaming the wooded boundaries of Fairlawn. He's home, free to do whatever he wants, the old man thought, but he acts like a fenced-in wild animal. I'll get to the bottom of this, or my name isn't Zachary Benton Travers! he vowed to himself.

The next day, the colonel had his favorite horse saddled and rode off, determined to follow Cord. Through field after field, over stream and sandy bog, down to the main road, up past Amelia's grave and back to the river, the colonel followed his son. The boy was good, damn good, at hiding his tracks, Zachary was forced to admit. The rumors must have been true about Cord living among Indians and taking up their ways. But he was still Travers' son, and his father knew his favorite boyhood haunts.

Just ahead in a field left fallow, Cord dismounted and let his horse graze. The colonel followed suit and quietly sneaked up behind his son.

"Finally caught up with me, did you, sir," Cord threw out, his back to the older man.

"Consarn it, boy, you mean you knew ah was followin' you all along?"

Colonel Travers had meant to be indignant, but the joke was on him and he knew it.

"Took me for a merry chase. All over the damn property."

He guffawed and limped toward the younger, stronger man.

"Help me set awhile, will you, boy? These old bones got a pretty fair shakin' on that nag of mine."

Cord went through the motions of spreading an old Santee blanket on the ground and giving his father a hand down.

"Why did you follow me?" Cord demanded quietly.

The moment had come, and Colonel Travers had rehearsed his speech over and over during the long morning ride.

"Ah've left you on your own . . . to make peace with yourself."

Cord flashed his father a quick piercing glance.

"That's right, boy. Ah know you've got troubles," Travers continued. "But it's time to get a hold of yourself, make somethin' of yourself . . ."

Cord looked away, wincing almost imperceptibly, but the colonel had seen it. He realized he'd hit a raw nerve and paused, switching tactics.

"You know, son, ah'm not goin' to be around fo'eveh. Ah'm not gettin' any younger. These brittle bones of mine barely hold me up."

What did the old man want? Cord wondered. His

manipulativeness was about as subtle as a beaver trap.

"What ah'm tryin' to say, boy, is you're a grown man now. It's time you really settle down . . . marry . . . have fine, strong sons . . . take over for me here at Fairlawn."

He glanced at Cord warmly and reached out his hand.

"That's all I evah wanted for you, Cord."

Cord sat there as if numb, but a whole siege of emotions passed through him. For a moment he reexperienced the flare-up of anger he had always felt when made to do his father's bidding. But those were the feelings of the child Cord had left behind so many years ago. He was a grown man now, his own man, as seasoned as his father . . . and, like his father, had lived, loved, and lost.

Cord glanced at the wizened older man and shot his own arrow at a well-known target.

"I don't think so, sir. You and I were just meant to be bachelors in our old age."

The colonel's mouth turned down in a thin arc. Amelia still stood between them. Cord had always been angry about his mother's death, but he'd never been cruel. The elder Travers regarded his son with new eyes. What had happened over the years that turned this impetuous youth, full of ideas, into a spiteful, sour stranger? Fearing that he might lose his newly restored son again, he grabbed at Cord's shirtfront, forcing Cord to look directly at his father.

"Tell me, son, tell me what's plaguing you so," the old man cried.

Without any display of emotion, Cord removed his father's trembling hands and stared at him, long and coolly. His impenetrable gaze revealed nothing, but the muscle of his jaw jerked spasmodically.

"I came back, didn't I, Father? Just don't push me. Don't ask any questions."

Abruptly Cord stood up and strode to his horse. He rode from the field as if the hounds of hell were after him.

With some difficulty, Colonel Travers got up, shaking his head sadly. He mounted his horse and set a slow, ambling pace back to the stable, worrying, thinking, planning all the way. He'd give Cord more time, but he wouldn't give up.

True to his word, the colonel held off, neither baiting nor sweet-talking Cord. But the situation did not improve. Instead, to the senior Travers' great alarm, the unhappy young man withdrew even further, looking for solace in draft after draft of cane whiskey. Finally Colonel Travers reached his limit of toleration.

During supper one evening, the older man, red in the face with chagrin, slammed down his knife and fork.

"You haven't touched a bite, boy. And, Aloysius . . ." The colonel signaled to a house slave who stood poised over Cord with yet another open bottle of whiskey. "No more."

The stern voice momentarily brought Cord out of his doldrums. In the three or so weeks he had been home, he hadn't heard his father use that tone. He hadn't heard it in fifteen years. With difficulty, he performed a mock bow of acquiescence in his father's direction. But his dark mood ruled his better sense and he couldn't resist grabbing the amber bottle from the slave's gloved hand, placing it on the table before him.

"Come now, boy," Colonel Travers said more lightly, "Delilah's prepared all your old favorites: shrimp and oyster gumbo, catfish stew, a nice country ham with chutney, boiled greens and sweet potatoes, even spoon bread."

For all his efforts, the colonel was rewarded with his son's mumblings about nursery fodder. The veins along the old man's temple stood out.

"Consarn it, suh, you're makin' it mighty hard to treat you like anythin' but a babe in the nursery!" the frustrated man roared. "Wanderin' all day like a displaced ghost, drinkin' at night, hopin' you'll get too drunk to think. But it doesn't work, does it, boy?"

Cord stared at his father, stung by the truth of his words. Was he that transparent, or did Zachary know something about suffering too? Cord reached for the bottle and poured himself another slug of the sweetly sour liquor, wishing his mind would blur and give him some relief from his haunting thoughts of Vesper. Damn her. Damn himself. Damn everything. He quickly emptied his glass and refilled it just as fast.

The old man gestured to Aloysius, who brought him his cane. He propped himself up out of the chair and shuffled over to Cord.

"Mah boy, mah boy, tell me what you're tryin' to fo'get."

Travers put a hand on his son's hunched shoulders, immediately aware of tense, knotted muscles.

"It can't be all that bad."

Cord lurched away from his father's touch. Seizing the whiskey bottle, the misery-racked young man lumbered out of the formal dining room with its high ceiling and sought refuge in the oak-paneled study. Even in the warmer months, a cozy fire blazed in the huge fireplace. Cord flung himself down in an overstuffed chair and stared into the flames, shackled by visions of Vesper, her hair streaming in his face as they rode together . . . her body pressed to his, creating an intense heat of passion . . . her hand stretched out to him, almost touching, then torn from him . . . the scarlet dress of Morgana, clinging, revealing, inviting . . .

Cord threw his glass into the fire and clawed his fingers through his hair in heartsore agony. And there was his father again, standing over him, a look of kind, curious pity in his eyes.

"It's time, son," the old man demanded gently, "time you told me what's eatin' you up inside."

The vast quantity of whiskey Cord had consumed finally took its toll. Unable to carry the burden anymore, he poured out the whole story. Colonel Travers took a seat near his son, and when the tale was completed, he sat forward in silence, his mind awhirl. He felt in awe of this man who had lived and almost died by his principles. Inwardly, he crowed with joy at his son's triumphs and ached in horror at his losses.

Cord also sat in silence, not knowing how his father would react. He half expected some kind of blustery retort about his masculine prowess. But Zachary surprised him, and Cord felt nothing but relief and gratitude.

"Ah understand now, mah boy. Ah understand. Give it a little more time, son. You'll see, it'll be better."

Damn right, it'll be better, the colonel gleefully thought, settling back in his comfortable chair. Now he had the power to make it better. He had memorized every last detail of Cord's tale, taking special note of Lucinda Moore in Washington, the aunt of his son's wife. His son's wife! His daughter-in-law! Rubbing his hands together, Colonel Travers wryly considered how he'd get his heirs from Cord yet.

But the old spinster was the key. Besides himself,

she was the only other person who seemed to care about Vesper's welfare and potential happiness. It wouldn't be that hard to pin this Miss Moore down. He'd just send a harmless little note to his good friend, Vernon Halley, senator from Louisiana. . . . The two Travers men stayed by the fire in companionable stillness, Cord bound by his bittersweet memories, Zachary dreaming of the future he would make happen with Lucinda Moore's help.

In the ensuing weeks, the colonel was pleased to see Cord's spirits pick up. The day after Cord had told his story, he promised his father he would start helping out with the business of the plantation. But he had firmly drawn the line when it came to any work with horses.

"I mean to start fresh, Father. That means no ties with the past."

"As you wish, mah boy," was the colonel's nonchalant reply, for the old gentleman's plan was in effect.

He'd already sent a messenger to Senator Halley late the previous night. It didn't take more than a week to get Miss Moore's address, and in the interim he had composed draft after draft of the letter he would send to her. Now he seemed to walk with a lighter, livelier step. He even considered putting away his infernal cane.

Each day he checked the incoming mail with an eagle eye, impatiently waiting for Miss Moore's response. Though Cord plowed through his chores, there was still a mechanical joylessness to him. Colonel Travers could barely contain his enthusiasm around his son, knowing that soon Cord's lackluster days would be over.

One sunny day late in spring, when the mockingbirds seemed to chorus in unusual harmony, the letter arrived. Nervously Colonel Travers examined the spidery handwriting on the envelope as if it might contain some clue to the lady's reply. He called for a mint julep and went out on the verandah. For once he was grateful to those damn savage alligators which roamed the back corner of his property. Cord had gone off into the bayou to hunt them, accompanied by the overseer and a small party of trusted field hands. He'd be gone all day, so the colonel was safe to read the letter.

When he had finished, he took off his wide-brimmed hat, savoring the moment by basking in the warm glow of the sun. So the peppery old lady had shed tears of delight upon reading that Cord and Vesper were alive. He chuckled over her description of what she had done to the negligible report sent by some low-ranking muckamuck from Fort Snelling, claiming the young couple had perished at the hands of Indians. Humbug, she'd thought at the time but had no one to tell.

She had firmly agreed to help reunite the aggrieved lovers and to involve no Lawrences in their doings. Rapscallions, she had called them, the whole nasty lot of them. She was on her way to *The River Siren* and would contact the colonel when she discovered Vesper's whereabouts.

Colonel Travers leaned back and laughed out loud. He had been right. Lucinda Moore was just the ticket he needed. He couldn't wait to meet the old gal, certain she'd have Vesper in tow when that day came.

The moist summer heat had invaded New Orleans, and Vesper's fourth-floor apartment was sweltering by midday.

"Vesper, it cain't be any worse down by de ribber," enjoined Daisy. "Mebbe we'll find a Gulf breeze nearer de water."

Even in a light muslin mourning gown, Vesper was too uncomfortable to refuse.

"Just let me get my shawl and parasol. But we'll stroll in the park, Daisy, not near the river," she added adamantly.

The lobby was brimming with activity and filled with people coming and going. Vesper sniffed at her handkerchief, which Daisy had drenched in rose water. Busy with all her paraphernalia, she did not see a spare older woman with a grizzled bun and dressed in a gray traveling suit coming toward her. Her shoulder bumped against the other woman, and Vesper quickly looked up to apologize. Instead she stood there speechless, with her mouth open and her eyes wide with disbelief.

"For heaven's sake," Lucinda Moore said. "What are you doing here, child? For a moment, I thought I was seeing a ghost."

She folded her long-lost niece in her arms and hugged her hard for just a moment, then peered at her. The scars of tragedy were visible despite her breathtaking beauty. There was a pale cast to Vesper's skin and the unmistakable evidence of painful defeat in her eyes.

"They tried to tell me you were dead. Bosh! I never believed that silly story for a moment. No niece of mine would give up without a fight, and anyway, I knew those Indians were your friends."

Vesper was completely stunned. She had never expected to see her aunt again, much less in the St. Charles Hotel lobby. But her delight at finding the old kindred soul of her girlhood was boundless. Staring into the familiar nut-brown eyes, Vesper felt as though she'd come home.

"B-b-but why are you here? And h-h-how did you find me?" Vesper stammered.

Lucinda bustled the pale young woman over toward a more intimate corner of the lobby where pairs of padded chairs were separated from each other by large potted ferns. Discreetly Daisy took a seat at a distance from the reunited relatives. The two women sat and, according to Colonel Travers' plan, Lucinda concocted her answer, trying to make herself sound like an excited matron gossiping at a quilting bee.

"Well, it's just an extraordinary coincidence, that's all it is. I wasn't looking for you at all. You see, I got the worst case of chilblains last winter . . . it was the coldest winter yet in Washington," she interrupted herself. "Then, this spring, I got a letter from an old friend of mine down south who invited me to take the cure at his plantation. Seems he has these hot springs on his land that cure everything, so he says."

Vesper had never heard her aunt chatter and carry on so. She searched the older woman's face, but all she could find was the brisk no-nonsense affection for her she'd always seen in her aunt's eyes. While Morgana had learned to be alert, almost suspicious of a newcomer's line, Vesper unquestioningly believed Lucinda, who had never lied, much less stretched the truth.

"But land sakes, child," Lucinda was saying, "where have you been? I was worried sick when I stopped getting your letters. I almost went to your father's house . . ."

Vesper started and a wild fear shot through her eyes.

". . . but I didn't. I wouldn't," replied Lucinda staunchly.

She had seen her niece's change of expression, and her heart softened even more toward this young woman who had suffered so.

Vesper took a deep breath and seemed to sink limply into her chair.

"I couldn't contact you, Auntie," she whispered. "I was too afraid . . ."

Her mind flew to Bledsoe and then to the image of Cord resolutely walking away from her.

". . . and then it didn't matter anymore," she ended brokenly.

The poor child, Lucinda thought. She's used up just about all the gumption she's got. The colonel's letter had reached the capital in the nick of time.

"I'm taking you under my wing, Vesper, and let's have no arguments. Now, tell me why you're dressed in mourning."

Vesper had no arguments left, and somehow Lucinda's matter-of-fact manner seemed to cut through the intricate cobwebs left of her life. Being with her aunt again was like rediscovering her innocent youth and, maybe, Vesper dared to hope, some perspective on the past.

"Oh, Auntie, I'm so glad you're here." Vesper sighed. "But please come up to my rooms first. Daisy?" she called to her companion.

Once there, the horrific tale poured out of her. Lucinda had heard two versions of it by now, from Colonel Travers and Raoul St. Martin whom she had cornered in his suite aboard *The River Siren*. But hearing the sad, shocking story from Vesper's own lips affected Lucinda to such an extent that tears flowed freely down the usually taciturn woman's cheeks.

Vesper was touched by her aunt's reaction. The only other time she had seen Lucinda Moore openly cry was the day Vesper's mother had died. Now as then, Lucinda held her sister's child to her breast and shared her misery.

"Thank heavens you had Daisy, child," Lucinda sniffed, wiping away her tears. "But I'm here now, to fight your battles with you."

"There's nothing left to do," Vesper said despondently.

"Oh yes there is, my girl. First things first," the indomitable woman stated. "You're leaving New Orleans and coming with me. You need a fresh start . . . gird your loins, the Bible says."

Vesper giggled, feeling like a schoolgirl.

"I can't, Auntie. There's Daisy to consider . . ."

A careworn look swept the animation from her face.

". . . and I must be here when Delgado sends his report."

"Nonsense," retorted Lucinda. "A bath in the hot springs is just what you need, and your mail can be forwarded daily to the colonel's plantation."

"But Daisy . . ." Vesper sputtered.

"Daisy is a free woman, Vesper Lawrence Travers," replied the older woman sharply. "You saw to that, and a very good thing, too. But a free woman makes her own choices in life, as I have done and you as well, Vesper."

Daisy stood in the shadow of the drapery while Vesper stared out the balcony window toward the river. "Free to make choices," Lucinda said. Was it really so? Vesper wondered. Lucinda was content with her life, however it looked to others. She had always been satisfied with her meager fare, balanced by a rich intellect and a strong sense of humanity. Lucinda Moore's boardinghouse, Vesper realized, was a breeding ground and haven for the young philosophers and would-be political reformers. Yes, Lucinda had made her choice.

What about her own life? Vesper had known the heights of ecstasy and the depths of agony. She had loved and lived with the man of her dreams. When she lost him, she had fought her way back, finding a strength and a will she never knew she had. Now she had lost him again.

She did have a choice, she realized. Maybe she could fight the battle again, once she could think clearly. Maybe leaving New Orleans was the right thing to do. Maybe Lucinda's hot springs would replenish her weary spirit. Vesper turned away from the window and a gleam of light crept into her dark violet eyes as she took Daisy's hand in hers.

"You know, Auntie," she said cunningly, "when Mme. Adèle made my mourning gowns, she saw Daisy's exquisite needlework on my other clothes. Ever since, she's been after me to let Daisy go so she could hire her."

Lucinda's thin face began to light up.

"Daisy would never leave me as long as she thought I needed her . . ."

Vesper paused.

"But I think Mme. Adèle truly needs her more than I do."

A huge smile broke out on Daisy's face and her dark eyes brimmed with happy tears.

"Thank you, Vesper, thank you. Ah feels lak ah got mah freedom twice in one life."

Lucinda's face shone like a beacon.

"Let's get you packed, my girl. The colonel expects me tomorrow!"

# Chapter Twenty-one

SADNESS AND JOY REIGNED EQUALLY AS VESPER AND Daisy exchanged their farewells on the curb of St. Charles Avenue.

"It's not forever," Vesper whispered in the young woman's ear as she embraced her one last time.

"'Course not, Vesper. Why, ah expect to see y'all wander into Miz Adèle's empo'yum to try on mah latest creation," Daisy joked with a sparkle in her jet-black eyes.

"Vesper," Lucinda called from within the fringe-topped surrey. "We can't keep the colonel waiting." In kinder tones she added, "It's time, child. Good-bye, Miss Cotter, and thank you for your loyalty to my niece."

"Yes, ma'am," Daisy answered shyly.

She started to bob in a quick curtsy, but then she saw Lucinda Moore's outstretched arm. The free woman of color stepped forward, smiling, and shook the proffered hand.

Vesper climbed up into the open carriage and waved at Daisy until she was out of sight. Sighing, Vesper settled back into the bouncy seat, leaving the crescent-shaped city behind. Her aunt patted her folded fingers.

"You're doing the right thing, Vesper. Believe me."

Vesper did believe Lucinda. There was no reason to doubt her advice. But one thing continued to nag at Vesper.

"Auntie," she asked, "when did you say you met this colonel?"

"During the War of Independence," cracked the doughty older woman.

Vesper laughed.

"You weren't even born yet, Auntie. Maybe you mean the War of 1812," she added, carrying on the jest.

"I've known many of our country's militiamen, missy, and supported several of them in my boardinghouse," said Lucinda tartly.

"Oh," Vesper said, nodding with understanding, "the colonel knew you in Washington."

"Let's just say," Lucinda replied curtly, "my dealings with him took place there."

Her conscience was bothering her. Lucinda Moore didn't like deception, but she was in the thick of it now and she'd have to play her part in Zachary Travers' little conspiracy very carefully.

She sniffed the air and sneezed.

"Vesper, I don't know how you can stand to breathe this air. Between the heat, the humidity, and the oversized flowers, I feel like I'm being cosseted in a hothouse!"

"Why, Aunt Lucinda, the South agrees with you

and you know it." Vesper caressed the peppery woman's wrinkled cheeks. "I've never seen your face so rosy."

"Maybe so, child, maybe so."

The dangerous moment had passed and Lucinda breathed more easily. Let her niece think she had the bloom of health. It was far more simple to explain that than the nervousness which caused her unusual glow.

Time passed swiftly, with the two women caught up in the lush beauty of the bayou. When the sun was at its zenith, the plantation came into view.

"It's magnificent," Vesper murmured. "Have you ever been here before?"

Before Lucinda had time to think of an answer to Vesper's innocent question, the arriving surrey was surrounded by a bevy of slaves, some to hold the horses, some to remove the baggage, one to lead the coachman to the stable, and one following in the wake of the colonel.

"Why, Lucinda Moore, honey, can it really be you after all this time?" the colonel jocularly inquired.

He spun the flustered woman around and bussed her soundly on the cheek. Lucinda started to flare indignantly when she remembered her role in this little farce.

"Why, Colonel, you're just as incorrigible as ever," she said, smiling through clenched teeth.

Vesper was astounded. This flirtatious belle was a side of her starchy aunt she never knew existed. And the colonel seemed to be completely captivated.

"Ah'm so glad you came. Ah can honestly say ah've thought of nothin' else since ah got yo' last letter."

For a brief moment, the older couple exchanged a

meaningful glance which was not lost on Vesper. She noticed the obvious spark between the two.

"Auntie," Vesper whispered into Lucinda's ear, half teasing, half pleased. "You never told me you had a beau."

"I most certainly do not!" hissed the spinster.

Here was another dangerous moment, Lucinda thought to herself. She had better take control now before the situation got entirely out of hand. Between that prancing old dandy and her niece's willful leaping to one conclusion after another, Lucinda would have her hands full.

"Colonel," she said in her most authoritative stentorian tone, "I've brought my niece with me. May I introduce Vesper Lawrence . . ."

She stopped herself before adding the name of Travers. Plenty of time for that, she thought, without further complicating matters.

Colonel Travers had steeled himself for the moment he would meet his son's wife. But now, with her here before him in the flesh, his emotions were too strong to contain. When Vesper stepped forward, the old gentleman bowed and took up her fingers, kissing them with a paternal intensity. He longed to take her in his arms and welcome her home, but he knew he dared not. Not so fast, he warned himself.

Vesper smiled sweetly at the colonel's formal gallantry. She liked him instantly without knowing why.

"Charmed," she murmured, withdrawing her hand from his gentle lingering grasp.

But it was he who was charmed. She was a bewitching creature, he admitted to himself. Amelia's beauty had been as delicate as the woman herself had been. But Vesper was a woman of substance, and her great earthly beauty was no less alluring than the tragedy of love and loss naked in her eyes.

It was no wonder that Cord had fallen in love with her. She was a perfect match for him, spirited, courageous, and hurting now without him. The colonel's heart warmed to his precious daughter-in-law, and he resolved even more firmly to reunite Cord and Vesper.

"Ah've arranged a little party in honor of yo' arrival," Travers said to both ladies. "Just a few guests ah thought would like to meet you."

Lucinda arched an eyebrow and shot the colonel a warning, questioning look. He merely smiled and took up an arm of each lady, escorting them into the house.

"But I'm in mourning, sir," Vesper reminded her host.

"You'll be fine, just fine, Miz Lawrence. May ah call you Vesper? Ah'm sure yo' aunt will make sure you won't be bothered by the wrong people."

The colonel winked openly at Lucinda while signaling to a house slave.

"Flossie, show Miz Moore to the Willow Room and Miz Vesper to the Magnolia Room. Until tonight, ladies?"

Lucinda bustled Vesper upstairs as fast as she could, away from the provoking influence of Colonel Travers.

"A bath and a nap in that order," she stated irrevocably, once the women reached their adjoining rooms.

Vesper complied, exhausted from the exciting turn of events in the last two days. She awoke much later to a brilliant sunset, the dying hues of purple and crimson staining the white flocked walls of her bedchamber. Next to her bed was a little silver tray with a plate of orange slices and thin fingers of corn bread. She ate hungrily.

The door between the bedchambers opened and Lucinda entered in her best gown. It was no longer stylish, but it fit well, and Vesper suddenly remembered when she had last seen her aunt wear it. It had been more than twenty years ago, the day her father had introduced her to Belle.

"Hurry, Vesper, guests are already arriving."

The young woman, refreshed from her sleep, chose one of her evening mourning gowns and performed her uncomplicated toilette. She coiled her hair in a low knot and placed a black lace square over her head. The simple scrubbing she had given her face produced a natural sheen to her cheeks and lips that rouge could never improve on. Her eyes glowed with an incandescent mystery that made Lucinda understand Raoul's fascination with the woman who came to him out of the depths of the river. If Cord had any similarity to St. Martin, the old lady reckoned, he wouldn't be able to resist the artless lure of his wife.

"I'm ready, Auntie," Vesper said.

"Just a minute. I see no animation in your face. This is a party you're going to, girl," reminded Lucinda sharply, imagining what it would be like when Cord and Vesper saw each other.

Vesper raised herself to her full height and, for the first time, regarded her aunt disdainfully.

"I'm quite capable of pasting a smile on my lips," she said coolly, then added with obvious distaste, "I've had years of practice at it."

Lucinda yielded the point and cast new eyes at her niece. She'd thought she had seen a new Vesper back in Washington when the impressionable girl had first fallen in love and discovered her native spirit. But here was yet another Vesper, cool and collected, quite aware of her own commanding presence.

"I just want you to be happy, Vesper," her aunt explained in all honesty.

She followed her niece down the long winding polished staircase and paused midway as Vesper stopped to lift her long skirt which trailed on the steps. At the same moment, the guests in the foyer and those ambling into the ballroom stopped to stare at the compelling figure in black poised before them. Her exquisite somber beauty caught their attention completely, and their small talk ceased.

In the silence that followed, Vesper looked directly into each face, as though she were searching for something or someone. At last, she spied the colonel with his white hair slickly pomaded and his cheeks red as ripe apples. What presence the girl had about her, the senior Travers thought. He glanced around at his friends and neighbors who were captivated by his daughter-in-law, caught in her spell. He swelled with pride and took a step toward the staircase. She broke into a dazzling pearly smile and continued her descent toward him.

As if her smile and step had snapped the enchantment, a buzz of loud whispering spread throughout the rooms. Who was she? passed from the mouths to the ears of plump matrons, flighty hothouse belles, and every man present. Several bachelors, young and old alike, clambered toward her in hopes of leading her into the ballroom. But Colonel Travers was there in an instant. He'd be damned, he swore to himself, if anyone danced with his son's wife but his son or, in Cord's absence, Zachary himself.

Extending his hand to Vesper, the old gentleman begged, "Will you do me the honor?"

She nodded graciously but remained still. Picking up her cue, the colonel selected a handsome, slightly balding man from the crowd of male admirers to escort Lucinda. The two couples then strolled into the lovely ballroom with its long gilded mirrors, parquet floor, and heavy crystal chandeliers. There were several dancers already enjoying the lively tempo of a quadrille. When the musicians saw Colonel Travers, they switched to a slower-paced waltz tune.

"Will you help an old man feel young again, my dear, and take a turn with me about the floor?" the colonel asked.

Though dressed in mourning, Vesper felt she couldn't refuse his sweetly phrased invitation. As they circled the ballroom a question formed in Vesper's mind which she strove to ignore.

"Is somethin' wrong, Miz Lawrence, Vesper?"

"What?" she asked, suddenly paying attention to her partner.

"You're frownin', mah dear. It must be mah two left feet . . . nevah could figure out the steps to these newfangled dances."

"Oh no, Colonel," laughed Vesper. "I was just thinking . . ."

Impulsively the words came tumbling out.

"By any chance, Colonel, is there a plantation near here owned by a Zachary Travers? I believe it's called Fairlawn?"

She could have bitten her tongue. What was the matter with her, asking such a question of a stranger? Pretty soon, she'd be blurting out her whole life's story. But the colonel was coughing and turning red in the face.

"Ah . . . ah think ah may have heard that name a

few times," he sputtered and began coughing again as if he had choked on something. He pulled out a snow-white handkerchief and dabbed at his forehead nervously.

"Vesper, Miz Lawrence, you'll have to excuse me. Somethin' in the air . . . eh, the evenin' breeze . . . excuse me."

He shuffled off toward the verandah, calling for his cane and leaving Vesper alone to find her aunt. The older woman's escort had secured two brocaded chairs at the edge of the dance floor and Lucinda beckoned to her from there.

"You can see everything nicely from here and nobody will bother you," Lucinda promised.

But Vesper was immediately inundated by questions about her mourning and requests to take punch, to taste the barbecue, even to dance. And to all the men, she politely declined. She was struck by the utter frivolousness of the party, and her mind wandered back to the last President's ball she had attended. She remembered how it felt to be openly admired and desired by men when all she could think of was Cord Travers.

She looked about her here in the colonel's less ornate ballroom at the flighty young girls doing their utmost to beguile the charming eligible gentlemen. Had anything changed? she asked herself. No, for she still found her thoughts were occupied completely by Cord Travers.

Her attention was caught by a shimmering blond young girl with a pale ethereal beauty who had come to stand shyly in the entrance to the ballroom. How sweet and innocent she looked, Vesper noted. She could hardly remember when she had felt that way.

The girl suddenly smiled radiantly, and Vesper knew her beau must be nearby. A tall, lean man with classic features and cheerless green eyes came to her side and tenderly wrapped her arm through his. Vesper started out of her seat and clutched at her breast. It was Cord, her Cord, and his arm was around another woman. What was he doing here, and what did this child-woman mean to him?

Vesper saw him lean down and whisper into the little blonde's ear. She blushed and hid her face in his coat, then looked up at him adoringly. With growing horror, Vesper realized the girl was in love with Cord. But was Cord in love with her? Had he succeeded in putting Vesper out of his heart?

Cord surveyed the gathering, looking right past Vesper. His eyes lit on his father, who had returned to the ballroom and stood among the older men, talking politics. Cord whispered again to the girl on his arm and escorted her over to the colonel. Vesper could see the confused hesitation in the colonel's eyes as Cord approached him.

But when she heard her husband address his host as "Father," she thought she would faint. Suddenly the room seemed to twist at an odd angle and a high-pitched, whirring noise squealed in her ears. She turned for support to Lucinda, but the woman had an odd mixture of worry and guilt written all over her face. Vesper stared at her aunt, uncomprehending. Lucinda looked back at her niece beseechingly.

"Vesper, child, it wasn't supposed to happen like this. We didn't plan it this way."

Vesper stepped back, stung by the shock of betrayal.

"We? You and who? The colonel?"

The truth had finally dawned on her.

"It's Colonel Zachary Travers, isn't it? How could you, Auntie," she demanded, "when I trusted you so?"

Her fragile world in shambles, Vesper raced past

Lucinda, the colonel, and Cord. She ran blindly into the study and slammed the door shut, alone with her pounding heart. She sank down before the fire, racked by soul-wrenching sobs, releasing all the pent-up feelings she had had since Cord left her on *The River Siren*.

The door opened slightly and Lucinda slipped in.

"Vesper," her aunt began.

"No! I'll hear nothing from you. You're no better than the rest of my family, manipulating and conspiring to get what you want. At least they were open about it," Vesper spit out, "but you . . . you're a hypocrite, pretending all this time to be on my side."

"Perhaps I deserved that," Lucinda admitted. "But I've always been on your side. I've always had your best interests at heart."

"To throw my defeats in my face? Is that in my best interest?" Vesper demanded.

"No, child," the older woman said softly. "Zachary and I only wanted to see you and Cord happy again."

Vesper laughed bitterly. "Cord seems happy enough. He's found someone else, hasn't he?"

"Now, listen to me, Vesper Lawrence Travers," admonished Lucinda. "Zachary told me his son has been mooning around here like a sick bull ever since he arrived. That doesn't sound like 'happy' to me," Lucinda concluded briskly.

"Don't you understand?" cried Vesper, at the end of her tether. "I've been hurt enough. Cord doesn't believe me and he doesn't want me anymore."

Lucinda knelt down and held the distraught woman in her arms.

"Fiddlesticks, Vesper dear. I say fiddlesticks. That young man is still in love with you. Mark my words.

He just needs a little more time. Hush, hush, now," she said soothingly.

But the words died in her throat as Vesper tore herself away from her aunt. With a last reproachful glare full of recrimination, she stalked out of the study and sought the privacy of the Magnolia Room, locking all doors.

Meanwhile, in the ballroom, Cord was stunned, torn between shock and anger, by Vesper's presence at Fairlawn. How in hell had she found her way here, and what was she after this time? Would she never leave him in peace? He gave his father a tight, furious look and did not like what he saw. He's trying to run my life again, Cord thought. I should never have trusted the old man, telling him everything.

Without completing his introduction, he grabbed his young lady by the arm roughly and led her onto the dance floor. She gazed up at him, slightly frightened but trusting, and he saw in her eyes the same sweet purity and innocence Vesper had possessed when they first met.

A Virginia reel started up. As he bowed, turned, and promenaded with a different woman each few steps, he realized he was looking for some piece of the Vesper he loved in each of them. Was he always to be haunted by his wife and the hurt she had caused him?

Abruptly he left the dance and his partner behind. He found a handful of whiskey bottles and headed out of the house, stopping only when he reached the old summerhouse. Quickly he downed half of the first bottle, but in his mind's eye he still saw Vesper, dressed in black, her face pale, beautiful, and agonized.

When she wasn't physically with him, she was always there in his mind. If he managed to blot out her memory, she invariably appeared in appealing flesh before him. The only answer he could find was in the bottles he had brought with him. He proceeded to drink himself into a numb fog.

Hours later, when the last guest had left Fairlawn, Colonel Travers went searching for his son, lantern in hand. He found him in the summerhouse, staring gloomily into the dark night, dead sober.

"Ah've somethin' to tell you, Cord," began the old man.

"There's nothing you can say I want to hear," Cord stated flatly. "I don't know what you thought you could accomplish by bringing Ve— my wi— her here, but it won't work."

"It can work, mah boy," insisted the colonel. "She's magnificent. The two of you belong together."

Cord snorted cynically. "Too much has passed between us."

The old man leaned forward on his cane and stared hard at his son.

"Ah know you walked out on her, son, but are you prepared to lose her? To let her walk away from you and find comfort in another man's arms?"

"She's already done that," Cord snarled.

"You're wrong, boy, just as ah was wrong twenty-odd years ago about your mother."

Cord looked up quickly at his father.

"What do you mean?"

Colonel Travers sat down heavily next to his son as if he bore the weight of the world on his shoulders.

"Ah should have told you the truth years ago. Perhaps ah wouldn't've been so hard on you or mahself. Perhaps you wouldn't've left Fairlawn so angry and filled with hate. Perhaps you wouldn't be on the verge of makin' the same mistake I made."

The force of his words struck home.

"Tell me the truth, Father. Now," Cord demanded.

"Ah was a young man driven by principle, just like you, son," the senior Travers began in a harsh voice. "But mah principles had only one name—ambition. Ah wanted to make mah fortune and ah wanted mah own dynasty. Then ah fell in love with your mother."

The colonel's tone changed and softened.

"She wasn't anythin' like me. In fact, she was everythin' I wasn't. Where I drove a hard bargain, she would be generous. When I spoke of money, she spoke of music and poetry. Where I was firm, she was soft and giving. Where I might hurt, she healed. Ah thought ah had everythin' the day you were born—money, land, power, and mah first heir."

He paused and took a deep breath.

"But ah was greedy and wanted more, and ah wasn't content with Amelia's gentle, lovin' ways. When it came to raisin' you, we fought like cats and dogs. She warned me to ease up on you, that ah'd end up chasin' you away, but ah didn't listen. Ah just threatened ah'd take you away from her. One day she packed the two of you up and stole off to the next plantation. It was easy to follow her, but ah went crazy when ah found you in the Warners' nursery and her cryin' in Booth Warner's arms."

Travers' voice cracked, and Cord silently offered his father a sip of whiskey to clear his throat. Barely audible, he continued.

"Ah called her a whore and worse and told her she wasn't worthy to be the mother of mah child. She came home with me because of you, but ah couldn't forget the sight of her in another man's arms. She tried everythin' to ease mah mind, but ah was just too bullheaded. Finally she left. There was a lightnin' storm and her horse bolted. She fell and broke her neck. Booth Warner brought her body back, but it was his wife Katie who told me Amelia had been three months pregnant with mah child."

Silence filled the air.

"Ah never forgave mahself. Consequently, ah drove mahself . . . and you . . . harder and harder. Ah made our lives miserable, son, and ah never admitted it to mahself till the day you left home. Amelia was right, bless her. Ah demanded perfection, and ah lost you both. You and ah are cut from the same cloth, Cord, but this family doesn't need two stubborn old mules."

Chastened by his father's confession, Cord looked back into his childhood, finally understanding the loud battles and alienating silences between his parents. He realized he was carrying on the same kind of warfare with Vesper. Like his father, he was driving away his only chance for love and happiness. Cord stared at old Zachary, mellowed by time, beaten by circumstances of his own making.

"I beg you, son," pleaded Travers with tears in his eyes, "don't let the past repeat itself. Don't destroy your future."

Cord clasped his father's hands in his, then rose from the weathered bench and stared up at the distant twinkling stars.

"I don't want to, Father, but I don't know. I don't know if I can trust her again."

# Chapter Twenty-two

THUNDER MUTTERED AND FRETTED THROUGH THE FOG-thickened morning air as Vesper marched across the misted emerald lawn of the Travers plantation. Her riding boots left clear tracks in the wet grass.

"Lawdy, miss," said the short, mahogany-skinned stablehand, his round face crinkling in a frown at her request. "You cain't be takin' a horse out this mo'ning. It about to rain sumpin' fierce."

Vesper's urge to escape the constricting trap of the house made her hard with the boy. She had slept little the night before, swept by waves of jealousy and made miserable by her aunt's betrayal.

"I told you to saddle me a horse," she gritted, her teeth clenched. Her riding whip lashed impatiently against her boot.

"Please, ma'am, de colonel, he beat dis heah slave

if'n any ob de horses git hurt. Hey, doan you do dat!" he shouted.

But he was too late. Vesper, unable to endure another shred of frustration, had leaped bareback upon a huge, smoke-colored stallion and urged him away in a ground-eating gallop.

"Damned old meddlers," she muttered to herself as the horse hurtled down a lane lined with live oaks that dripped gray-green moss at every twig end.

How dare they try to force me through this pain again? she demanded. She had lost Cord once at the hands of murderers, and only her memories of him had allowed her to survive. Then she had lost him again on *The River Siren*, where his anger and distrust had blurred even her memories of their shining love in the Indian Woods. That deep hurt was still with her. She battled with it every day. And now they were forcing her to lose him again, this time to a pastel-faced miss with adoring eyes and clinging little hands.

"I'd just as soon go back to Washington and marry Augustus Bledsoe as have my heart trampled again," Vesper swore out loud to the uncaring landscape that was dissolving before her eyes in wind-tossed flurries of rain.

Her horse balked at a bark of thunder, and then rushed on. Vesper did not attempt to direct him. His wild headlong flight mirrored perfectly her hunger to escape.

"The human heart can only endure so much," she cried to the encroaching storm, angry and despairing sobs breaking from her.

The heavens opened up, pouring endless sheets of wild water down upon the weeping woman. The stallion was slowed by the slippery ground. The earth was turning to mud, making the footing more and more treacherous.

A sizzling fork of lightning split the sky, and Vesper screamed as it hit the thick branch of a nearby oak. Her horse reared in panic. She clung with both arms around his tense neck as the jagged branch flew toward them, missing her shoulder by inches. Horse and rider stood still for a moment in the pouring rain, recovering from their near disaster.

"It's all right, boy," Vesper murmured, stroking his quivering flank. "It's all right."

They stood in a hissing circle of rain. Peering about in all directions, Vesper realized she was completely lost. She could see nothing but tree shadows against a curtain of misty gray and white. One direction is as good as another, Vesper thought defiantly, urging the horse on.

He tried to obey, but his hooves had stuck fast in the ever-thickening mire. Damn, Vesper thought, pushing her dripping hair back from her face. The horse tried to rear, whinnying in panic. Vesper slid herself down from his slick back, falling to her knees in the slushy mud.

"Easy, boy," she shouted, praying the terrified animal wouldn't break one of his legs in the struggle.

She pushed through the mud toward him, reaching to try to free his hooves. But the ground gave way under her boots, and she was trapped in the greedy clay where her floundering only forced her in deeper. Her shouts for help were all but drowned out by the stallion's fear-filled neighing and the coursing waters.

Then Vesper caught sight of a man on horseback coming toward her. "Help me," she cried.

He dismounted and, carefully skirting the soft patch of mud, grasped her under both arms and wrenched her out of the muck, setting her to one side. She watched gratefully as he managed to free her horse as well. She was shivering with cold and relief when his voice came to her over the pounding of the rain.

"He's free now. Get back up and follow me."

Cord's voice! Cord had found her in the storm. Vesper's heart cried out to him. Whenever she could not save herself, he was always there. In a trance, she mounted the waiting stallion and followed her husband's voice to wherever he would lead her. Through the downpour, Vesper glimpsed a ramshackle hut.

"It's an abandoned slave cabin," shouted Cord. "We can take shelter there."

They led the horses onto the wide covered porch and tied them to a splintered railing. Cord eased open the front door, which groaned in protest, and gestured for Vesper to enter. Inside the gloomy one-room house, the roar of the storm quieted to a soothing hush.

"You're shivering," he said to her.

He bent and picked up a coarse woolen blanket draped across a crude cot. Standing behind her, Cord wrapped her tall shaking body in the dry cloth. Vesper felt the warmth of his massive hands through the blanket and sighed unconsciously as he took her arms and turned her to face him.

"How did you manage to land in Fairlawn's worst swamp in a thunderstorm?" he queried as he dried her face with a corner of the blanket.

There was a tenderness in his eyes he couldn't quite disguise. Vesper couldn't tell him that his romance with the little blonde had made her sick with jealousy, so she countered instead with a question of her own.

"Why did you come after me at all?"

He tried to shrug casually, but Vesper could see the effort it took him.

"I, uh, seem to have an instinct about you," Cord

rumbled. "After all this time, I still sense when you're in danger."

His words warmed her, for she felt that the deep unspoken bonds between them were unbroken. There was a sweet giving in her luminous amethyst eyes as she looked into his face.

Cord swallowed as his eyes locked with hers. She was still the vision of his wondrous woman of the Indian Woods, the other half of his naked soul. He shook with wanting her.

"Cord," she said in a low voice, the words tumbling out of the deepest recesses of her being, "I've waited so long. Please. Please love me."

She was in his arms, giving herself up to the most frenzied caresses she had ever experienced. He tore the wet garments from her, his frantic, insatiable mouth tasting every inch of her silken flesh. He laid her on the blanket-covered ground, and she heard his worshipful, unbelieving whispers over and over.

"Vesper. Vesper."

Her whole body burned with need, the flames flaring brighter with each lave of his tongue. The ache to find him again overcame her. She slid her palms down under the waistline of his trousers, easing the damp cloth over his lean hips, and traced with hungry delight the long, muscular lines of his powerful thighs, the sculpted rounds of his buttocks. She slid her fingers through the crisp golden hair surrounding his rampant manhood, and breathed his name.

"Oh, my darling," he groaned as her fingers closed on the core of him.

He loomed over her, looking down into her face adoringly.

"You are mine alone," he growled.

"Only yours," she whispered as he entered her and she was lost in the pulsing rhythm of their love.

They bucked and plunged and rocked in a restless agony of desire, battering down all walls of separation and mistrust that had grown between them. Higher and higher they rose, until, with a cry of gladness breaking from each one, they reached the pinnacle and were one.

Vesper lay on her side, pressed against her husband from head to toe, her skin joyfully drinking in the touch of his. Her memories had not been wrong. The ecstasy of their lovemaking was sheer wonder.

He smoothed the long black tendrils of her hair that clung wetly to his arm and chest. Then he cupped the face that nestled under his chin, stroking and caressing her soft cheek, her thick curls, as he stared out over her head.

"You never gave yourself to any other man, did you, my Vesper?"

"I couldn't," she whispered into the hollow of his neck.

She trembled with gladness. He loved her. Their bodies had taught him what his mind had refused to admit—that they belonged together.

"I've been a fool," he said quietly.

She kissed his calloused palm as it wandered tenderly over her face.

"It was an easy mistake to make," she offered. "I didn't look exactly respectable the first time you saw me on the boat."

"Yes, but then I kept making the same mistake, despite all your efforts to stop me."

"It would be easier to stop a rampaging bear in its tracks than you, once you've made up your mind," she said with a teasing glint in her eye.

"You're not the first person who's accused me of being stubborn," he said, shaking his head at his own blindness. "Suppose you tell me now what happened to you. I promise to listen without resorting to any . . ."

His face tightened for an instant, and Vesper knew he was remembering how brutally he had treated her.

". . . any more violence."

His look of self-disgust made Vesper want to cradle him in her arms and soothe away the pain. But he met her pitying expression with a steady glance.

"Tell me," he said.

Haltingly the story spilled out. She skipped nothing, from the terrible loss of their child to Bledsoe's threats, her bargain with Raoul, Daisy's revelation, and the details of her plan to humble her husband's supposed murderer.

"Oh, my darling," Cord cried when she finished, "I would give anything in my power to have spared you all this."

He held her against him, wrapping his arms around her as if he would never let her go.

"My brave, brave girl. You faced down dangers that would have crushed most people."

Vesper thrilled to the pride in his voice. For too long she had feared she would never have his respect again.

"Each time I thought that I couldn't go on," she told him, "I remembered you and all you had taught me. Somehow those memories gave me the will to continue."

He shook his head.

"Don't give me the credit. You've become everything I knew you could be, and more."

His admiring smile darkened.

"It was all for me that you became Morgana, and then, when I met you, I punished you for it."

He faced her unflinchingly.

"Can you forgive me?"

Her eyes glowed with unshed tears of happiness.

"I've already forgiven you," she said.

Their lips met in a kiss that sealed their love forever. Cord's searching mouth explored the elegant curve of her jaw, the corners of her eyes, the soft side of her neck. His hands washed over her waiting skin, bringing her to pulsing life.

"You used to love this," he murmured.

He traced the intricate whorls of her ear with a hot tongue tip.

"I still do," she assured him, her eyes fever-bright as his evocative touch set her trembling.

"And this . . ."

He insinuated his thigh high up between her legs and moved it back and forth in a sinuous rhythm. Vesper arched against him with a yielding moan.

"You have a . . . a good memory," she managed.

"I've never forgotten a single moment we spent together," he assured her passionately as he pressed the length of his heated naked body to hers. "When I thought I had lost you, my memories were all that kept me going."

His words spent themselves against her skin, between her breasts, as he lowered his head to take a pointed nipple in his mouth. Fiery darts of pleasure raced through Vesper as he pulled and sucked. Her body twisted on his, inflaming him as well.

His mouth traveled lower, softly brushing over the quivering round of her belly, back and forth across the sensitive tops of her thighs. It seemed as if a many-petaled flower deep in her body began to unfold at her husband's tender giving caresses. Involuntarily she moved her body against his lips, bringing him to the core of her womanhood.

"Darling," he groaned.

Slowly he tasted of her cherished sweetness, stealing from her what little control remained. She was his, she was all his, the flower within her opening wider and wider. He covered her writhing body with his own, and slowly slid inside her waiting moistness, letting the rain of sensation envelop him. So close were they that he felt her pleasure as his own, and she his. Intertwined in flesh, intermeshed in spirit, Cord and Vesper returned to the valley of endless love each had dreamed of for so long.

She slowly returned to earth from the high reaches of ecstasy, her body feeling melted against Cord's pliant warmth. She had found this utter fulfillment only in dreams, Vesper thought mistily, since she had lost Cord.

Gently he kissed the tears of joy that shimmered on her dark lashes.

"It's not the same as it was," he rumbled.

Startled, she asked, "No? We were everything I remembered."

He settled her in their old position, her head lying on his chest, her body nestled at his side, her long inky locks wrapped around his neck.

"We've lost our innocence, my darling," he explained. "I used to feel that nothing could hurt us. Nothing could come between us. But now we've both known terrible hurt and grief. We've changed, my darling, and I think we're wiser for it."

He bent his head to kiss her slender fingers.

Vesper recalled those far-off sunlit days and realized that he was right. She looked at his tousled bronze hair, a rush of tenderness sweeping through her. My darling, she thought, what does metal gain in the fire? It becomes tempered, tested, stronger than ever. We're surer now, she realized. We know the value of what we have because we almost lost it forever.

Her hand tightened convulsively in his. She looked up into his face, desperate to make sure she'd never be parted from him again. He read her as easily as he always had, seeing the depths of longing leaping out of those marvelous crystalline amethyst eyes. His powerful arms took her, welded her to him, and she clung to him with all the fervor of her fears and needs.

"I'll never let you go again," he promised, his voice a fierce whisper in her ear.

"Never," she echoed gladly.

They lay clasped together while the driving storm outside pelted and swayed. Finally it slowed, coming to a hushed halt. A ray of sunlight penetrated the umber gloom of the cabin. A single bird sang its sweet release from the wild shower of rain.

Vesper and Cord rose and dressed, gathering up their wet things. They kept intercepting each other's wondering little smiles, as if neither one could believe their good fortune. The newly rinsed air smelled delicious, rich with scents of bark and leaf, as they mounted their horses and turned their heads toward home.

"My father will be overjoyed," Cord said finally, breaking their long, reverent silence.

"And Lucinda will purse her lips and try not to tell me she told me so."

Then a shadow passed over her face.

"We may really be in danger, Cord. I've been playing with fire, threatening Augustus Bledsoe."

She shot her husband an alarmed glance as they led their horses along the sodden bank of a dark rushing stream. She felt the year-long nightmare begin to shred the edges of her happiness.

"Before," she explained, trembling, "the danger didn't seem to matter as long as you were avenged. But now . . ."

"We'll call it off. One letter will do it. As long as Bledsoe doesn't know who put the bloodhounds on him, you'll be safe."

He shot her a reassuring look.

"You're not alone anymore, my darling. Remember that."

Vesper relaxed at her husband's logical suggestion, his firm voice, his easy calm. The nightmare receded again, and the joy remained.

Privately, Cord promised himself that Bledsoe would hang for his crimes. In all conscience, Cord could not leave such a monster loose in the world, to prey on other innocent victims. But none of this showed on his face as they rode up Fairlawn's broad oak-lined avenue.

In Colonel Travers' cozy book-lined study, the two old conspirators were enjoying a glass of sherry by a cheerily blazing fire when Cord and Vesper, hand in hand, entered. One look at the younger couple's blissful faces was enough to assure the schemers that their plan was a complete success.

"You've reconciled," announced the colonel, trying to control the tears of joy forming in his rheumy blue eyes. "I'm glad of it, my boy. You made the right choice." He set down his wine and rose to give Cord's shoulder a congratulatory clap.

"It certainly took you long enough," added Aunt Lucinda tartly, "but it's none the less welcome for all that." Her brisk nod to Vesper held a world of pleasure in it.

The colonel took Vesper's free hand in his and drew her to him so that he could kiss both her cheeks.

"Mah dear," he said after he had bussed her, "you're the daughter I've always wanted, and ah know you'll be very happy together."

Vesper's voice had tears in it as she said, "Might I call you Father?"

"It would make me very happy if you did," he returned gallantly.

"Zachary," Lucinda broke in, "this is all very well, but these young people must be starving. They've been hours out in that storm."

"She's right," the colonel told Vesper ruefully. "She's always right, isn't she?"

Vesper laughed, sending her crusty aunt a fond look.

"Yes, I'm afraid it's so."

She pulled Cord up to where Lucinda sat in her characteristic upright pose.

"At least, let me introduce you to my husband before you sweep us out to table."

"Well, I'm very glad to meet you, young man, as I'm sure you must—"

Her speech was interrupted as Cord leaned down and, with a twinkle in his green eyes, gave her wrinkled cheek a smacking kiss.

"Thank you, Aunt Lucinda," he said in his deep voice. "I hope you don't mind my calling you Aunt, ma'am, but you brought Vesper and me back together, and that makes you family in my book."

Lucinda had to clear her throat several times as she struggled to regain her customary composure. There was a suspicious dewiness in her eyes as she answered, "You're a fine, upstanding man and I'd be proud to be your aunt."

She sniffed.

"Now let's go to dinner before I make a complete sentimental fool of myself."

Arm in arm, the quartet went to a feast that would include many a champagne toast and cheerful reminiscences.

# Chapter Twenty-three

THE ROSY GLOW OF DAWN ILLUMINATED THE PEACEFUL sleeping face of Vesper Travers. Her husband gently disengaged her arms from about him. Cord gave her lovely form one last adoring look and kissed a naked alabaster shoulder before he dressed as quickly and noiselessly as he could. A smile stole over him as he thought of the surprise he would bring her. He tiptoed from his bedroom, boots slung over his broad shoulder.

When Vesper awakened alone, two hours later, she sighed. She rolled her body into the long hollow Cord had left and buried her face in his pillow, inhaling his scent. Of course, he had chores to do, she chided herself when she found she was wishing him there with her. Soon she too would be rising at dawn as they reestablished their marital teamwork.

But for this morning, she thought, she could luxuriate. Slowly and completely she stretched her naked body in the pale gilding of sunlight streaming in through the casement window onto the glowing velveteen patchwork coverlet. The outdoors seemed to call to her.

Vesper pulled on a simple warm dress of rose chintz trimmed with white lace at the collar and cuffs. She grabbed a light shawl as she swept out of the room, intent on rediscovering her love for nature. Too long had she been imprisoned behind the mask of Morgana.

The soft morning mist that bathed southern Louisiana most of the year was turned to pearl by the diffuse sunlight. In this moist and glowing world, each leaflet, each pebble, each blade of grass, was edged with a silver-gold light. Vesper strolled along the shining expanse of lawn and imagined the new house Cord would build for them, a new paradise for horses and gamboling children, rich and fulfilling.

She strode along the perimeter of the plantation, enjoying the company of the moss-hung oaks and the sawtooth-edged palmetto trees, with all their feathered and furred inhabitants. The air was soft as a caress. Once she bent over a set of pointed-toed tracks in the mud, and was almost sure the pawprints were muskrat. She turned quickly at the sound of a bush rustling, and caught a glimpse of a white-tailed deer as it leaped away into the olive-brown swamp. Vesper felt such joy in these simple sights. Each discovery brought her closer to the happy bride she had once been.

A branch snapped suddenly and twigs crackled underfoot. Vesper stopped, puzzled. The animal sounded too heavy to be a deer. She frowned. Alligators didn't usually move from the riverbanks into the underbrush. There were no bears here, were there? Belatedly she noticed that the birds had stopped singing. Alarmed, she whirled toward cover, but her woodland skills were rusty. A fetid hand clapped itself over her mouth and she was dragged away, struggling, into the pathless swamp.

Cord felt the past months of misery falling from him like brown forgotten leaves as he urged his frisky black-maned stallion up the glistening avenue to his father's home. He threw a proud glance back at the lovely mare he'd just purchased for Vesper. Cord smiled. The new horse was a real lady, slender, graceful, and spirited. She'd be a match for Vesper.

Under the whispering oaks he galloped excitedly, pleased with this first purchase. He would rebuild the herd and rebuild their lives. Cord waved cheerfully to Aunt Lucinda, who was waiting for him on the marble steps of the portico.

"Vesper isn't with you?" she queried in a tight voice as he tied up the horses.

He frowned. "I left her sleeping early this morning."

"She's nowhere about," Lucinda said in worried tones. "No one's seen her all morning. We assumed she was with you."

The growing dread in her voice matched Cord's sudden instinct of danger.

"Something's wrong, Lucinda," he told her. "When did you last see her?"

She had to hurry to keep up with his big strides as they entered the house. In a rare display of emotion, Vesper's aunt placed a shaking hand on Cord's arm. "L-last night," she stammered. "Oh, I hope, I hope . . ."

He patted her hand comfortingly as his mind

worked frantically. Then his eyes lit on the silver salver holding the newly arrived mail. Riffling through the pile, he found a letter addressed to Vesper.

"Do you think . . ." began Lucinda in hushed tones.

"We'll soon know," Cord rumbled as he tore open the envelope, only to find another one inside addressed to Miss Morgana.

The pair exchanged worried glances. Cord ripped open the inner letter and quickly scanned its contents.

"Damn," he swore.

The letter crumpled in his fist as he hit the salver and sent the rest of the mail flying.

"It's a warning from Joaquín Delgado in Washington. Bledsoe's uncovered Vesper's plot and is on his way here," he said tightly.

Lucinda peeked at the letter's date. "It was mailed over a week ago."

They exchanged alarmed looks.

"He's got Vesper," Cord gritted. "I'm going after her."

He raced for the door, a voice inside him wailing his wife's name.

"Hurry!" Lucinda called after him, clutching at her heart with a bony hand.

Outside, Cord grabbed his rifle from his saddle and easily picked up Vesper's tracks as they meandered to the edge of the lawns and onto the tree-lined plantation margin. She had been alone and moving slowly. Then he came to a jasmine bush smashed in on one side, a shawl caught in its broken branches. He bent to examine the ground, reading easily the signs of Vesper's scuffle with her two captors.

Cord looked up at the path of crushed foliage and roughed-up ground left by his wife's fierce struggles as she was dragged away. A towering wave of fear reared up inside him.

They had several hours' start on him, and he knew Bledsoe was capable of any horror. What might be happening to Vesper this very instant? With the immense strength he'd garnered from all his solitary years in the wilderness, Cord forced his fears down. He had vowed never to lose his wife again. He would find her.

In that moment, Cord shed the look of a civilized man. His stance became the crouch of an Indian hunter. His face tautened. His eyes looked sharp as a hawk's, reading the swamp as if it were an open book. With fierce concentration, he started down the kidnappers' trail.

Vesper hadn't made it easy on her two captors. Her furious struggles and muffled shrieks had slowed them so much that they'd finally knocked her unconscious. Before the rifle butt had connected with her head, the last thing she'd heard was one frustrated kidnapper say to the other, "Hit her easy, Bart. Bledsoe'll have yore hide if she's hurt 'fore he gets her."

At dusk, she awoke to find herself in a tiny, dank cabin. Its crude log walls dripped with the moisture of the bayou she could glimpse from the single small window. When she tried to bring her hand to her aching head, Vesper discovered that she had been chained hand and foot to the wall. Horrified, she made out other sets of rusty manacles dangling from two of the other walls.

Her captor's words rang menacingly through her mind. Bledsoe! He must have cornered Delgado and traced her. This fearful place could be no other than the infamous slave cabin Daisy had described, where the Butcher broke runaways.

Vesper's heart thudded painfully in her breast. She was truly helpless now. At any moment her nemesis would pull open the primitive door and carry out his unspeakable threats. She remembered his lurid promises in the little St. Louis inn. Now he had far more reason for his rage.

Cold perspiration beaded her scratched forehead as icy panic threaded through her veins. Then she remembered Cord's words.

"I have an instinct about you. I sense it when you're in danger."

A picture came to her of his grim tracker's face examining her trail. He would find her, Vesper realized, heady with relief. But, came the disquieting thought, would he find her in time?

The groan of old wet wood made Vesper startle. Augustus Bledsoe stood in the doorway, holding a flaring lantern in his meaty fist. His belly bulged out from under a grease-stained leather vest and his widely planted legs were encased in knee-high muddy black boots. On his face was the familiar and hateful gloating leer.

She watched with a sinking heart as his expression turned to shock. Augustus Bledsoe had just recognized the notorious river siren who attempted to unmask him as none other than Vesper Lawrence Travers. She forced herself to stare back at him as evil flames began dancing in his little pig eyes.

"What an unexpected surprise," he said slowly, his fat lips parting in a triumphant smile.

There was a painfully long silence as he walked up to her, running his eyes appraisingly up and down her chained body and finally back up to her eyes.

"I expected to meet you next in hell, Vesper."

He hung the lantern on a nearby hook and came closer to her. Augustus Bledsoe licked his lips slowly.

"You won't escape me this time."

Slowly he drew off his black gloves, flexing and unflexing his thick fingers.

"After tonight's work, I'm sure I'll join you down below."

Her heart was pounding so loudly she could hardly breathe.

"What do you mean?" she managed to croak.

"If you know who I really am, then you know what I use this cabin for, don't you?" he snarled.

"Torture!" she gasped.

"Every sleepless night your boy Delgado put me through, I'm going to take out on your pretty hide. You'll beg me for death after an hour or two, but you'll have to wait until you've paid for everything."

The anger flaring unleashed in his eyes told her that he meant every word.

"Or maybe I'll just leave what's left of you on the bank out there, for the alligators."

Keep him talking, Vesper thought frantically. Give Cord time to find me before . . . Her mind balked at the rest.

"I've never seen you so upset, Augustus," she forced herself to say with some semblance of calm. "It must have been quite a shock to you to find that some victims can bite back."

She stretched her mocking smile taut to hide the shivering of her lips.

"Why, you unspeakable little snake, I'll grind you into the dirt," he shouted in a rage.

It was the first time Vesper had ever seen him completely out of control, and the sight sickened her. His plum-colored scar puckered and lengthened down his cheek as he screamed out his fury.

"Do you have any idea how close you came to destroying me? It will take me years to repair the damage and silence the whispers. You filthy little baggage, you dared to undermine Augustus Bledsoe? It is I who pull the strings, I who call the tunes that they all dance to."

He was mad, Vesper realized, maddened by his drive for power. He wanted her dead because she had revealed to him that he was vulnerable. She pulled futilely at her heavy chains as he approached her.

"I could run the whole country if I chose to," he claimed insanely, "and look what crawls out of the woodwork to reveal my secrets."

He grabbed her chin in a bruising grip, his fingers digging into her tender flesh. She was forced to confront his raving bestial face, twisted in an ecstasy of rage. His hand gripped lower, enclosing her slender neck. Vesper's instinctive cry of protest was choked off as darkness began to descend upon her senses. At least I won't suffer long, came her dim thought as Bledsoe's hand tightened. I never wanted to leave you, Cord, Vesper cried inwardly. Red-black stains swam before her eyes.

The kidnappers had been careless, and Cord found their trail easy to follow. As he loped through the shadowy swamp he prayed that he'd reach his Vesper in time. In the velvet-gray light of dusk, he spotted a crude cabin, guarded by two rough-looking men. With practiced ease, Cord melted into a tangle of weeds, approaching the hut unseen.

He waited until one guard's back was turned and then sprang upon the other. Noiselessly he swung his rifle butt and knocked the man unconscious, catching him before he hit the ground and rolling him under a bush. Then Cord bound the man with vines, tying his arms and legs together.

The compelling urgency for haste was a litany in his mind as he crouched low and stalked the second man. Anything could be happening inside those crude walls. Cord forced his hands to remain steady as he raised his rifle again. The other guard was quicker and received only a glancing blow. He grappled with Cord but was no match for the ferociously determined frontiersman. Soon he had met the fate of his fellow.

Now the path to Vesper was clear. Flinging open the cabin door, Cord froze at the sight of his precious wife strangling in the brutish grip of Augustus Bledsoe. Cord's dominant voice rang out.

"Bledsoe, your fight is with me."

Releasing Vesper, the Butcher whirled around. His eyes bulged as he recognized Cord Travers, an enemy he'd thought long dead. Bledsoe bellowed frantically for his men as Vesper's eyes fluttered open and fixed with unbelieving joy on her husband.

Cord gave Vesper a smile of passionate relief before he said to the panicked older man, "You're wasting your breath, murderer. I made sure that, this time, it will be a fair fight between us."

Slowly Bledsoe turned to face Cord, and the flickering lantern light seemed to make his bulky shadow loom frighteningly larger to Vesper.

"Unchain her," Cord demanded.

He cocked his rifle and raised the barrel until it pointed directly at Bledsoe's heart. The sound of the gun's hammer seemed to unnerve the brutish kidnapper. Sullenly he obeyed Cord's order, taking a key from his vest pocket and unlocking all four of Vesper's manacles. She took a tentative step toward her husband, then another.

Suddenly she was jerked back as Bledsoe pulled her against him and held a knife to her throat. Vesper bit back a scream as she was dragged backward toward the door. Cord dared not shoot. He followed the pair as closely as Bledsoe would permit. Vesper was forced to the dark bank of the moon-spangled bayou.

A wind sprang up and racing clouds hid the moon. Bledsoe cursed, stumbling on the slippery mud, and Vesper tore herself from his arms, hurtling toward her husband. He pulled her to him with one powerful arm and tried to take aim at Bledsoe, scrambling and slipping in the mire.

Under the cover of darkness, the bulky man managed to crawl to a small flatboat and set off down the bayou. Helplessly Cord whirled his rifle toward the water as he heard the boat being launched. The moon appeared again and Bledsoe's hunched figure on the water became visible. Cord took aim and fired.

Flocks of disturbed birds shot out of the trees, squawking and circling. From the slime of the riverbank, primitive hulking forms lurched and glided into the still waters of the bayou.

Cord fired again. Bledsoe ducked, but the bullet winged his shoulder. The impact knocked him off balance, and he rocked crazily in the pirogue before falling heavily into the water.

Excited by the taste of blood, the waiting alligators converged on Bledsoe's flailing form. Moonlight glistened on their rows of needle-sharp teeth as mouth after voracious mouth yawed open. With instincts born in the prehistoric mud, the monstrous predators moved in for the kill.

"Oh my God," Vesper breathed.

There was one hoarse scream. Then came the

sound of frenzied splashing as the water seemed to boil with the lashing tails of the hungry reptiles.

Cord wrapped his precious Vesper in his arms and turned her head away from the ghastly sight.

"Don't look, my darling," he said. "It's all over now."

# Epilogue

It was spring at Rancho Rio del Oro and the emerald meadows were lush with Dresden-blue spears of wild lupines and vivid wafer-thin disks of California golden poppies. It had been a rainy winter on the Sacramento River delta and the land was bursting with new life. The air was rinsed clear and fresh as a tumbling mountain waterfall. Small white ruffs of clouds chased each other across the vast aqua bowl of the sky. Against a distant backdrop of the snow-capped Sierra Madre a long whitewashed adobe ranch house with a red-tiled roof sprawled comfortably, trailing a bright shawl of magenta bougainvillea.

Across a luxuriant pasture of their land, a couple raced their palominos neck and neck. The woman glowed in the molten sunlight like a figure from an ancient legend, her magnificent mane of ebony hair flying in the wind, her gentian eyes brilliant with happiness. Her consort, a bronzed god with leaf-green eyes, rode his stallion as if he and the horse were one. Under the canopy of an enormous arching white-barked sycamore, they reined in their horses and dismounted.

"You still can't beat me, even on Zephyr," Cord called out gleefully.

He grabbed her shoulder and spun her around.

"So pay up, Mrs. Travers."

Laughing, Vesper raised her mouth for his kiss. His lips were cool from the rushing spring air, and their hot search sent marauding shivers through her. Shamelessly she pulled him down to the ground.

Placing her mouth at his ear, she whispered, "I think it's high time our little Zach had a sister, don't you? Maybe a little Lucy?"

She nipped his earlobe teasingly.

"Both Grandpa Travers and Great-aunt Lucinda tell me they want another grandchild to spoil, and you know they always get what they want."

Cord's fingertips suggestively traced the row of buttons down the front of his wife's muslin riding shirt.

"We'd better get started right away," he growled.

His fingers pulled the buttons from their holes, exposing her beautiful naked breasts to the spring breeze. Cord and Vesper looked at each other, hearts racing. She ran a tongue tip between suddenly dry lips.

"Touch me everywhere," she demanded hoarsely.

She groaned with pleasure as his massive hands slipped into her riding trousers and cupped her bare buttocks, pressing her against his aroused loins. Vesper clawed at his clothing, desperate to find his gold-pelted flesh. He chuckled at her eagerness, though his excitement was easy to read in the wild way he ran his palms over her creamy skin.

"You're in such a hurry, my little vixen. I'm not going anywhere."

When her fevered movements didn't slow, Cord grabbed her wrists and held them widely apart. He looked down into her protesting face and very deliberately ran his tongue up one breast, over its rosy tip, and down its snowy slope. Feeling her excited shudder, he slowly repeated his action on her other breast. She quivered all over, tossing her head from side to side.

"Let me go," she cried. "I want . . . I want . . ."

He shook his head in mock protest as he released her hands.

"Whatever happened to that shy little innocent I had to teach everything to?" he teased as he undid her last button.

"I grew up!" Vesper answered as she removed his last piece of clothing and rubbed herself against him sinuously as a cat, luxuriating in the scent, the warmth, the textures of him.

They reveled in each other, pleasing themselves like seasoned gourmets at an exquisite, voluptuous spread.

"Oh, Cord. I love you so," Vesper gasped.

An inarticulate growl was his only answer as his rampant manhood plunged into her waiting center. Ever onward they raced, the rhythm of their love a transcendent dance of joy. At their apex, they spun in a shower of dazzling golden shards, lost to all but each other. They were complete. They were one.

Cord and Vesper lay quiet in each other's arms. The delicious breeze eddied playfully along their dewy flesh and flicked the emerald grass tips around them into a softly rippling sea. As they gazed upward into the swaying leaves of the sycamore, a profound gratitude filled their hearts, as it so often did now after their lovemaking.

For Cord and Vesper Travers had come through the cruelest currents of the river of life. Against all odds, with only their love to guide them, they had emerged, wholehearted, together, into the Golden State.

# TAPESTRY ROMANCES